Judah could short out all her circuits. Turn her into a gibbering mass of wanting.

Sophie had learned that. And she loved every minute of scorching to a crisp.

But not now.

The tip of his finger brushed the edge of her shirt.

"Why are you always touching me, Judah?"

He smiled. "I like touching you, Sophie. That's why. Just…because." His gaze held hers.

She didn't say anything. She couldn't, not faced with the sadness in his eyes. She didn't have it in her to move away at the moment from the lost, damned look in Judah Finnegan's eyes. It was that glimpse into the dark corners of his soul that got her. Every blasted time.

Dear Reader,

Welcome to another fabulous month of the most exciting romance reading around. And what better way to begin than with a new TALL, DARK & DANGEROUS novel from *New York Times* bestselling author Suzanne Brockmann? *Night Watch* has it all: an irresistible U.S. Navy SEAL hero, intrigue and danger, and—of course—passionate romance. Grab this one fast, because it's going to fly off the shelves.

Don't stop at just one, however. Not when you've got choices like *Fathers and Other Strangers,* reader favorite Karen Templeton's newest of THE MEN OF MAYES COUNTY. Or how about *Dead Calm,* the long-awaited new novel from multiple-award-winner Lindsay Longford? Not enough good news for you? Then check out new star Brenda Harlen's *Some Kind of Hero,* or *Night Talk,* from the always-popular Rebecca Daniels. Finally, try *Trust No One,* the debut novel from our newest find, Barbara Phinney.

And, of course, we'll be back next month with more pulse-pounding romances, so be sure to join us then. Meanwhile...enjoy!

Leslie J. Wainger
Executive Editor

Please address questions and book requests to:
Silhouette Reader Service
U.S.: 3010 Walden Ave., P.O. Box 1325, Buffalo, NY 14269
Canadian: P.O. Box 609, Fort Erie, Ont. L2A 5X3

Dead Calm
LINDSAY LONGFORD

Published by Silhouette Books

America's Publisher of Contemporary Romance

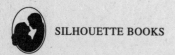 SILHOUETTE BOOKS

ISBN 0-373-27315-0

DEAD CALM

Copyright © 2003 by Jimmie Morel

Visit Silhouette at www.eHarlequin.com

Printed in U.S.A.

Books by Lindsay Longford

Silhouette Intimate Moments

Cade Boudreau's Revenge #390
Sullivan's Miracle #526
Renegade's Redemption #769
No Surrender #947
Dead Calm #1245

Silhouette Romance

Jake's Child #696
Pete's Dragon #854
Annie and the Wise Men #977
The Cowboy, the Baby and the Runaway Bride #1073
The Cowboy and the Princess #1115
Undercover Daddy #1168
Daddy by Decision #1204
A Kiss, a Kid and a Mistletoe Bride #1336
Baby, You're Mine #1396

Silhouette Shadows

Lover in the Shadows #29
Dark Moon #53

LINDSAY LONGFORD,

like most writers, is a reader. She even reads toothpaste labels in desperation! A former high school English teacher with an M.A. in literature, she began writing romances because she wanted to create stories that touched readers' emotions by transporting them to a world where good things happen to good people and happily-ever-after is possible with a little work.

Her first book, *Jake's Child*, was nominated for Best New Series Author, Best Silhouette Romance and received a Special Achievement Award for Best First Series Book from *Romantic Times* magazine. It was also a finalist for the Romance Writers of America's RITA® Award for Best First Book. Her Silhouette Romance *Annie and the Wise Men* won the RITA® for best Traditional Romance of 1993.

Sometimes life throws you totally off balance. If you're lucky, you find angels along the way. I did. My very own funky, funny, fantastic angels, Cathie Linz, Susan Elizabeth Phillips and Suzette Vandewiele, kept me flying through the storms. They saved me with their laughter, their support and their concern. How did I ever get so lucky?

I want to thank some special people at Silhouette, too: Karen Taylor Richman, Leslie Wainger and Tara Gavin. I don't know why you didn't throw me overboard. But I am blessed by knowing you.

Without all of you, the baby would have remained abandoned in the manger.

To My Readers

This is a book about hate, love and redemption. We live in a world that has too much of the first and too little of the second. But I still believe in the possibility of redemption, and so, with hope and faith, I write of love triumphing over hate. It's my small attempt to shine a light into the darkness of fear.

ACKNOWLEDGMENTS

So many people were generous with their time and their knowledge on this book. As usual, I dived headfirst into subjects of which I was ignorant. These generous people helped me along the way. I am indebted to them. From the Greatest Class Ever of Manatee High School, Bradenton, Florida: Bruce Malcolm, CEO, Trilithic; Jeannette Floyd, funny lady extraordinaire, and Kerstin Knos, for help on Florida adoptions; Kaye Sneary Wood, for her research on Vietnamese customs; and Jim Vandelly, whom I will always remember for his performance in *You Can't Take It with You*. Others who gave incredible help were Xuyen Ich Hinh, for his extensive help with Vietnam questions and language; Beth Schemenauer, aka Big Beth, *the* surfing queen; Bill Ritis, ever ready with anecdotes of a Russian childhood; Jacalyn Schauer, for her constant attempts to keep me supplied with pens and make sure I wasn't by myself on holidays; and her cousin, Dr. William Gossman, Asst. Professor of Emergency Medicine at Chicago Medical School; Margaret Watson for the "felony flirting" line; and Josh Polak. The helped me take an idea and give it reality. All errors are, alas, mine.

Chapter 1

The biggest shopping day of the year was a killer, all right.

Sophie sidestepped a trail of plastic syringe tips.

Torn plastic wraps from hastily opened four-by-four gauze pads drifted in her wake. One step away from a full trot, she jammed her hands into the pockets of her medical jacket and grimaced at a blood trail dotting the black-and-white tiled floor. Third time that night.

Overstuffed with turkey both fowl and Wild, two good ol' boys had duked it out in the Emergency Room hall earlier. Then they'd thrown up on her socks. "Damned shame waste of good likker," one had said morosely. Boozily consoling each other, they'd left in the firm grip of one of Poinciana, Florida's knights in blue.

Following the blood trail, Sophie automatically checked out the ER. All five treatment rooms were filled, the waiting room out front was packed to the corners with sniffling, bleeding people, and they all wanted her attention.

Now.

Five minutes ago.

Behind her, a bucket clanked against the floor and water slopped against her, trickled inside her lace-trimmed green socks. She swore under her breath and stopped, the bells on her shoelaces jingling.

"Sorry, Doc. Damned thing slipped." Billy Ray Watley's stringy ponytail swung with his quick grab for the cart. A yellow Caution—Wet Floor sign smacked against the wall. On the other side, the sign warned, *Cuidado—Piso Mijado.* He shot her a worried grin.

"No problem, Billy Ray. Don't sweat it."

"Your Christmas socks are ruined." He jiggled the cart, his ponytail a pendulum to his jitters.

"Not really." Even with soapy water squishing between her toes, she smiled. An effort after fourteen hours on duty, but Billy Ray was one of their own.

She reached down and plucked at one soggy sock. The bells clinked flatly. At six this morning, filled with energy and cold pumpkin pie, she'd pulled on orange socks. With turkeys prancing around the cuffs.

By four in the afternoon, the turkeys had yielded to plain white. She'd meant to save the jingles until midnight. No sense rushing the season, but she'd run out of her white socks. It was going to be a five-sock-change day before she could get out of here, thanks to Billy Ray, the barfing good ol' boys and the teenager from the motorcycle accident.

Dumb kid. No helmet. No sense. She straightened and felt the pop and crackle of every vertebra in her back.

Billy Ray dunked his mop into the cleaning solution, wrung it dry. "I'm cleaning this mess up, Doc, I am. Don't worry."

She gentled her voice and tapped his arm. "You'll handle it."

"Yep. Getting it done. Billy Ray'll stay on top of it." The slap-slap of his mop erased the spill of water, the spots of blood. "Busy night." He nodded toward the examining rooms, scratched his nose. "Busier than last night. I like busy nights."

"It'll get busier before morning."

"I liked that pumpkin pie you brung us, too. Real good pie. Whole lot better than cafeteria pie." He dipped his head, peering at her from beneath his hair.

"Glad you enjoyed it." She shook her head and, bells jingling, headed toward the last examining area of the observation room.

Like the scrape of fingernails across a chalkboard, a shriek ripped from one of the treatment rooms down the hall and halted her in her tracks. The eerie keening lifted the hairs on the back of her neck. She grimaced. "That the gunshot?"

"Nah." Billy Ray shifted uneasily, lanky arms and legs in constant motion. "The woman. You know."

"Right."

Shattered and broken beyond recognition, the woman had been found earlier in the evening by the Poinciana cops.

Sophie had stitched and bandaged. She'd listened to whimpers in a language she didn't understand.

She understood pain, though. No translator was needed for that language.

Billy Ray sent her a quick glance, then concentrated on his mop. "Real bad, huh?"

"It is." Sophie heard the melancholy jangle of her bells as she shifted, half turning away from Billy Ray to check out the treatment room.

She'd put casts on the woman's frail, small arms. Taped ribs. Sutured the long gash that cut whitely through hair matted with blood and sweat. Under different circumstances, Sophie imagined that the woman's hair would have been a swath of glossy black, a source of pride. Maybe she'd been pretty, this small Asian woman who kept calling for something that Sophie couldn't provide.

The woman sure as hell hadn't deserved this.

Nobody did.

Now, still unconscious but moaning and calling out, the woman waited for an empty hospital bed upstairs. Sophie had done what she could. Nothing more she could do now.

From the first, the plaintive wails in an unknown language had pierced Sophie. Horrible to be unable to ease the pain. Worse to be powerless to answer the woman's anguished cries.

Sophie balled her hands into fists inside her pockets. Not in her hands any more. In someone else's.

Maybe the start of the holiday season would be a good omen for the woman. Maybe she'd get a miracle.

Probably not.

Over the doors to the waiting room behind Billy Ray, Christmas lights mingled with leftover paper pumpkins.

Peace on earth, goodwill toward men? Right. Well, she could damned sure use a little goodwill toward women.

"I hope she's gonna be okay. She gonna be okay?" Not meeting Sophie's eyes, Billy Ray continued to work the strings of his two-foot-wide mop back and forth.

"It's anybody's guess, Billy Ray. We'll find out. Who's checking on her?"

"Ms. Cammie."

"That's good." Sophie sighed and risked a glance back at the entrance to the emergency room, to the doors that led away from here, away from this mingled tragedy and comedy.

Outside the glass panels, red and green bulbs glittered along the swaying fronds of palm trees, reflected in the dark puddles underneath. Then the doors slid open and sweet-scented night air floated to her with a promise of escape, of air free of disinfectant and alcohol and despair.

That air teased her with the hope of fleeing this place where laughter was coming harder and harder these days, and when it did, it had an edge of desperation that crept insidiously into her spirit, stealing energy and joy with it. Silly socks weren't much of a Band-Aid.

The curtain at the far end of the hall billowed, flattened.

Jerked back into the moment, Sophie shrugged and strode off, her muscles tight across her shoulders, the cuffs of her wet socks clammy against her ankles. "Gotta go."

Another wail shivered through the hall.

Billy Ray plopped his mop on the cart and scurried down the hall. His raspy voice trailed behind him. "I'm keeping an eye on things."

The desperate keening of the beating victim still ringing in her ears, Sophie shoved open the far curtain and glared at the newest patient.

In front of her, Santa sagged on the examining-room table. Blood dripped from his shoulder onto his seen-better-days polyester fur trim. His belly drooped over a cracked plastic black belt, and he clutched his fine acrylic beard with a lean, callused hand. A nurse had already cut him out of part of his suit, and a saline drip snaked down over his smooth tanned shoulder.

For a second Sophie paused, puzzled by a faint sense of familiarity. Something about the tilt of Santa's head.

The reek of liquor filled the room.

He snugged the beard closer to his face, his long fingers disappearing into the crisp curls. Chilly blue eyes met hers impatiently. Warily.

Santa with an edge.

Not dying.

Just drunk and damaged.

Sophie shook her head and picked up the chart. Three wise men with frankincense, gold and myrrh would come waltzing through the door next. And they'd probably be two-stepping with the Easter bunny.

"Hey there, Mr. C. Rushing the season a little, aren't you?" She flipped open Santa's chart and scanned the nurse's notes.

"Look, sugar, I don't have all night."

Sophie snapped the examining-room curtain shut. The rings rattled and skittered along the dividing rod. "Incidentally, that's *Dr.* Sugar to you, Claus."

Santa tugged at his beard, adjusting it around his face. Shifted one black-booted foot irritably. "I've got things to do, places to be."

"Of course you do. And all before midnight, I'll bet." She smiled sweetly, acid etching her words. No sidewalk Santa reeking of gin was going to give her grief. Not tonight.

"Nah," he grunted as she brushed by him and reached for the blood-pressure cuff. "No midnight curfew until the end of the month. Just working the elves overtime tonight."

"Working's what they call it these days, huh?" She pumped up the blood-pressure cuff and watched the numbers. One-thirty over eighty. He was in better shape than he looked.

From behind the beard and the cloud of white hair, his unfriendly eyes met hers.

Eyes that were almost sober. Their hostility caught her off guard.

Once more that sense of the familiar teased her brain.

Snapping on gloves, she inspected the jagged red line that began at the edge of his neck and disappeared under the ratty faux velvet of his suit. "Knife?"

Santa nodded, grunted a second time as he shifted uncomfortably on the table.

She touched the wound. A long, shallow cut. "Nasty bunch of elves you hang with, Claus."

"Yeah, they can get testy. Like a lot of people." His gaze held hers, and some emotion she couldn't name stirred in the pissed-off blue depths.

With a flick of her hand, she stuck a digital thermometer in his mouth.

As her hand fell away, his gaze still held hers, and he tightened his mouth around the thermometer. It rose slowly, toward the ceiling.

A snotty challenge in the tilt of that whisker-hidden chin.

And that fast, triggered by his take-no-prisoners arrogance, by the heavy smell of alcohol on him, by too many cases gone wrong today, her exhaustion slid over into irritation.

She wanted to smack him.

Zipping down her veins like a skater on speed, her pulse skittered and jumped. This two-bit Santa with an attitude was getting under her skin, pushing buttons, making her jumpy. Damn him. This was *her* turf.

"Okay, Claus, let's get the rest of your vitals." Sophie picked up his wrist, counted his wrist and peripheral pulses, did her ABCs. Airway, breathing, circulation. Looking him over, assessing him, she focused on her job instead of the lick of anger that crisped along her skin whenever his eyes caught hers.

His heart beat steadily under her fingers, his skin hot to her touch even through her gloves. On his index finger the oximeter glowed cheerily. His fingernails were pinked up, not cyanotic blue.

An image of the Asian woman's bruised face flashed through her mind, and she wanted to tell this Santa off the street that he was wasting her time, that she had really sick people needing her out there in the waiting room. She wanted to tell him to go home, stick a bandage on his wound, and sleep it off.

The strength of her reaction startled her.

She inhaled deeply and moved to his back, lifted his jacket. "Easy, will you? I'd like to salvage this damned outfit, if you don't have any objections?" he snarled around the thermometer.

She managed not to grind her teeth. "Certainly. Whatever you say. I'll give it my best shot."

Slotting the thermometer to the side of his mouth, he sent her a quick look. "Best shot? You working the comedy clubs in between stitch jobs?"

"Be still. Please." She eased the jacket away from his ribs where blood had caked it to his skin. This rag-tag Santa shouldn't have been allowed away from whatever place passed for his North Pole. The tatty fabric brushed against her arm, and once again the smell of liquor rose pungently, gagging her.

Eau d'ER, they called it. Poinciana County Hospital's Friday-night, any-night cologne.

"Don't want to lecture you—" she began.

"But you're going to anyway, aren't you?"

Her teeth clicked audibly as she shut her mouth.

She was seriously tempted to slap the cold stethoscope up against his broad back. But, earning her pay, she warmed the disk and ordered, "Breathe in, Claus. Hold it." Checking for temperature and dehydration, she pressed her finger to his skin. Oddly, the sleek skin and ridged muscles of his back didn't fit his air of dissipation. Her eyes narrowing, she tapped his back with her hand, checking his lungs, moving around him to check the bronchial breath sounds under his armpits, around to his chest. "Exhale."

And her busy brain went on autopilot, thinking, observing.

His chest moved easily with his long sigh. With the thermometer still in his mouth, he was finally, blessedly, silent as she quickly finished the basics.

Tapping his belly, she listened for fluid accumulation, not expecting to find any, but still checking. His stomach was flat, the muscles taut and elegantly shaped. The trace of a scar curled around one rib.

Caught by surprise, she hesitated as she stared at his lean, sharply defined abs. Santa's smooth, hard belly was a six-pack, a world away from what he'd been drinking. The tiny hip-hop of her pulse embarrassed her. A sudden flush of heat in her face kept her silent, her face turned away from him.

Damn. She was a well-trained, thirty-four-year-old physician, not some fifteen-year-old star-struck by the school jock. All speechless and hormonal.

Swallowing, she cleared her throat. "Looks like you'll live. Pulse rate's good. Blood pressure's terrific. The stitches will leave a scar, but not too bad. However," she paused and jotted a note on his chart before continuing, "you might want to find a better way of spending your evenings, Claus."

One fuzzy white eyebrow winged upward. "Figured you couldn't resist the lecture." The thermometer wobbled with his mumbled words.

She tapped her pen on the chart. "I have to call in a police report. But I'm sure you know that."

Annoyance steamed off him.

"Too bad, Claus, but them's the rules. You pays your money and you takes your choices." She tried, she *really* tried not to relish his annoyance. A chat with Poinciana's cops would do him good.

She snapped the thermometer out of his mouth and chucked the cover away.

"Sure you had time to get a good temp reading?" His scowl would have terrified small children and rabid dogs.

"What?" She scowled right back at him.

The fabric of his pants shushed along the examining table as he turned toward her, white beard twisting over his good shoulder. "God knows I don't want to rush you."

"Oh, I took all the time I needed." She slammed a lid on the gremlins of temper wriggling free.

"Yeah, I noticed. Weren't in any hurry, were you?"

"Of course not." Under the beat of temper, her voice stayed cool, a tiny edge of malice icing it. "We pride ourselves here in the ER on our excellent, painstaking care. You'll live to slide down another chimney, big guy."

She took out the basin and grabbed towels and gauze pads to clean the area around his neck. Cammie, the best ER nurse around, had already laid out the Neosporin and irrigation syringes.

"I'm going to clean out the wound before I stitch it. This will take a few minutes."

"Hell."

His beard fluttered with his breath, the strands wisping against her cheek as she leaned toward him. Inside her damp sneakers her toes curled, another tiny, unnerving response.

She took a step back. "Gee, hate to inconvenience you. You think you can spare us that much time?"

"Just get on with it, will you?" Not a question. An order.

"My pleasure." She pinched her lips. "Gotta tell you, Santa, you really need to work on your people skills."

"You think?"

"Unless you're a whole lot different around happy little

children, yeah, that's what I think. You're mighty short on charm, Claus. Didn't anybody spell out the job requirements?''

''I do just fine, thank you, Doc.''

''Not in denial at all, are you? Got a real clear picture of yourself, do you?''

His mouth twisted in the thicket of acrylic beard.

She grabbed the 60cc high-pressure syringe and the bottle of sterile water from the Mayo stand beside the examining table. Holding the towel under his shoulder, she began irrigating the wound, tidying up and moving the 4x4 sterile gauzes quickly over the area.

The tight muscle along the top of his shoulder twitched once and then was still.

''So what happened, Santa? On your way to a party, had too much to drink and you took a walk on the wild side?''

''Anybody ever tell you you talk too much?''

''Doing my job, Santa, that's all.'' She flung the stained gauze into the container and bent closer to his shoulder, angling the high-intensity lamp directly onto his neck.

Under the stink of liquor, his skin smelled clean, confusing her. He smelled way too good for her peace of mind. Too clean and fresh for a sloppy drunk. Sophie touched the edges of the wound, checking the depth. ''Your drinking buddies roll you?''

''I was careless.''

Probing gently now, she cleaned the last of the blood away. ''Stupid, more likely.''

''Yeah. Probably that, too.'' His hard-edged eyes flashed her way. ''But mostly careless.''

''Too bad. Carelessness causes a lot of trouble.''

''I'll make sure I write that down so that I don't forget. Next time.''

She looked up at him. ''Hey, Claus, do the ER a favor and make sure there isn't a next time? Save us all a lot of time?''

Even masked by the scruff of beard, his mouth was tight with resentment.

But his eyes followed her every movement. "Filled with sympathy and compassion, aren't you?"

"For those who need it? You betcha." She glared back at him for a long second before returning to her work. The sharp edge of contempt in his eyes bothered her, but she wasn't sure why. What she did know was that he was ticking her off. And once more that disturbing sense that she was missing something here peeked out of the shadows. "You want to know if I have compassion, buster? Sympathy? Up to here." Head down, she motioned to her chin. "But you? You're a waste of my time, you and all the other bozos who make messes because you're careless or just looking for a good time. I have to do the clean-up after you've had your fun. And sometimes, Claus," she poked him in the chest, "sometimes I get damned tired of deliberate self-destruction. I don't have the patience for it. There are people out there," she gestured vaguely toward the world beyond the curtain, "people with real problems, problems they haven't caused, and you've just created a paper-producing, time-consuming mess that I'm not in the mood to deal with." She slapped the irrigation needle and bottle down on the tray. "Not tonight."

"Long speech. It's a wonder you didn't pop a gasket holding all those words in this long."

"No speech. Telling it like it is." Finished with the irrigation, she yanked the edge of the beard around his jaw. "Beard's got to go, Claus. I can't stitch the wound with this mess dangling in the way."

He turned. His face was suddenly too close, his warm, coffee-scented breath mingling with hers, the strands of his beard tangling with her hair. He reached up, those long fingers separating the commingled strands, and his palm brushed against her cheek, lightly, accidentally.

Then, as if he weren't aware of his movement, as if his fingers moved with an unwanted will of their own, he tucked her hair behind her ear, a curiously personal touch that rippled all the way down her body to her toes, curling them in her damp green socks.

She blinked.

He frowned, dropped his hand.

Sophie spun to her feet. The stool wobbled and rolled away, careened into the wall. Like a crazed horse, her blood leapt and bolted through her veins.

Behind her, Santa cleared his throat.

Snapping open the supply cabinet, she pulled out cotton swabs and rubbing alcohol. As if it had a memory of its own, her ear still tingled where he'd touched. She stared blindly at the objects in her hands.

Coffee-fragrant? No smell of liquor on his breath? Alcohol stink only on his clothes?

She glanced back over her shoulder. His eyes were tired, bloodshot. Drifting shut, but focused.

That didn't fit either.

Caught up in her irritation, she'd missed that sharpness.

And there was that damned, niggling sense that she should *know* him.

Not wanting to look at him, not wanting to be stranded in the unsettling ocean of his gaze, she pivoted and began pulling at the sticky edges of his beard, lifting it from his neck. She rubbed the alcohol-dampened swabs along his jawline, working swiftly, loosening the glued-on beard until it fell free.

And all the while her hands skimmed along his jaw and chin, she thought about the contradictions and that warm, intimate scent of him.

Tossing the blood-soaked mass of beard and swabs into the waste container, she turned and saw his face, fully, for the first time.

"Nice bedside manner, Dr. Brennan." Santa was motionless.

"Oh, hell."

His face was one of those southern Florida faces she'd come to recognize, long, all bones and angles. His blue eyes watched her carefully now, eyes she really, *really* should have recognized staring at her from a face that had given her sleepless nights for months.

"Swell to see you haven't lost your gentle touch," he said. *Not a drunken bum after all.*

"Why didn't you say something as soon as I walked in?" Her throat was tight, squeezing shut.

"My name's on the chart. You should have seen it. I wondered if you knew who I was."

"I didn't look at the name. Detective Finnegan." A sigh, the name slipped out as she stared at him.

"Yeah. Me. In the flesh. Alive and well. Disappointed, Sophie?" A flame that burned cold, challenge flickered in his chilly eyes.

After that first appalled glance, she couldn't look at him. Still, she was proud of herself. Her hand didn't tremble. She hadn't flinched. But Finnegan would have heard a thousand things in the sound of his name. Even during their short time together a year ago, his ability to analyze every little bit of body language and nuance of voice had astonished her. Even then, even under the awful circumstances that came later.

On that disastrous Christmas Eve that changed everything between them.

Oh, yes, even then Detective Finnegan had been good at reading between the lines.

Both hands bracing him on the table, he leaned closer, so close that it was all she could do not to lean back as he murmured, "I didn't know you were on duty, Doctor."

She wouldn't move an inch. Not for Finnegan, she wouldn't. Not for anything he threw her way. "Why? You would have gone to a different hospital?"

"Hell, yeah. I don't care if this *is* the only hospital in the county. If I'd known you were working ER tonight, I would have driven myself one-handed down to Sarasota instead of coming here. But here I am. And here you are. Fate's a bitch sometimes, isn't she?" His thin mouth tightened. "So, Dr. Brennan's on duty the day after Thanksgiving."

"Where else would I be?" She made the mistake of looking up.

"At Home Depot? Picking out a tree?" The tubing lifted with his shrug. "And if I'd had the least bit of luck tonight, another town? Another state?"

With jerky movements, she lifted the suture tray from the counter and placed it near the stretcher. Damn Judah Finnegan. Taking a deep, steadying breath she faced him, her smile as false as the tatty fur on his Santa suit. "I'm needed here." In spite of herself, that year-old pain spilled out. "Besides, you look as though you've done enough celebrating tonight for both of us."

"Appearances to the contrary, I don't do trees, Christmas, or jolly." Aggression radiated from every line of his long torso. "I'm not really a holiday kind of guy."

"No, I suppose you wouldn't be. Not under the circumstances." She tightened her mouth and stared down at the suddenly foreign needles and antiseptic, a fine tremble now vibrating from her to the plastic tray.

"No, not under the circumstances."

"But time passes. Things change. People change. Life goes on."

"Not for all of us." Gripping her chin with one hand, he forced her to look at him. Too thin with all those severe angles and hollows, his face was still compelling in its strength, a strength even she had to acknowledge. "And how tacky of me to bring up Christmas, huh, Sophie?" His fingers were cold against her flushed skin. "But I had to know. I would have bet a thousand dollars you'd forgotten. After all, hey, it's been a year."

"Really? You think you know me that well, Finnegan? How nervy can you get?" She jerked her head free.

"Pretty damn nervy when the occasion calls for it," he said, tapping her with controlled ferocity on the chin. "But hell, yeah, sugar. You bet I've got your number. I think you put that episode with my partner out of your mind the minute you left the hospital last Christmas Eve. I wouldn't have expected anything else, not from you. Not after the run-ins you and George had already had. You had it in for him from the get-go—''

''Never—''

''Sure you did. You and George were oil and water. Yeah, he was loud and crude. A jerk sometimes. But that night, hell. *That* night the patient was more than just another drunk who'd screwed up on Christmas Eve.'' He leaned forward until his face was all she could see. ''*That* night you couldn't wait to run the blood test. Because it was George. Because he bugged you. Because he was mouthy and vulgar. You prissed up like a prune every time he came within five feet of you. It was George. It was personal.''

''No!''

''Shoot, sugar, your little butt was just quivering with righteousness. I thought you were going to cheer when the test proved Roberts was DUI.''

''He wrecked his cop car. He hit a light pole with the squad car, for God's sake. He was lucky—'' She stopped, appalled, wishing she could take the words back.

''You think he was lucky?'' Finnegan smiled, a smile as bitter as any she'd ever seen. ''Yeah, Roberts was lucky that the suits would probably let him ride the desk for the last three months before his retirement. Sure, he was going to be disgraced, demoted. His pension cut. Hell, you're right. He was lucky.'' He paused, and then, as smoothly as a surgeon's scalpel, he added, ''Personally, I never could figure out what the big deal was. Sure didn't seem to me like he had any reason to go home that night and eat his gun.''

Instruments clattered on the tray she held.

''Or didn't you know what happened to Sgt. George Roberts?''

''I read about his suicide in the *Herald* the next day.''

''And what did you think, when you read that bit of news? Anything? Feel bad about how you'd handled things? Wished you'd done anything different?''

"What I felt or didn't feel isn't any of your business. I did what had to be done."

"Did you?" Soft, soft the accusation.

"You bet I did." She'd walk across glass before she'd let him inside her soul to know how she felt about that night. Any doubts or second thoughts were hers and hers alone. "Now get out of the rest of your suit, Detective. I can't stitch you up like this."

"Oh? I thought you could do anything. I thought you knew everything. You sure seemed damned certain you knew best last year. No doubts. No hesitation. Just a 'gotcha' for George."

In the face of his bitterness, Sophie fell like a drowning woman on the raft of professional competence. She motioned to the green suture kit. "I'm going to numb the area before I sew you up."

"Why bother?" With his free hand, he jerked apart the Velcro tabs along the front of his Santa suit. "Just more needle sticks." Shark-like, his teeth flashed as he shrugged off the padded belly and jacket, letting them fall in a blood-red pile on the floor. "Besides, you might enjoy it too much."

"I might." She saw the rest of the old scar that curved down over his ribs and flat stomach to the tight semi-circle of his navel. "But I'm the doctor and you're the patient. Guess you'll have to trust me, won't you?" She smiled in return, a smile as controlled and taunting as his had been. But her stomach twisted in knots.

"Trust you, Sophie? Lord, that prospect makes me shake in my boots. But stitch away. If you can stand it, I can." He winced as she dabbed cold antiseptic along the line of the wound. "But hurry up. I have to get back to a stakeout."

"Right," she said, her grim face reflected back to her from the shine of the table. "Right. Whatever you want, Detective."

She bent forward, and as she did, he whispered into the curve of her ear, his warm breath sliding around the rim and curling deep inside her. "In case you were wondering, Dr. Sugar, I've already filled out the police report. This was a job-related injury." Contempt lifted the corners of his mouth. "You don't have to worry that I'm getting away with anything."

For a moment she paused. There were things she could say, *should* say. She wouldn't. He was her patient. She'd give him the same care she gave everyone. The same care she'd given his partner last Christmas Eve. She could do that. And then he'd be gone.

She stitched. Silently. She didn't trust her unruly tongue.

And the entire time she felt the burn of his eyes on the back of her neck as she bent to her task. Doggedly she moved the curved needle through his skin and wondered why in the name of all things good, Judah Finnegan had landed in her ER tonight.

She dressed the wound. Silently.

But even as her brain registered the animosity that rose like shimmers of heat from him, she was aware, too, at a tactile level, of his sleek skin and the supple muscles beneath it. Aware of the heavy stillness between them, a stillness and silence that would take only a movement, a word to turn into something…reckless.

She smoothed down the last piece of tape and took a deep breath. Almost home free.

As if she'd spoken aloud, Finnegan moved suddenly, his thigh brushing her hip.

She stepped back, a shade too quickly, but he remained seated.

"Done." She handed him the list of instructions. "I need to go over these with you. One of the nurses will explain—"

The curtain flew open behind Sophie. She turned, relieved. "Oh, good, here's—"

"Dr. Brennan!" Cammie stood there, the chubby shine of her face flattened with tension.

Just over Cammie's shoulder Sophie glimpsed Billy Ray's

ponytail swinging against the back of his shirt as he hovered in the hall.

"Room 4. Code Blue."

The beating victim.

There would be no miracles tonight.

Sophie dropped the instructions on the examining table, shoved her pen into her pocket, and pointed a finger at Finnegan. "You. Sit. Stay!" Her coat billowed around her as she ran to catch up with Cammie, who'd already disappeared.

The muttered "woof" behind her didn't even slow her steps.

Finnegan eased off the table. He watched her race down the hall, her shoes jingling.

Sophie's curly hair bounced wildly against her white medical jacket. Dark brown with the glow of fire. Not red exactly but not brown either. There was a word for it. *Russet.* Yeah. That was it. The gray material of her skirt bunched and pulled against the length of her thighs as she darted between oncoming techs, hands out, warning them out of her way.

Long, smooth-muscled thighs.

His fingers curled around the curtain. When she'd leaned in close to him, she'd smelled of cinnamon and pumpkin.

And antiseptic.

In a full-out run behind her, a tech followed with a crash cart.

Electricity buzzed along his skin. Whatever was happening was bad. He understood that sudden crackle in the air—like ozone before a storm. He'd smelled it on stakeouts gone sour.

It was always bad.

He watched as Sophie and her colleagues entered a room at the end of the hall and shut the door. For a second everything down the long corridor slowed down, became too quiet, one of those moments between a breath, a moment between life and death. Irrevocable what the next tick of the clock would bring.

He knew that too.

And then, as if everyone had inhaled, exhaled, movement and noise resumed. Only an occasional furtive glance at the closed door revealed the enormity of the moment.

Finnegan glanced at the examining table in back of him. Nothing there that he needed. Nothing more he needed or wanted in this place. Shrugging, he pulled the curtain silently shut behind him and walked toward the exit, stepped out into the night and took a deep breath of his own, sucking the damp air deep into his lungs.

Life and death. A thin line, nothing more than a second or a wrong turn, a wrong word, separated the two.

An hour later, heartsick and exhausted to her bones, sweat beading her forehead, Sophie returned to the examining room and shoved the curtain aside.

A pile of red velvet and bloodied white acrylic lay puddled on the floor of the empty room.

Chapter 2

In a cold, driving rain at two in the morning, they found the baby lying in the manger of the Second Baptist Church, directly across the street from Beth Israel, the only synagogue in the tri-county area.

"What the hell," Finnegan muttered as rain spat into his eyes and seeped down the neck of his yellow slicker.

"Lord have mercy." Tyree Jones squatted and reached under the rough wood roof of the manger. His broad dark hand touched the cradle, hesitated. Rain dripped from the edges of the straw spilling over the edges of the cradle. "Shoot, man, it's a baby, that's what."

The spotlight in the shelter shone down on the baby. Chocolate-brown eyes stared back at them.

"I can see it's a baby, Tyree, an Asian baby, in fact. The punk knifed my shoulder. Not my eyes. What's a baby doing here?"

"All right, I'll play." Tyree's forefinger brushed against the baby's cheek. "What?"

"Damn it to hell, Tyree. Get the kid out of there. It's got to be freezing." Finnegan rolled his shoulders, easing the ache of the stitches, and stooped down beside Tyree.

"She's not an *it*, Judah. She's an itty-bitty baby girl, that's what she is." Tyree said as Finnegan bent over him and scooped her up with one hand, tucking the pink Winnie-the-Pooh sheet around her. "What a pretty girl you are, too, honey," Tyree cooed. "Now why'd somebody go off and leave you here all by your lonesome, huh?" Tyree poked his face close to the silent baby.

Coming at them sideways now, the rain sliced against Finnegan's face and drizzled under his slicker. "Go back to the car and get the blanket. She needs to be kept warm—"

"Judah," Tyree said patiently as he rose to his full six feet three, "I have babies of my own. I know what to do."

"Yeah, reckon you do, all right." Holding the baby in a football grip, Finnegan shot him a wicked grin.

"Well, shoot, that too." Tyree grinned back and loped toward their unit parked on the sidewalk. "Making babies is part of the *re*-ward, you know?"

"Kids? A reward? I don't know. All those late nights and early mornings. Diapers and all that—"

"Be the same if I still worked patrol. I'd still have late nights, early mornings. More fun my way," Tyree called back as he dashed toward their unmarked car.

Finnegan hunched forward, keeping the baby under the manger roof and near the warmth of the spotlight. "Got a story to tell, don't you?" he said to her before looking off into the shadows at the sides of the church.

Rain glistened against the stained-glass windows. The branches of the huge banyan tree on the right side of the church lifted with the wind. Rain drummed the wide leaves and streamed to the ground. "You sure didn't walk here by yourself."

Considering him carefully, the baby's eyes followed his face.

"Not very talkative? Can't say I blame you." Judah

looked toward the unit, turning carefully so he wouldn't slop water from his slicker onto the baby. "Not a fit night for dogs to be out. Much less you." He looked away from the solemn face. Sheesh. Somebody dumping a baby on a night like this. On any night. What a world. First the undercover Santa lookout earlier in the evening, now this. No wonder a cop's job was never done.

In the blaze of the car's dome light, he could see Tyree speaking into the mike, shaking his head.

Huffing back, Tyree pulled the cotton blanket out from under his slicker and tossed it to Finnegan. "Nobody's reported a lost baby tonight. Nothing but an anonymous call into dispatch saying we should check out the prowlers at the Second Baptist."

"Prowlers?" Judah looked off into the darkness of the wind-whipped trees and back down at the unprotesting lump in his arms. "Funny kind of call, don't you think? No prowler left this package."

"Nope. Probably the mom. Not wanting to leave our little darlin' completely alone."

"You're figuring it was the mom, then?"

"Most likely. Some kind of twisted maternal instinct."

"Could be. I don't know." Judah stared back at Tyree's face gleaming with rain and shadowy reflections. "*Prowler?* That's an odd word choice, isn't it? I think a mother abandoning her kid would refer to the kid as 'my baby.' 'My child.' Something, anyway, that would give a heads-up about an infant. But not *prowler.* It would be interesting to find out who made the call."

"Going to worry it like a dawg with a bone, aren't you? I swear, you think too much sometimes, Judah." Tyree swiped rain out of his eyes. "Anyway, my man, whatever, whoever, our orders are to have li'l missy here checked out at our fine medical facility. Guess we'll be making another run to your favorite establishment." He sent Finnegan a sly, sideways look. "Some nights just don't get any better, do they? This one's been a world-beater. Got to play Santa, saved a baby, and now you get to revisit your favorite doc.''

"We haven't been riding together long enough for you to go there, Tyree. Back off.''

White teeth sparkled as the big man gave him a huge grin. "So? I got my opinions. You gonna beat me up because I say what I see, Judah? You with that baby slung under your arm like you're ready to gallop into some end zone? Huh? You think you can take me?'' His grin glinted again as he did a little two-step in the rain, his arms moving in a smooth rhythm. He tapped Judah lightly on the chest, the shoulder. "Bring it on, then.''

"Oh, go to hell, Tyree.'' Hunching over and draping his slicker across the baby, Finnegan stomped off toward the car. "It's a wonder Yvonna hasn't whomped you upside the head, you know that?''

"Hey, I'm Yvonna's sweet-talking man.'' He slid under the steering wheel, fired up the engine, and slammed the door.

The baby jerked in Finnegan's arms. He laid his hand lightly across her forehead. Too warm.

"Sorry 'bout that, baby girl. Didn't mean to spook you.'' The low velvet of Tyree's words moved through the darkness, easing the sudden tension. Not looking at Judah, Tyree added quietly, "We got to talk about George sometime. You know we do.''

"No. We do not.''

"Fine. Be a jackass. But I'll still be your partner.''

Finnegan clipped his seat belt in place and settled the still-silent child into his arm. "That can be changed, too, Tyree.''

"Partners share, Judah. That's all I'm saying. We've partnered for four months now. And you don't share. Ever. Hard enough being a black cop in this town without wondering if my partner's gonna be at my back.''

For a long moment there was only the hiss of the heavy tires and the sound of the rain beating against the windows. Finnegan ran the back of his forefinger over the baby's cheek and stared out at the neon lights sliding past in the darkness. The slap-slap of the windshield wipers punctuated the silence.

He sighed. "I've got your back, Tyree."

"Okay, then." Tyree let out a sigh of his own. "Didn't mean to push so hard."

"Yeah, you did." Finnegan scooched down farther into his seat, adjusting the quiet infant against him. "You realize you're plumb irritatin', don't you?"

"Hell, yes." Tyree's smile was quick and open. "Part of my charm."

"Whoever said that was a damned fool."

"Hey, man, don't you go insulting my Yvonna, hear?" They slid to a stop under the protected entrance of Poinciana's ER. Water spurted onto the side windows. "Not if you want any more of her potato salad."

"Well, there you go then. Obviously Yvonna, a woman of brilliance and charm of her own, has adopted you as her very own charity case, Tyree. That's the only explanation." Yanking the hood of his slicker up with one hand, Finnegan hoisted the blanket over the baby, tucked her under his rain gear and slid out of the car. As he did, he added, "But in spite of her unfortunate taste in husbands, I sure do admire that woman's potato salad."

At his sudden movements, the baby waved its tiny fist under the blanket, gave a burp of movement and then lay still again as Judah shouldered his way through the ER doors.

He saw her, of course.

It had been that kind of night from the start. One screwup after another. Why should he expect anything else at the end of a lousy day?

A flicker of movement caught his gaze, nothing more than her arm rising to her forehead, but he slowed. He wanted to look away, felt the urge so strongly that he almost believed for a second that he was walking toward the desk and the crowd of people in front of it.

But something about her gesture checked him, rooting him to the floor.

Unable to look away from the figure at the end of the hall, he watched her.

And resented her because he couldn't look away. Resented the power she had to compel his attention.

Resented her most of all because he didn't *want* to look away.

They were standing close together, Sophie and another doctor, the man stooping down to her. Her head was bowed. She'd jammed her hands into her pockets. From time to time she nodded as the man jabbed his finger in the air. With each nod, her dark hair bounced, swung forward, hid her expression.

It was the slump in her shoulders that held Finnegan's attention.

Exhaustion.

Defeat.

He understood defeat, its nasty-ass gut-punch. That's what his eyes read in the sag of her shoulders, in the brace of her sneaker against the wall behind her.

He just hadn't figured cocksure, bold-as-brass Sophie Brennan for someone who'd ever look this defeated.

This diminished.

All the sparking, combative energy had drained away, leaving her small and helpless, the bells on her goofy socks silent.

Suddenly, as if he'd whispered in her ear, Sophie's head jerked upright. She looked straight at him for a long moment.

Judah held her gaze, willing her to blink.

She didn't.

The infinitesimal lift of her chin was the only sign that she saw him.

No, he thought. Not helpless at all. Not Sophie.

"*Hola,* tall, dark and battered. Back so soon? It's only been three hours. Got something else you want sutured?"

"No thanks. And it's been four hours." He glared down

at the woman tapping him impatiently on the arm. The picture ID clipped to the pocket of her blue scrubs gave him her name. *Cammie Esposito*. The same short, round-faced nurse who'd rushed Sophie out of the examining room earlier.

"What in the world do you have there? Not somebody's pet poodle, I hope? We don't do pets. Even for good-looking *hombres* like you, *amigo*."

He pushed his parcel toward her. Once more a miniature fist pushed free of the blanket and banged his hand, a soft graze of skin against skin.

She lifted the edge of the blanket. "Oh, my." All teasing gone, She took the baby from him and turned abruptly toward Sophie and the man still with her. "Dr. Brennan, you'll want to see this."

Sophie's clear voice rode lightly over the relative quiet of the ER. "Sure, Cammie. Be right there. What's the problem?"

"A baby."

"A *baby?*"

He watched as Sophie pushed off from the wall, watched as she straightened her shoulders, and he recognized the effort. Like the last embers flaring in a gust of wind before dying out, she suddenly glowed. Even her hair gleamed now with that touch of firelight he'd noticed before sparking in the dark curls.

Her hands were still jammed in her pockets, though.

He noticed that, too, and wondered about that bit of body language and what it might mean.

Details.

His preacher daddy had been a humorless man with meanness bred bone deep. All his passion had been spent in an adoration of God that left no room for love of humankind. But he'd said one good thing to Judah. Judah didn't believe in anything else his daddy had said, but he'd never forgotten the old man's beautiful voice, sonorous, one of those hypnotic magic voices that could fill the pews of their small church, pronouncing, "God is in the details, Judah," he pronounced. "Don't you be forgetting that. You pay attention, hear?"

Then the preacher man had slapped him twice, once on each side of his face. Hard enough to leave a bruise. "Hear me?"

Judah heard.

And he'd remembered.

In his experience he'd concluded it was more likely the devil he discovered in the details. Still, he'd found that bit of instruction to be one of the few useful bits of his father's legacy.

If Tyree knew it was Judah's pa who'd taught him the basic rule of being a detective, Jonas suspected Tyree would hoot about that, too.

George had known.

With a quick tap on his arm, the nurse interrupted the melancholy flow of his memories. "What a doll. Girl?"

He nodded.

"*Oye, muy bonita. Pobrecita.* What's the story?"

"It's…*she's*…" he corrected himself, "*she's* been outside a while. Don't know how long, though." He rubbed his hands along the side of his slicker and water sluiced off, dripping to the floor and splashing against his jeans. "It's a rough night. Don't know anything about babies, but she seems okay. A bit warm, maybe. Quiet."

"*Sí,* this baby's come to the right place."

Judah shifted as Sophie reached him.

"Detective." Her expression dismissed him.

The hairs along his arms rose lightly as her scent reached him. "Doctor," he replied politely.

Her gray-blue eyes glittered momentarily, then flickered to the bundle. "What brings you back this evening?" Her tone was cool and crisp.

"Morning, actually," he said, matching her coolness.

"So it is. Do you need our attention again? Or have you

managed to keep yourself out of harm's way for a few hours?''

''I'm not your patient this time.'' He pointed to the nurse's blanket.

Sophie leaned toward the bundle, peered inside the blanket, and that scent that wasn't perfume, wasn't exactly soap, wasn't anything except *her* filled his nostrils.

Funny, he thought, amused by his body's awareness of her. An awareness he didn't want, but there it was. That old devil sex could rear up and trip a man when he least wanted it.

Or expected it.

He'd thought this past year had made him immune to the very particular appeal of Dr. Brennan.

On edge, he gestured toward the baby. ''Well. She's all yours. I'm out of here.''

Sophie's warm hands brushed against him as she lifted the baby out of the nurse's arms and cradled her. Sophie's face went soft, as soft as the curves of her breasts where the baby lay, and he thought he saw sadness in her eyes as she touched the baby gently and said, ''Ah, you're a little love, aren't you? Let's go see how you're doing, sweetie-pie.'' Her hands moved lightly over the baby, automatically evaluating, examining.

Finnegan turned around, ready to make tracks for the outside as fast as his size elevens would take him.

''Not so fast this time, Finnegan. We need some information first.''

Damn. ''Whatever you say, doctor.'' He gritted his teeth and swung back to her.

''What can you tell me about this baby?''

''Diddly squat. We found her at the Second Baptist Church, in the manger, under its roof. Nobody else was there. She doesn't look abused, she doesn't look like a newborn, but of course I'm not the *doctor*—'' he let the word take a bit of ice ''—and that's all the information I have.''

Sophie's gaze flickered from the baby to the nurse. ''You know what I'm thinking?''

"Makes sense," the nurse responded as she stared at the baby and then down the hall. "Might explain what the woman kept crying out, I guess."

"Awful big coincidence otherwise."

"Still, it could be coincidence. It's not as though she's the first Asian patient here in Poinciana."

"And not the first beating victim, either. We're getting a lot of them lately." Anger rippled over her face. "And not just our Asian population. Boy, this is lousy. What in heaven's name is happening to Poinciana?" Her eyes were huge, dominating the soft roundness of her face.

Judah shook his head, fighting for clarity. He was finally free of the baby, but something she'd said had struck him as important. He shook his head again. Got it. "Coincidence? What coincidence?"

Sophie's mouth tightened as she glanced from the baby to him. "A patient we had earlier."

He forced his brain to focus. "A patient?"

"A woman. Beaten."

"What happened?"

"She died."

"I see." He scratched the bristles on his chin. "You think this is her baby?"

"I don't know, Finnegan." Her sigh echoed his own fatigue. Her gaze returned to the baby. "It's all such craziness."

"You'll get no argument from me on that score."

"Really? How remarkable." Her quick glance mocked him. Taking the warmed blanket from the nurse, she passed him the one in which he and Tyree had cocooned the baby. "This little girl looks all right. We'll give her a thorough work-up and then—" She frowned. "Children and Families will take over. You know how the system works. It's the way it is."

"Yeah. I reckon." Every inch of his skin twitched with the need to go home, collapse on his bed and sleep for a day.

Or a week. How many hours had he been on duty? When was the last time he'd slept? Last night? The day before?

Every cell in his battered body craved relief from the fizzing running through him when he was around Sophie. He didn't know which he wanted more—sleep, or just a release from the tension she created in him.

Every instinct he owned urged him toward her.

It had been like that from the first moment he'd seen her, jogging down Palmetto Avenue, her hair clumped together by a green clip on top of her head, beads of sweat pooling in the small triangle at the bottom of her throat. Beneath fire-engine-red frayed shorts, her thighs and calf muscles pumped and thrust.

And heat had licked through him like a flash fire.

He hadn't even thought about what he was doing. He'd simply nudged the squad car over to the curb, letting it roll forward with her for a few minutes until she finally glanced his way.

She'd sent him a smart-alecky grin, saluted with a quick hand to her forehead, and shot off, her legs like slim pistons flickering in the late August heat as she disappeared into the path that curved along Poinciana River.

That was how it had started.

Dangerous, being this tired and this pissed off. Remembering. Remembering never led anywhere good.

A faint stirring of adrenaline roughened his voice. "Do I have permission to leave now, Doctor?"

Even as he spoke, she was already walking away toward one of the examining rooms, her head bent to the baby.

The nurse, *Cammie,* he made himself remember, sent him a quick smile and a thumbs-up.

And once more he found himself treated to the fine sight of Sophie Brennan's butt, its curves shaping the jacket to her, the jacket moving with each hip sway. He swallowed. His mouth was dust-dry, the night's fatigue vanished momentarily in a rush of blood.

"Look, but don't touch, right?" Tyree's smooth amusement snapped his head around. "Caught you, didn't I?"

"What?"

"My, my, aren't we grouchy? Guess doing without will make a man…irritable."

"I was thinking, Tyree."

"Sure you were, Judah. And I'll bet you a nice, green hundred-dollar bill I know exactly what you were thinking." His grin widened, crinkling his whole face. "Looks like it wasn't the first time, too."

Judah scowled at him. "Button it, Tyree."

"Can't blame you. The doc sure is one fine-looking woman." He laughed. "But don't tell Yvonna I said that, or I won't be getting so much as a sweet kiss for a month."

"Serve you right."

"Nah, you don't know Yvonna. She can be one tough lady when she puts her mind to it. She can make my life real…interesting when she wants to."

"Yeah?" Judah listened with one ear, his attention still on Sophie.

"Anyway, c'mon. Another call came in while you were in here."

"Right." Judah's gaze stayed on Sophie as she hovered over the baby, her every movement visible through the still-open curtain.

He couldn't get over her—foggy-headed, he couldn't find the word he wanted. *Protectiveness.* Yeah. He rubbed his head again. That was the word. She seemed so protective of the tiny scrap of life he'd brought to her.

Not cold at all.

Not at all the way she'd been with George.

And none of the prickliness she showed him.

One more puzzle piece.

But he couldn't make sense of any of it until he'd had a couple of hours of sleep.

"Hey, Judah. Heads up. We're needed over on 15th and

Oak.'' Tyree tugged at him, and with one last glance, Judah left, the glass doors snicking shut behind him.

"Detective Hunkster has left the house." Cammie poked Sophie in the ribs.

"What?" Sophie lifted her stethoscope and patted the baby, her palm lingering and warming the tiny chest.

Cammie pointed to the exit. "The detective with the hormones and the 'tude."

"Oh." Lifting the baby, Sophie curled her over one shoulder, close to her neck. She looked toward the exit. The baby mewed softly and nuzzled closer. "What a sweetheart you are." Reflexively she cupped the baby's bottom, swaying slowly from side to side, rocking the infant.

She could barely make out the faces of Finnegan and his partner. A gust of wind puffed out Finnegan's yellow slicker. Rain striped down his faded jeans, and he yanked the slicker closer to him, rolled his shoulder and vanished into the darkness.

His shoulder had to be hurting him. Anybody with any sense would have stayed and taken the pain scripts. But the stubborn idiot had chosen to assert himself and leave her ER instead of doing the sensible thing.

For all she cared, he could fall down in a heap if that's what he wanted.

Absently she crooned to the warm baby.

Still, Judah had looked like the burnt end of a match when she'd walked up to him and Cammie. Stubble shadowed his cheeks, and black circles pouched the skin under his eyes. He'd looked like a hundred miles of bad road, as she'd heard one of the local doctors say.

Faded jeans, a look of weary dissipation, and that attitude. Attitude to burn.

But sexy.

It was in the eyes, she decided. He had that look about him that women talked about in hushed tones. The kind of man who would be hell on wheels in bed. The kind of man who could leave a woman smiling in the morning. Oh, no question. She knew exactly what Cammie meant about hormones. Judah Finnegan fairly reeked of pheromones and sex.

Dirty, lowdown, wonderful sex.

She'd felt the flutter of her pulse every time she'd thought of him during this past year.

He was exactly the wrong kind of man for a woman like her.

Even without their history.

Sergeant George Roberts might be dead, but even a year later his presence was a powerful ghost.

The night Roberts had killed himself he'd also killed the tenuous *something* building between her and Detective Finnegan.

Maybe if they'd had more time together first…

Maybe if they'd slept together…

No, she didn't think so.

If they'd slept together? Impossible.

She'd known from the beginning that Judah was a man who kept his emotions under tight control. That had been part of the attraction. He was so different from her that it was tempting to see what it would take to make him lose that reserve. A buzz-cut, reined-in kind of guy, he wasn't a man easily given to showing his emotions. Or handing out forgiveness.

Except with Roberts.

Cammie tapped her arm. "Want me to call the Department of Children and Family Services?"

"Yes, please." Sophie looked away from the empty glass doors. "Until we find out where our little angel belongs, that's our only choice. I hope the woman who died wasn't her mother. I hope that somewhere out there is someone who's looking for this beautiful baby." Near her breast the tiny mouth moved damply, tugging at something deep inside her. "This little girl doesn't deserve to be thrown into the system. Be passed around from foster home to foster home." Sophie found her arms curling possessively around the infant. "She needs parents, Cammie. A mother."

"All the babies do. It's not our decision, though." Cammie looked away. "If her parents or relatives can't be located...you know how it is, Dr. Brennan. Like you told your cop. That's where she'll wind up."

"I do. It's a hard world sometimes, Cammie."

"It is. Nothing we can do about it. It is what it is."

Sophie shifted the baby to her other shoulder, settling her in snugly. "How long have you worked at Poinciana? Have things changed so much?"

Cammie shrugged.

"Because in the two years I've been here, it seems as though we're seeing a lot more gunshots and beatings. Abused babies and kids. Or is it my imagination? I haven't checked the hospital statistics." Sophie tried to smile past the ache in her heart. "I know what you said earlier, but tell me it's my imagination and the result of too many long hours, Cammie. Please. I need to believe that."

"Poinciana's a good town. People are good here. Most of them are. But, *sí,* things have changed. There's a different feel to the town these days. All this graffiti springing up everywhere, overnight, it seems. Kids hijacking the Santa kettles. And these fires at places of worship, for heaven's sake. Sometimes, I am afraid. It doesn't feel like my town anymore. Not the Poinciana I knew."

From the corner of her eye Sophie glimpsed stringy hair. She turned, snuggling the baby closer. "What is it, Billy Ray?"

"I wanted to see the baby. They said the baby was here." He edged around the curtain into the examining room. "Is the baby all right?"

"Yes."

His face scrunched up in something that she thought might be relief. "Okay, then. I was wondering, that's all. What's going to happen to her?"

"She'll stay here for a day or two for observation. We'll see if anyone can identify her." Even saying the words felt so wrong to Sophie that she stumbled over them. "If she's healthy and we haven't found her family, then Social Services will come and take her to an out-placement home."

Billy Ray twisted a strand of his hair. "That's okay. I guess. She's safe, isn't she?"

"Sure she is." Sophie held up the baby girl so Billy Ray could see her.

Sleepy brown eyes peered over the edge of the light blanket as Billy Ray leaned farther into the room. He chewed his lip. "She looks okay then. Okay. I gotta go finish my shift."

And as abruptly as he'd appeared, he vanished.

Sophie watched him lurch away. "Did Billy Ray seem more Billy Rayish than usual? Or is that my imagination, too?"

Cammie laughed and reached for the baby. "He's been Billy Rayish all night long. There's a full moon. I'll take the baby up to pediatrics and then alert Social Services. I see Dr. Bornes is finally here. You can head for home now, can't you?"

An inexplicable reluctance kept Sophie's arms around the fragile bundle. She stared down at the silky eyebrows and wide-open eyes watching her. "Oh, you decided to wake up and join the party, did you, sweetheart?"

From the safety of her blanket, Baby Doe reached up and caught a curl of Sophie's hair and gripped for all she was worth, holding on as if she'd never let go, holding on as if she had understood every word Sophie and Cammie said.

Holding on to Sophie as if she were a lifeline.

"Cammie, I'll take her up to Peds. And hold off on the call to Children and Families, okay?" she said abruptly and headed out the door.

With every step Sophie took down the long hall, she felt that tiny grip grow more powerful.

Felt those tiny fingers close around her heart.

Chapter 3

Hours later, as night melted into gray pre-dawn, Finnegan found himself at the beach off the island.

He hadn't slept.

Earlier, Tyree had dropped him off at the station. Judah had waved him off, fired up his bike and taken off into a world filled with drumming rain. Blending with the roar of rain and wind, the Harley six-cylinder engine throbbed beneath him.

They were off-duty. It was time to go home.

He meant to go home.

He really, *really* meant to go home.

But he'd thought about the baby. Laying there in the manger for over an hour before they'd taken it to the hospital. He shook his head and slewed rain drops off his helmet. Not *it. Her.* Taken *her* to the ER.

To Sophie, who'd cradled that baby to her as if the tiny mite was her own.

Sophie, whose pale skin and big eyes had swallowed her

face and whose scent lingered treacherously in his nostrils. A Judas of the senses, that perfume that was only Sophie.

Streaking down back roads and over bayou bridges, he'd lifted his face to the rain, let it wash over him, and he still smelled *her,* the scent of woman underneath the cinnamon and antiseptic.

Even with the sensory memories flooding him, the memory that sent a shiver of foreboding down him was the one of Sophie holding the baby.

An hour before dawn, with rain blinding him and Sophie's scent filling him, he'd braked hard, tires screaming against slippery pavement, and headed west over one more bridge.

To the island.

To her house.

To Sophie.

He told himself he could interview her there just as well as at the hospital or the station house. No problem. He was cool. She didn't have any power over him. He was immune. The interview would be official, nothing more.

A less honest man would have believed it, too.

Even so, even knowing he was being a damn bonehead, he crouched over the Harley and rode its rumbling engine into the storm wind. To Sophie.

The thought of her name brought her face in front of him, mixed the remembered scent of her with the clean rain smell and sent his blood skipping and slipping through his veins.

He didn't pretend that the pulsing in his groin had anything at all to do with the throbbing of the bike beneath him. He didn't want to *see* her again.

He wanted to...

And so he'd whipped the bike around and damned himself for a fool as he flew onto the bridge, coming down with a hard bounce that jolted him to the top of his aching shoulder.

Now, a surly gray sky shrouded gray surf thundering onto the beach. Storm-driven salt spray stung his face, clung to a two-day stubble and dripped down his jacket. Gritty with sand and sleeplessness, his eyes burned as he peered through rain and mist at the surf.

She was out there.

Far out on the horizon where the Gulf of Mexico blurred into the sky, he could see the narrow stripe of black against gray that was Sophie.

She hadn't slept either.

Hunkered down, nothing more than a shadow in shadows on the beach, he watched as she rose from bended knees. She crouched over the board, riding the power, waiting. Her small hands gripped the side of the board. Then, balanced, steady, she stood upright, arms flung out parallel to the board.

He inhaled.

Breathtaking, that small shape out there in all that darkness, facing nature's might. He clasped his hands tightly against his knees.

Watched.

And waited with her. Forever, it seemed, in those moments as he watched powerless.

Behind her the wave hung for a long time. Dark at the base, black in this light, its crest all white foam and shivering green glass.

He thought she hesitated as the wave came up under her. She was in the backwash. She bent her knees again, curved forward, and the wave took her, enveloped her like a careless lover. Threw her forward, sent her board spiraling up into the sky and covered her with boiling white water that splashed high into the sky.

Lunging to his feet, Finnegan scanned the distance and couldn't see her, couldn't find that sleek head bobbing in the water. He covered the three yards to the water without realizing he'd moved.

Surf roiled around his knees, clawed at his chest.

Far beyond him her board floated on the surge of a small wave and vanished into a trough.

He couldn't see her anywhere in the pounding waves.

He yanked his shoes off and hurled them toward the shore

behind him, struck out toward the deep. There, right between two waves, he could see her board again, could see now the wet white of her face as she crawled onto the board and slumped. Strands of heavy wet hair hid her face.

Unseen, treading water, he rose and fell on the waves, their bodies joined in the great rhythm of the gulf.

She struggled to hold onto the board, her arms trembling with effort.

Or he imagined the effort. He wasn't sure.

Finally she brought her knees under her.

And waited again.

His eyes never leaving her, Finnegan sank beneath the water and moved slowly toward the shore behind him until his feet scraped against cold sand.

He hauled himself up the incline of the shore. Turning back, he saw her stand.

Behind her, bigger than the wave that had taken her under, a wall of water raced toward him. His throat tightened and in the roar of the waves that filled him, everything went silent. He wondered if her heart was thumping as hard as his. He yelled at her to let the damned wave pass, to wait for a smaller one, not to try this freakish thing leaping out of the Gulf.

The wind caught his shout, shredded it into nonsense.

Half crouched, arms balancing her, Sophie caught the edge of the monster and hung there, for hours it seemed, in the pre-dawn sky. Against the cold sand, his toes buzzed with the power of the wave. He could sense the thrust of the wave as it grew, its glassy green stretching, stretching, filling the horizon with shivering power.

Then, in one perfect moment, it crested, spitting white against the gray sky.

Puny against the glassy green, she rode its momentum all the way to the collapsing crash of soapy foam.

Over the surf noise, her laugh rang with triumph, a bright, bell-like sound, as she trudged to the sand with her board.

Arousal ripped through him. His skin rippled with it. He

could smell it in the air, coming off him like bands of storm waves. He couldn't even hear the surf over the roaring in his ears. His wet jeans flapped against his legs as he strode toward her. Even his fingertips thrummed with the need to—what?

Mid stride, he stopped, took a deep breath. A second one.

He forced himself to stroll toward her and was appalled at the struggle it took.

He'd been stupid.

Was being even more stupid. If he had an ounce of sense, he'd turn and run for the hills before she saw him.

But he didn't.

Instead, water slopping at his heels, he approached her. Blowing off the Gulf, wind plastered his wet clothes to him. He should have been cold to the bone.

He wasn't.

How could he be cold when his blood was pumping so damned hot through him? He half-expected to see steam rising from his every footstep. A pressure cooker of intensity, looking for an escape valve.

Burning even the roots of his wet hair.

He wouldn't have been shocked if he'd swung around and seen a string of black, scorched footprints following him in the sand.

Flopped on the wet sand and facing the storm surge, she didn't see him approaching her.

It gave him that extra second he needed.

It gave him the element of surprise he wanted.

Relief washed over him and left him feeling like a yellow-bellied coward as he pitched his voice lower than the booming waves. "Sophie."

She leapt to her feet. The board bounced to the sand, kicked up a shell. "Finnegan? *Finnegan?*" She was breathing hard, her breasts lifting with her questions. "What—where did you come from? *And why?*" Strands of wet hair clung flatly to her head, lay against her cheek as she stared at him. "Judah. *Here?*"

"Yeah. Me. Here." He stooped and picked up her board, handed it to her.

"Thanks," she said automatically, her face crumpled with confusion. She held the board close to her, and that pulse in her throat was going ninety miles an hour. "You—"

"Scared you?" He'd like to scare her, just a little, just enough to make her drop that brittle mask she wore around him. He wanted to see her without all that clever self-possession, just once.

"Scared? No, no, you startled me. That's all. I thought no one was here." She lifted the board, tamped it onto the sand. "How's your shoulder?"

He shrugged. He hadn't thought about his stitches once since he'd arrived at the beach. "It's okay."

"Good. Do you need any pain meds?"

He must have made a sound.

"No, tough guy, I guess you wouldn't. Need anything, that is." She bounced the board hard against the sand, shifted. "So, Finnegan, exactly how long have you been here?"

"Long enough to see you eat pie on that wave."

She glanced toward the Gulf, gave a small, delighted smile. "Big waves for the Gulf. I hadn't expected anything like this." From the east behind her, light was beginning to stain the sand, tint the water a softer shade of gray. "That beast stripped my rash guard off, right over my head and arms. Gone." She paused before turning her attention back to him. "I hit the backwash. It popped me right off. I couldn't hold it."

"Too bad."

"That's surfing for you." She looked out at the Gulf. "You play in God's ballpark, you pay the price." Absently she rubbed her elbow, calm as all get-out.

Except for that pulse going like a bat out of hell.

Hair flattened against her head, she was a sleek, otter-like silhouette against the lightening gray in her shiny black neoprene. He wanted to sluice the water dripping from her hair with his hands, he wanted to slide those same hands, wet with salt water, down the smooth, shiny curves of her, he wanted to taste that tiny pulse beating like a trapped butterfly under her skin—

She glanced back at him, frowned, the little pulse beat going lickety-split. "So. You've been here a while."

"I have."

He knew the second she regained control. It was caused by a tone in his voice. Or the look on his face. But the confusion softening her face disappeared, the restless shifting back and forth ceased as she registered his comment. She narrowed her eyes. With a quick assessment, she considered his wet clothes, sopping hair, and the seaweed still clinging to his worn jeans. "Looks like you ate pie yourself."

"Not me. You couldn't pay me enough to go out there at this time of day. I sure do admire a shark's efficiency, but I'm not right fond of having breakfast with them. Or being their breakfast. Didn't you know this was feeding time, Yankee Girl?"

"Not much of a risk on this coast. Different if we were down in the Keys."

"There's always a risk."

"Hey, Finnegan, life's full of risks. Don't you know that?" Her laugh was a ripple of sound that furred along his nerve endings and made him catch his breath.

"Remember a couple of years ago? That huge migration of sharks in the Gulf off Tampa? Hundreds of them?"

She shrugged. "Surfing's a controllable risk. I like surfing these fat storm waves. They're as close as I can get to Hawaii. I like dawn patrol. And I like taking risks." She ran her hands over her hair, spraying water onto his bare feet.

"Do you now?" The drops burned against his skin. An errant scent drifted to him and it took him a second to realize that it was the scent of her skin flavored by Gulf and an unknown tension.

"I'm an adrenaline junkie. Otherwise, I'd have chosen some other profession."

"And here I've been thinking it was pure compassion that put you in your doctor whities."

The wind carried the light sound of her laugh behind them, to the east and the still-shrouded sun. "Oh, come on, Finnegan. You know exactly what I'm talking about. Cops feed off that rush. Isn't that fine testosterone rush why most of them go into the job? Isn't it why *you* became a fine boyo in blue? And don't try to play the innocent," she mocked as he hesitated. "Because I know better."

"I never thought about it."

"You should...think about it."

"Are we still talking about cops and robbers? Because all my fine detecting skills pick up something else here," he drawled.

"Really? How perceptive of you." She wrung water out of her hair, sent it spattering again onto his feet. "By the way, where are your shoes, Finnegan? Or are you the original barefoot boy with cheek of tan?" Her eyelashes sparkled with drops of water. Giving off a heat of their own, her eyes glittered.

"I'm a Florida cracker. Of course I'm barefoot." He gave in, yielded to temptation and that siren heat. Reaching out, making himself move slowly, he brushed his forefinger along the edge of her lashes, let it skate slowly down her cheek until his finger rested in the hollow of her neck, just above the zipper of her neoprene vest.

The leap of her vein against his finger sent a painful pulse straight south. He stepped closer, stepped into the heat rising from her.

"Where did the seaweed come from, Finnegan?" Her breath puffed against his chin as he dipped to her face.

"Same place you did, Dr. Sugar."

She stepped closer. Against him, through his clothes, through his jacket, she was a cold, supple shape moving in his arms.

And then, with a breath, hot skin everywhere his fingers slid. Cold neoprene and hot skin.

Unbelievable, the heat radiating from her.

From her cheeks, from the lobes of her ears.

All that silky skin should have been cold, blue-tinged.

Yet it blistered the palms of his hands as he cupped her face and tasted the salt lingering on her eyelashes. Dimly he wondered, *why?*

But the clean, salty smell of her skin spun him away from his memories of the night and its ugliness, sent him spiraling into a place where there was light and peace. "Delicious," he murmured, absorbed in the scent and taste of Sophie.

He thought she would hesitate, expected her to step back, figured she would push him away. He hoped she would. But her eyes darkened, the pupils huge as she curled one black-clad arm around his neck and pulled him to her.

"Share, Finnegan," she murmured into his mouth, her lips soft and pliant, as soft and pliant as the woman standing on tiptoes and stretching herself against him, one thigh slipping between his legs. "Nice," she said. "I'd forgotten how nice touching you could be. I didn't remember."

He spread his legs and made room for her, let her come as close as wetsuit and soggy jeans would allow, and as he did, she reached up with her other hand and slid her fingers through his hair, holding his face still as she sipped at the corner of his mouth and sighed.

He wanted to believe it was a sigh of pleasure.

But deep in the sigh, he heard the sadness.

He hesitated, his fingers fumbling with the broad tab of her zippered vest. "This isn't a good idea."

"I don't know about you, Finnegan, but this is the best idea I've had in weeks."

He brushed her cheek with his thumb, trying to get his thoughts in some kind of order. "But—"

"If you stop now, Judah, I swear I'll hunt you down and kill you. And no jury on earth would convict me." Her voice was low and breathy as she slipped her hand between their bodies, closed it over his, tugged down, the slippery material opening as he slid his hand inside and found softness and heat, found the hard bump of her nipple.

And lingered, tugging, entranced by the contrast of cold suit and flushed skin.

Touching her, he remembered again how it had been for him the first time he'd seen her, the rush of wanting, the physical ache of needing to touch her.

Touching her, he could forget the past, could escape the prison of his soul by losing himself in her.

That was what he wanted most on this dismal, storm-wrecked morning, escape was what he'd craved and hadn't known he needed.

Here, with her smacked up against him, he didn't have to think about the creeps spraying graffiti around town, didn't have to think about the jackasses stealing from the Christmas charity kettles. He didn't have to think about the baby left in the manger, didn't have to think about George. Didn't have to *think*.

That was the blessing. It had been a lifetime since he'd felt anything, not anger, not joy. Nothing. But with Sophie in his arms, he could just *feel*.

This, he thought as he moved his mouth along the long line of her neck, this salvation in Sophie's scent, touch, in the very texture of her skin under his seeking fingers, *this* was the light in the darkness. "Closer," he muttered against the slope of her breast. His chin scraped against the metal zipper teeth as he nudged the vest opening wider. "You're not close enough. I want you *closer*." He cupped her butt with one hand and pulled her tightly to him.

From that first moment, he'd known it would be like this.

In this moment, only Sophie. Beginning and end of thought, of regret, of anger.

Right now. Alpha and omega.

Now.

Sophie.

She tasted the hunger in his lips and fed on it, felt his seeking fingers at her waistband.

"Two-piece?"

"Yes," she exhaled into his ear. "Easier to get into." She wiggled her fanny, and felt him shudder against her. "And out of."

"Excellent." He flattened his palm into the curve of her back.

She twisted upward. "Good hands, Finnegan. Ah, but you have good hands." Her brain turned to mush as he edged a forefinger between the tight fabric and her spine.

The adrenaline rampaging through her had a focus now, and she leaned into it, just the way she would lean into a wave. Judah's lean form. Judah's hands on her. The movement of his hard body against her took all the energy the surfing hadn't touched and channeled it, a straight line from him to her. She should have grabbed Finnegan instead of her surf board, she thought muzzily as his thumbs met in her belly button and pressed, circled lower.

How long had it been since she'd been touched like this? She couldn't remember, oh, he was taking her breath away, she couldn't breathe....

Her knees buckled, and he went with her, their knees bouncing on the packed sand, but she couldn't turn him loose. Her fingertips hummed with the sensation of his hot skin against them.

His hands were on either side of her face, framing it and holding her still. "Inside. We need to go inside."

"Too far," she gasped.

"I can run." He pulled her to her feet and lifted her off the sand, snugging one arm under her behind and staggering to his feet.

"If you think so." She locked her legs behind his waist and buried her face in the crook of his neck, breathed and went dizzy with the feel of his skin against her cheek. "Go for it, tiger."

He lurched with her up the slope of sand and sea oats

toward the shadowy house. The rise and fall of his chest matched her own. "Damn. How much farther?"

"Two hundred yards. More or less." She nipped at his ear and ran her hand down from his belt as far as she could. "Not much farther, big guy." His arousal surged against the heel of her hand, and she moved coaxingly against it.

He stumbled. She slid down his body. The soggy fabric of his jeans rubbed against her, sent sparks shooting through her.

"We're not going to make it," he muttered, frustration in every syllable.

Laughing, she let all the night's misery drift away in the wind. "You don't have to look so grim."

"You don't know the half of it." He still held her snagged against him as he marched her backwards toward her house.

"Really?" she whispered slyly. "How…impressive."

Stomping onward, he glowered at her. "What? What?"

"Nothing." She stroked her hand down the hard front of his jeans, felt him throb into her curving palm.

"Oh."

"*Oh,* indeed." She laughed again. She could never have hoped for this kind of ending to the horrible night. In Finnegan's arms, all the destruction of the ER melted away.

Here was *life. Here* was pleasure. She moved her flat palm against him again. *Here* was power. His.

Hers.

Laughter kept bubbling up from deep inside. Her body fizzed and sparkled, everything inside her coiling and tumbling. And still he marched her relentlessly backwards, bumping against her, struggling with the waistband of her suit bottom as he kept moving. Trapped by his arms, the sides of her open vest bent back under her arms.

The wind blew against her bare breasts, tickling her with sand and cold. Her nipples brushed against his wet shirt, hardened.

"This is crazy, Sophie." But he didn't stop. Didn't stop touching, didn't stop moving her back to the house, his bare feet tangling with hers at every step, his pants legs flapping against her bare calves and knees.

Sensation *everywhere*. She was drowning in touch and smell. Drowning in Judah.

Careening backward, she tripped on the root of one of the pine trees and fell, a dizzying swoon of gray sky and his blue eyes.

Landing on the cushion of pine needles with Judah coming right after her, his arms still wrapped around her, she couldn't stop laughing at the silliness of it all. Oh, she'd needed this, this laughter, this touching, *this*. How could she not have known how much she needed his touch? She slid her palms under his wet jacket, let them slip down wet skin, traced the contours of muscles, felt their response to her touch. Some rawness in her soul eased under the balm of touching and being touched and laughing.

And in some distant place in her brain she pictured them tangled together on the beach, a mess of sloppy wet clothes and sandy bodies and she laughed again.

"What's so funny, Sophie?" His tongue traced the curve of her mouth, gently, dampening her lips, and the wind touched them, too, and everything in her shivered with delight.

She just wished Judah didn't look so grim.

So lost.

She didn't want him lost. She didn't want emotion now, not his, not hers, only this physical exhilaration that blanked out memories and thought and everything except *this*.

"Easy," she murmured. She smoothed the frown between his ocean-blue eyes. "It's not the end of the world."

Not answering, not meeting her gaze, he lowered himself over her, fitting his pelvis against hers, sliding his arms under her. "Any chance of getting this damn bottom off?"

"Finnegan, if I've learned one thing in this life, it's that there's always a chance." She squirmed encouragingly, every nerve ending in her thighs and belly quivering with pleasure, with life. "If there's a will, there's a way."

Tomorrow would come soon enough.

And in the meantime, here was Judah, filling her world with taste, with touch, with himself.

Easy, for the moment, so easy to let herself forget the ugliness. So tempting, this surrender to feeling, to the physical anodyne of what they were doing. Surrender to the power, to the wave of pleasure.

There were worse ways to end a day.

Chapter 4

He should have gone home.

Even as Judah slicked back the tangled hair hiding her ear and tasted her, he knew he should get up from the heat of her body, the salty tang of her skin, and leave.

He knew it. Like fingernails scraping down a chalkboard, his brain screeched warnings. Yet he lingered in the illusive comfort of her arms.

Stayed.

And hated himself.

Weakness, this craving to touch and taste. He despised himself for the need, for the loss of will. He hated this weakness that mewed *stay* when he knew he should flee as if the hounds of hell were on his heels.

Weakness.

And yet...

He stroked the slight swell of her flattened breast and lost himself in the warming whiteness of it, spellbound by the rose flush that crept upward from his touch.

A murmur. A sharp inhalation. Hers. The subtle accommodation of her hips to him fascinated him, whispered to the maleness in him, sang a silent siren song of movement and scent and urgency.

"This doesn't make sense," he said.

"You're wrong. At the moment it makes all the sense in the world."

"You? Me? No." His brain kept jabbering and screeching, a discordancy of mind and logic against the need for touch and taste. "This is stupid." He braced himself on his forearms, his hands framing her face and made himself look at her, forced himself to breathe the cool air and not her scent, made himself look at the woman who'd caused George's death.

Dark streaks against white sand and green pine, her hair fanned out from her round face. She looked back at him, knowledge and sadness and sympathy blurring the blue-gray of her eyes.

"Don't look at me like that, Sophie."

"How am I looking at you, Judah?" Quiet as sunlight moving across a wood floor, her voice feathered over him. "I'm only—"

"Don't," he said again.

"Don't what, Judah?"

"Just…don't."

"Ah, Judah." There was something like regret in that barely heard exhalation, something too much like pity.

From the corner of his eye, he saw her palm lift toward him. Before she could touch him, he fanned his hand across her face, stroked the skin at the corner of her eyes and drew her eyelids closed.

He hated her for the way she made him feel. Hated her for the sympathy in her eyes. Hated her most of all for the understanding glimmering there, an understanding so close to pity he couldn't bear it. She had no right to see straight down to whatever passed for a soul in the darkness of his heart.

And yet he wanted her. *Wanted* her. Hated her. And de-

spised himself. A sickness of body and mind he didn't want
to escape.

In that moment when the wind ceased, when all he heard
was the pounding of his blood in his head, he learned a truth.

Despite logic, despite loyalty, despite everything, he was
going to have Sophie Brennan.

He didn't want to think about how he was going to live
with that choice. Not with her soft and yielding beneath him.

With a quick, fierce movement, he pulled open the fastener
of her pants. Her hands were right there on top of his, urging
the skintight material down. Caught in the immediacy, he
gritted his teeth and struggled with his jeans. Their hands
bumped, tangled. She pushed his bumbling fingers aside. He
pushed right back, hands and fingers melding in a dance of
their own.

"Wait." She lifted her pelvis and shoved the fabric past
her belly.

"No." Cool, damp, that skin suddenly under his palm. He
dipped his mouth to her navel and blew softly against her.

Her belly fluttered beneath his mouth. "Ah," she said, a
tight, sharp sound of surprise.

He flattened his hand against her and pressed, his fingers
stroking, testing her inner heat. "Here?"

"Oh, yes. There is good. *There* is perfect. *There…ah.*"
One of her hands tightened in his hair, the other slid between
them, seeking him as he continued pressing and stroking.
"Oh, yes," and she surged upward, riding the rhythm of his
touch as she'd melded with the storm waves. Urgency
swamped finesse and he was clumsy, pushing and probing,
the blind eye of need driving him into her. Awkward in his
haste, no grace in the hurrying, no skill in his movements.

A sixteen-year-old would have had more control.

But she was in the moment with him, just as urgent, just
as needy. The impatient sounds of her breathing merged with
his, spoke to him in the silence.

He felt the wet denim of his jeans snick open, felt her
warm hand, exploring, moving against his belly. Not shy, not

delicate, her hands were those of a woman used to touching and examining, accustomed to the feel of the human body. Knowing. Confident. Incredibly seductive, that confidence. Behind his eyes a red haze burned. Then she freed him into the small curl of her hand and he bucked, thrust against her.

Need. Ugly.

Hunger roared through him, primal, finally blanking the monkey chatter in his brain. "Now," he ground out through teeth clenched against the pleasure racing through him. "Now."

He lifted her hips higher, positioned her, but she was ahead of him, already moving into him, her body welcoming and warm.

"Don't—" She shifted, her body opening and taking him deeper, toward the limits of his shaky control.

"You want me to *stop?*" The muscles in his arms trembled. But he stopped. He would have sworn he couldn't have. But he did. Head lowered, teeth clenched against a suddenly dry mouth, his whole body shuddering, he said again, "Stop? Is that what you're saying?"

"No. Not that. Heaven help me, not that." Her laugh was rueful, a coil of tension deep inside her that vibrated unbearably through him. Rising upward, she framed his face with her hands. "*Don't* stop. That's what I was trying to say." Her head dipped into his shoulder, and she felt her breath against his skin as she murmured, "Don't be careful with me. I don't want politeness."

"Believe me, manners are the last thing on my mind." His thighs quivered with the effort needed to stay unmoving. "What…do you want?" He heard himself and was stunned. He couldn't say her name. Drowning in her, he couldn't say her name. Didn't want to. "Tell me."

"The storm wave. Wildness. The deep blue sea. Can you give me that? I need—" She nipped at his skin, the scrape of her teeth a tiny command that slammed him over the edge.

Nothing but sensation in this moment, nothing but the blessed relief of skin against skin, touch and taste. Her body milking his, his palms sliding over the hot skin of her thigh, his touch sending shudders through her, through him.

Sex.

Simple. Something clear in his life for a change.

Sex.

He surrendered to it, to her, letting the reins of control whip through his hands, letting himself sink into the whirl-pool of sensation that was this woman.

And he didn't care in that moment of release as his body pumped into hers in pure sensation, didn't give a damn as he collapsed against her, that he couldn't look in her eyes.

That he wouldn't let himself say her name.

His cheek resting on the damp hair at her temple, he breathed in the light scent of her sweat, the salty air of the Gulf.

Overhead he sensed the movement of clouds, heard the angry squawk of seagulls.

For the first time in months, everything in his body and brain had stopped. He felt like a shell shimmering on the sand, abandoned by the tide.

Empty, washed clean.

And he wanted nothing more than to go to sleep, to slide into that darkness and stay there, unmoving.

The wind came off the Gulf and raised goose bumps everywhere Judah wasn't. Sophie shivered, but she didn't move. She couldn't. She needed a minute to *think.* She couldn't believe what she'd done. She'd just *taken,* dived headlong into the moment with no thought of consequences. She'd come off the waves with her anger and confusion not eased by the wild surf, and there was Judah. Frowning, hostile, but he was there, draped in seaweed and sending off waves of energy that bounced against her own unsettled emotions, his energy smashing against her own. Wind against current, the ninth wave of surfing, the big wave, the one surfers waited for.

Unthinking, not caring why he'd shown up, not wanting

to think about the reasons for his anger, she'd simply reached out and clambered aboard the wave of their energy, ridden it to the end. It had been worth it, too, every second of that intensity.

Stupid?

Sure. Of course it was. No protection. All the questions about their relationship. The torturous mix of emotions. And in the aftermath, this loneliness and emptiness. But for those few minutes... She turned her head slightly and stared at the sand. Did she regret what she'd done?

Yes. *No.* Maybe.

She groaned.

At the sound, Judah shifted against her, moved away. Minus the blanket of his body, she was cold. Her teeth clicked together. Wrapping her arms around herself, she sat up. Her scalp itched with sand and dried salt. At least there weren't any mirrors close at hand. Fine. She'd made her bed. She'd lie in it. So to speak. She pulled her top closed.

Beside her, she glimpsed Judah's movements as he struggled to ease himself back into salt-stiffened jeans.

"So." She stood up, caught the quick, sideways glance he threw her way. He was embarrassed. And now she was, too. Hideously embarrassed. And defensive. What had she done? And why?

Well, she could answer *that* question. She shoved her hair out of her face and took a deep breath. Could the aftermath of her craziness get any more humiliating?

"You must be wondering—" He cleared his throat.

"What must I be wondering, Judah? Tell me?"

"Why I'm here. What's up."

"I think that question's been pretty well answered."

He frowned, looked away. Then, taking a deep breath, he continued doggedly. "Why I'm *here*. You know what I mean."

"I don't know why you showed up on my doorstep. Tell me. Why did you come all the way out here, Judah? Not for a quick romp on the beach after a crazy day, I'm guessing? Delightful though it was. Or perhaps not so delightful?''

''I'm sorry—''

Palm up, she slapped his chest. ''Don't take that highway, Judah. I mean it. What happened, happened. *Sorry* doesn't even enter into it.'' She tried to scrape her hair back from her face, tried to sort through the mess of emotions rolling over her like an avalanche. One was as impossible as the other. ''There were two of us here. Nobody forced anybody to do anything. Let it go. I'm going to.'' She sighed in spite of herself and turned toward the house.

His hand closed around her upper arm. ''Can you?''

She jerked her head up. ''Absolutely. You think I can't?''

''There might be problems.'' His frown deepened.

''There are always problems. With everything.'' She laughed. ''Haven't you learned that, Judah?'' She heard the curl of something in her voice and realized she was losing it. ''But as for the particular problems I think you mean, they're not issues.''

Dark red slashed across his cheekbones.

''As for any other concerns, you don't have to worry about those, either. Medical personnel get stuck with needles more times than I can count. We're human pincushions. So we're tested all the time. There. All better?'' She smiled sweetly. ''And what about you? Do I need to worry?''

''No.'' His hand remained tight around her arm. ''You don't. Not about that.''

''Well, fine, then.'' She made her smile bigger, as bright as she could. ''Two consenting adults having themselves a fine old moment of bliss then. Everything's kosher, right? Or should I say 'right as rain'? Hard for a Yankee girl to keep up with all the gee-whillikers phrases.''

''Don't be snide. You're babbling, you know.'' His grip tightened. His frown had vanished. ''Not like you to babble, Sophie.''

''Oh, you finally remember my name?''

His frown flashed. He dropped his hand. Took a step back.

"Yes, I noticed, *Judah,* that you couldn't seem to say my name. I noticed, too, that you couldn't look me in the eyes. Cops aren't the only ones who pay attention to body language, Judah."

He shook his head, started to speak.

"If you say 'I'm sorry' again, I swear I won't be responsible."

"All right!" He threw up his hands. "I'm not one damned bit sorry!"

"Fine!" Her temper crashed against his. "Because I'm not either! So there." She stomped off, anger blazing away the cold.

He followed her slowly. "We sound like a·couple of four-year-olds, you know."

She stopped at her screen door and faced him. "We do. You're absolutely right. But I don't want to talk about this, Judah. I really mean that. It happened. It's over. I don't want to get involved in some kind of beat-it-to-death discussion of the whys and wherefores. Not today. Please." She gripped the frame of the door. Evidently humiliation and embarrassment were going to have no limit this morning. "If you can just leave, go away, go do your cop business, I'll be a happy woman. I can't deal with any point-by-point analysis, okay?"

"Isn't that usually the guy's line? And you've always liked to talk." His eyes were busy, watching her every movement.

"Judah, it was fine, earth-shaking. You were terrific. Nobody better. Okay? Okay?" Her voice rose and she yanked the door open, wanting nothing more than the comfort of her own space. Silence. She needed silence and solitude. "Is that what you want? A nice round of applause?" She gave three quick taps of her palms together. "There. All better?"

"No."

"What then?"

"I didn't plan what happened."

Her laugh broke free, a little manic, a lot frantic. "That was pretty obvious."

"That," he tilted his head toward the beach, "happened.

But *that* wasn't why I rode out here. I'm here on cop business, Sophie.''

Her laugh stuttered. "What? I don't understand? What business?''

"I need to ask you some questions.''

"About?''

"The beating victim you treated last night.''

Her eyes met his. "Oh.'' The cloud of exhaustion she thought she'd escaped in the waves, then in those strange moments with Judah, settled around her again. "Of course. She wasn't your case, was she?''

"No. But I have some questions about her.''

Tapping the doorframe lightly, she stared at him. "All right. Come on in.''

On the porch, she brushed sand away, let it sift to the wood planks. Behind her, she heard the brush of his hands against his jeans, heard sand drift from his clothes.

Ridiculous. Judah, here? In her house? After what had just happened on the beach, they were now going to talk business? Insane. She'd tumbled into Alice-in-Wonderland country. "I'll make tea.''

"I drink coffee.''

"I don't have coffee.'' She led him through the huge, open living room back to the kitchen. "Tea. Plain, no herbs, no choices. Can you deal with that?''

"If I have to. Tea's a pretty sissy drink for a tough cookie like you, Dr. Sugar.''

She whirled. Her sand-gritty hair slapped her cheek. "Don't push it, Judah. Not this morning. Drink your tea. Ask your questions. Leave.''

He prowled her kitchen, not touching anything, just roaming, checking out the territory. *Guys.* One way or another, they had to mark their territory. She leaned against the sink, deliberately making herself motionless, not going with the rhythm of his movements, not giving into the agitation ratcheting through her.

Not subtle. She knew from the lift of his eyebrow that he'd

read her message. But he kept moving around, and it was all she could do to make herself stay in one place, not to become a shadow cursor of his restlessness. As he watched her shift, a tight smile picked at the corners of his mouth.

Oh heavens. *His mouth.* Sophie shoved away from the sink. She grabbed the teakettle from the stove. *Judah's mouth. His mouth, moving on her, touching her.* Images flashed in her mind. *What had she done?* Her face flamed. She shoved up the faucet lever, letting water gush into the kettle, splash onto the floor.

"Nervous?"

"Don't flatter yourself, Finnegan." She snapped the gas knob to full flame.

"No tip-toeing around for Dr. Brennan. I'm impressed."

"I said I've talked as much as I want to about what happened. I wasn't kidding, Judah. Sex is sex. I'm no sixteen-year-old virgin."

"And I can't tell you how happy that fact makes me." He shot her that look again. "A woman of much experience, are you?"

"Enough." If possible, her face burned brighter. Let him think whatever he wanted to think. She didn't care. Of course she didn't. "I won't pretend nothing happened. I just *don't* want to get into this discussion. Can you get that through your thick head? Or is all this persistence part of being a cop? And for Pete's sake, can't you stay in one place? You're making me dizzy!"

In the stubble and angles of his face, a real, honest-to-God grin finally flashed. "Yeah. I can see that." A snarky lift of one eyebrow mated with the grin. "I'm guessing, oh, three? That about right? That much experience?"

The whistle of the kettle saved her. She took two mugs from the dish drainer by the sink, plopped tea bags into them and filled the mugs with hot water. "Here."

He took the napkin and spoon she thrust at him. "Sugar?"

"What? What?" For a weird second, she'd thought he meant something else. "On the table. Sit. Drink."

"You have a real flair for giving orders, *Sophie*." There was that flash of something unnerving in his eyes. "But I'll stand. Thank you. If you don't mind?"

"Sit. Stand. Jump out the window. I don't care." She gulped her tea, felt its warmth right down to her toes. The tea-bag tab dangled against her nose. She wanted Finnegan out of her house. She wanted a shower so badly she could scream. What was going on in his head? He kept swinging back and forth between this strange kind of teasing and the cold, judgmental Judah who'd first appeared after— After she'd filed the DUI report on his partner. That had changed everything.

She gulped again, too quickly. Coughed. "About your questions?"

"Right." He cupped his mug with both hands. Cop mode now. No grin. No sly comments. No electricity jittering at her. "You treated the woman when she came in, right? Do you remember her?"

"Don't patronize me, Judah. Of course I remember her." Sophie sank into the nearest chair. She placed her mug on the table, watching the amber liquid swirl in the purple mug. Very carefully, she lifted the tea bag out and wrapped its string around the bowl of her spoon, squeezing until the bag was drained. She laid it on the table. Moved it. "She died."

"Hell. This day just keeps getting better and better. What a damned mess."

She lifted her head so fast she almost saw stars. "There's an understatement."

Over his mug, his bleak gaze met hers. "Like you said, it wasn't my case. I hadn't heard what happened to her. But she's the reason I need to get some answers from you. I don't like coincidences. I thought it was weird that me and Tyree found that baby at the church the same night you had your beating victim."

"You found that baby at a church?" Sophie stared at him. "How odd. Where?"

"The Second Baptist. In the manger." He shrugged. Tea slopped down the side of the mug. "Damnedest thing."

Sophie felt her heart give a quick little jump. Felt a softening in her very bones. "In the manger?"

"Right. Anyway, what can you tell me about her?"

"The baby?" Sophie couldn't stop thinking of that small face with its calm brown eyes.

"No."

Even in her distraction, Sophie noticed that he was on the prowl again, playing with her blinds, tugging at the Halloween tea towel dangling from her stove.

"The woman. Was she conscious when she was brought in? Did she say anything to you? There was squat all on the report. Just where she was found on the street in a residential area. Nothing more. Nobody's canvassed the area yet. Been one of those nights."

"Full moon. The holiday." She stood up. Lifting the kettle, she refilled her mug. "The ER was a war zone."

"I'll bet. Anyway, did you find any identification on her when you examined her? Anything?"

"No. You think she and the baby are connected, don't you?"

"I'm curious. Like I said, I don't like coincidences."

"Cammie and I wondered about that." Sophie sipped her tea and let her mind wander to the past hours. "The baby is Asian. The woman was. Didn't necessarily mean anything since we have an increasingly large Vietnamese population. In the little time we had to think about things, we wondered. The baby's in the pediatric ward." Swirling the tea, she stared at Finnegan. "It's a shame."

"It's always a shame. Violence. Hate."

"Death."

"Yeah." For the first time since he'd come into her kitchen, he was motionless. "People are vicious."

"Some are."

"Most."

"That's a grim world view. A sad one."

"It's reality. I'm a cop. I see what people can do to each other."

"I do, too. But I don't think the lunkheads make up the majority."

"You're a fool, then."

"Really? You're full of compliments tonight, Judah, aren't you? Today, I mean. A silver-tongued devil. One compliment after another. Will my ego ever recover?"

Something that might have been amusement gleamed in his tired eyes again, softened the creases at the corners. He lounged against the sink. "I think your ego will survive."

She laughed in spite of her annoyance. She'd had worse jabs thrown at her in med school, but for some reason Judah's comment still stung. Clearly having a moment or even sixty of wild sex together hadn't thawed his view of her. And that was why his slow, deliberate statement hurt. "I'm a fool because I believe people are basically pretty decent? Because I don't think humanity's a lost cause?"

"It's the world I see every day." He rubbed the mug across his forehead. Pale plumes of steam drifted across his face. "A lousy world."

"It's not mine."

"Well, there you go, Doc. You got your point of view. Me? Every day I see what people can do. And they never cease to surprise me with the evil they can come up with. Seems they don't even have to put their minds to it." He shut his eyes and breathed in the steam from the tea. "Under the right circumstances, each of us is capable of anything."

"If that's how you feel, then how can you do your job? Why don't you give up? In the face of all that evil, what's the point?"

"Hey, I do my job. I go out and do my job. That's all. That's what they pay me to do. I collect my paycheck. There's no other point."

"I don't believe you. I don't believe the man I knew could live like that. Not the man who still holds me responsible for his partner's suicide. That man cared."

"You really are a fool, aren't you, Doctor Sugar?"

"And you have to go on the attack, don't you, Detective Finnegan? When the knife cuts too close to the bone?"

Abruptly he placed his mug on the counter. Went on the move again. Literally.

This time she followed him. "So tell me, Finnegan, why *did* you become a cop? If you don't see any point to it?"

With one long finger, he lifted the corner of the opened newspaper on her center island, let the pages rustle back in place. "Tell me about your vic."

"Oh? Can't answer my question?"

"Come on, Sophie." He slapped down the spoon he'd picked up. "Tell me about the vic."

"Funny how we distance ourselves, isn't it, Judah? Cops call their people 'vics,' 'perps.' We say 'the gunshot,' the 'bleeder,' the 'crispy critter.' Our language puts space between us and the people we treat. The people you arrest. We create that safe distance. For us. So we don't have to feel pain. So we can walk away at the end of our shift. And every time we do, it makes seeing the human in front of us that much harder."

"I see them. I see what they do. I don't want to get to know them. I've got no desire to understand them and offer sympathy. My job's to catch them if I can and stick them behind bars so they can't hurt anyone again. That's what the city pays me to do. I earn my paycheck."

"I don't see how you can get out of bed each day and go to work if that's what you truly believe about your job."

"I don't want to know why a rattler strikes me. I don't need to understand its nature. I kill it. And then it doesn't crawl out and bite me in the ass."

She shook her head in frustration. "I don't understand."

"Yeah. That's pretty obvious."

She poked his forearm and was aware again of the tensile strength that lay beneath the skin. "I know you cops are cynical as hell, but under all that machismo—yes, in their own way the women cops are full of macho too," she added as his eyes met hers. "But under all that stuff you guys carry around with you, cops usually have a sense of being one of the good guys, one of the guys making a difference. Sure, it's always you against the world, and I get that. It's the hunker-in-the-bunker mentality. We have it in my job. But—" and she poked him in the ribs again "—here's the deal. All the cops I've known believe what they do is important. They have to believe in *something*. Knights in blue, fighting the good fight."

"All the cops?" Judah's eyes flashed to hers, he didn't move, and, that fast, George was suddenly there between them, that ghostly presence as real and as dangerous as if he were standing there with Judah in her cluttered kitchen where a pot of brilliant red geraniums splashed their color against a white wall.

Her pulse sped up, danced around as the moment stretched out.

And then, in a flat, hard voice, he repeated, "Tell me what else you know about your vic, Sophie. You don't want to talk about what happened on the beach. I don't want to argue world viewpoints. I want to know about the vic. That's all. Tell me about the vic."

Over his shoulder through the red-and-white blinds of her kitchen window, a glimpse of smoke-gray skies and then his cop face filled her view, that energy crackling all around her, slamming against her.

Chapter 5

And that was that.

She let all that male hostility and energy whirl around her, let him wear himself out against her silence.

She couldn't summon the strength to deal with Judah and their ghost, not both at the same time. Not today.

Like staccato gunshots, his questions banged into her. "Did anyone come to check on her? Someone who knew her? Were there any phone calls asking how she was doing?"

"No. No. And none," Sophie finally reported. That was how it felt. Like giving a morbidity report at the hospital. That clipped, that objective. Stripped of emotion. Facts, nothing else. No opinions, no second thoughts. "The body hasn't been released yet."

Judah's questions, unlike those of the committee, were impatient, ricocheting off the walls.

"C'mon, Sophie. There must have been *something*." He took a step closer and all the air in the room went swooshing out of her lungs. "Unless you're deliberately holding back on me?" He placed one hand flat on the table and leaned into her space. "Are you? Holding back?"

She took a breath. "Why would I do that, Judah?"

He didn't answer, just fixed her with that stare that made her feel as if she'd run a red light, embezzled hospital funds, and kicked a dog.

Or killed someone.

"You want to take a step back, detective? I need to get something out of the refrigerator."

"Really?"

"Absolutely."

"You don't lie worth a damn."

"I'm not lying." She crossed her arms.

"Of course you are." He studied her. "It's in the eyes, Sophie."

"I want a glass of juice. And toast. I need to get the bread and orange juice out of the refrigerator."

"Sure you do. But in a minute. Let's finish this. I'm almost done." He didn't budge.

And for once she couldn't summon up the nerve to push past him.

"Fine. Whatever you say. But I have places to go. You know how it is." She threw his words back at him. "People to see. Things to do." She kept her arms folded.

"I'll bet."

Nope. This wasn't like reporting to the hospital committees. This was a whole new kind of bad. Whip-snapping between her and Judah with every piece of information she gave him, this tension wore her out. Every comment came flying at her loaded with at least three different meanings. And all because of his partner, the man who'd bailed out of life and left everyone else holding a bag full of guilt and misery.

Complicated.

Not how she liked to deal with people. She liked simple, not this underlying sense that she was walking through a minefield in the dark. The casual observer would have seen nothing more than Judah pacing and heard only questions about the woman who'd died. But the crackle and pop came from the slant of his eyes in her direction, the quick glances and the curl of his voice around her name every time he said it. From the way he used his body, leaning in toward her, placing an arm on the table and cutting off any avenue of escape.

She felt like a mouse with its heart beating fast under the watchful eyes of the cat. Judah was no tame tabby. A farm cat, an alley cat, but no declawed house puss, that was for sure. She resented him for making her feel as though all the power lay with him. She wasn't used to that sensation.

He touched the counter with his palm, let it slide down the edge, looked at her, and her damned brain spritzed out with the memory of his palm sliding over her. She shifted restlessly. His eyes met hers, lingered while he said, "All right. So no one called about her, no one came to see her. Was she clean?"

"Drugs, you mean?"

"Yeah."

"She wasn't a druggie. Her tox screen was clean."

"Did she look like she'd been living on the streets?"

"She wasn't homeless."

"How do you know?"

"Her nails were manicured. Does that work for you?"

"I'll let you know."

"Give me a break." There had been tension earlier. Last night. It had shot them into those go-figure moments on the beach. But the nature of the tension had shifted. The old hostility was back, but it had altered somehow.

She didn't like the change. It was worse this time because of the pictures snapping in and out in her head. Because of what she'd let happen. No, not *let*. She'd *wanted* to make love with him.

But they hadn't made love. Whatever they'd done, it hadn't been that.

Why hadn't she thought? She'd simply reached out for

what she'd wanted. Taken what she needed in the aftermath of the lousy night in the ER.

Taken.

And told herself it would be all right.

She'd believed it, too.

She was wrong.

Because it wasn't all right.

It was all wrong and uncomfortable and she didn't like feeling vulnerable around him, not with the damned ghost of George hovering between them.

"Think, Sophie. Think about her shoes, her hair, her jewelry. Anything. You're smart. You must have picked up something. As ER head, you would have been on top of every little detail. I don't reckon anything would have gotten by you. Right?"

"Gosh, Judah, you want me to go find a bright light you can shine in my eyes? I'm not one of your usual suspects, you know. Or perhaps you didn't realize you were treating me like one of your *perps?*"

His footsteps slowed. He frowned. "I'm not treating you like a perp."

"Really? Funny, because I feel as if you're two steps away from bringing in the handcuffs."

"Did you see any on the beach?" He sighed. "Hell, Sophie, I'm collecting information. Asking basic questions."

"You have a damned intimidating way of asking questions, then, is what I think."

"This is only a friendly interview, cop to witness. Anything else is your imagination." He chuffed a breath of air in what she thought was intended to be exasperation, but she didn't buy it. Not for one second. Especially not with his cat-got-into-the-cream expression. The man knew precisely what he was doing to her. He liked making her jumpy. He liked *keeping* her jumpy, that's what it was.

"You know something, Judah? I've been a rational woman all my life. Not a violent bone in my body. But, oh boy, you tempt me.'' The word tumbled off the tip of her tongue and fell between them.

There was a long silence, a silence loaded with possibilities and memories.

He could have said anything. He could have destroyed her with the lift of an eyebrow.

She'd stepped on a landmine and all she could do was wait for the explosion.

And then he asked, so gently that she almost threw her mug at him after all, because it felt like kindness and a kind of pity and she didn't want him to see her vulnerable, not now—

''Why would I try to intimidate you, Sophie?''

''Because you can't help yourself? Because you're a natural-born skeptic?'' She drummed her fingers against her leg. ''No, that can't be right. You always know what you're doing. I have to assume you're bringing on the attitude for some reason of your own.''

''What reason would that be?'' He leaned forward.

Because you still blame me for George's suicide? Because you can't forgive me for his weakness? Because you're still judging me? she almost blurted out.

But she stayed silent. Those were the questions he wasn't about to answer. Not today, anyway. She edged to the side.

A mistake. The heat of his body engulfed her, and before she understood what she'd done, she'd taken a step back, needing to put distance between them.

An unsettling idea after this morning, that she needed distance. Her insides still quivered when she remembered what had happened, remembered the unbelievable *intimacy* of what they'd done with each other. And every time those images flickered in her brain, her body sparkled, went hot.

It had seemed right at the time.

So right.

In the aftermath, though, she wanted that distance. Without it, Judah would walk right over her.

Curious, this instinct to keep him at arm's length, because

she wasn't a woman who built walls or analyzed her relationships.

Straightforward, cards on the table. What you see is what you get. That was her motto. It had worked for her, too. Until now.

Until Judah, this Rubik's Cube of a man. Not easy at all.

Or, she thought, watching his unblinking eyes in the gray light, he might not walk over her. *Was* he making her feel like a suspect he was grilling? Or was he right? Was it all coming from inside her? Was it his attitude? Or was he tapping into a sense of guilt?

Was that the source of this uneasiness?

Her brain seized the idea and galloped away with it.

Deep down, did she have doubts about her decision to push for the blood test on George? She'd said over and over that she didn't. No sirree. No doubts on her part. But…

Had she shoved some ugly little doubts into some closet in her mind? Doubts Judah was picking up on? Was he opening the door and saying, in effect, ''Y'all want to come on out into the daylight and play with Sophie's head for a while?''

It made terrible sense.

Because something was being triggered. In fairness, she couldn't lay all the blame at Judah's feet. But every time he pushed her, she overreacted. She knew she wouldn't have acted this thornily and warily with anyone else—not with the grungiest, most argumentative patient who ever walked into the ER, not with the most arrogant doctor on staff.

So, *were* his relentless questions about the woman who'd died making her question what she'd done a year ago?

And that, ladies and gentlemen of the jury, was the dead elephant in the middle of the living room. Had she made her decision to order the test too quickly because George had ticked her off with his constant innuendos and needling? Some twisted self-righteous payback?

Oh, God. She felt like throwing up.

Even the idea that she could have let her annoyance and

dislike interfere with the man's treatment shook her to her core. Could she have been that petty? That unprofessional?

She'd been so sure that night a year ago, so sure all the nights since. No doubts. Until Judah had showed up tonight in the ER, she hadn't doubted herself, not once.

Had she?

Not until today.

She shook her head.

She'd had her nightmares, but those hadn't been about George. Judah's face, cruel in judgment, had stalked her through the dark alleys of sleep, not George's.

Had she been in denial? Had the dreams revealed doubts she wouldn't allow to the surface?

Two long fingers snapped in front of her eyes. "You still with me, Sophie?"

"What? I didn't hear you." She brushed his hand away impatiently. "And don't snap your fingers at me. It's annoying."

"I thought it might be. Reckoned I needed something drastic to snap you out of your spell. Thought you'd gone to sleep standing straight up." Once again an unexpected glint of mischief flicked across his face.

"You don't even have to work at being annoying, do you?" She jammed her fingers into her hair instead of pulling it out by the roots. "All right. Repeat your question. Please."

"You don't know what or who she was calling for?"

"No." Sophie forced her mind back to the evening in the ER. She'd sort out these other thoughts later, without the distraction of Judah's presence. "We didn't have an interpreter at the hospital. She could have been saying a name, she could have been calling for help. There's no way we would have known. She wasn't really conscious, but she kept making the same sound. It could have meant anything."

"Do you know yet what killed her?"

"Not for sure. There'll be an autopsy, of course, and then we'll know definitely." Sophie stared at the blinds, at the stripes they cast against her walls even in the dim light.

"Liver, ruptured spleen. Internal bleeding everywhere. All bad stuff."

Abruptly she moved to the blinds, yanked them all the way up. "She was so small, you see. She didn't have a chance." The cord dangling from her hand, she swung back to Judah. "She was beaten to death. That's it. She wouldn't have died if someone hadn't treated her like a punching bag." She released the cord. The plastic knob smacked against the window. She turned back to the view of water stretching far and away. Her back to Judah once more, she shoved the faucet lever up and let the water run over her hands. "We found nothing in her clothes. They were moderately nice, not pricey, not cheap. Like the stuff Belker's carries."

"What do you mean? I'm not much of a shopper."

She tilted her head and looked at the two-day beard stubble, at the shock of hair several weeks past haircut time. "That's pretty obvious."

"What?"

In spite of everything, she almost smiled. "Heck, Judah, a platypus has a better sense of style than you do. You're into all that basic Southern guy stuff. Jeans. White T-shirt. Blue T-shirt when you're feeling adventurous. The occasional baseball cap, but at least you wear yours bill forward. Of course everyone else is wearing theirs bill back, so you could argue that you're sort of carving out a retro look."

"Clothes are clothes. Mine are comfortable." His mouth went all stubborn. "Jeans wash easy."

"A little defensive, are we?"

His frown was fierce and all male intimidation. "I'm not defensive. I know what works for me."

She resisted the impulse to soothe. "Whatever you say. But, no, you wouldn't know about Belker's. It carries stylish clothes for the price, Judah. Good quality marked down. This was a woman who knew value for her money, and she was careful with herself and her appearance. She would have lived somewhere. Probably in an apartment. A house? If so, I'd guess a rented one."

"What makes you think she was a renter?" Once again he stepped too close, stepped right into her space.

Not looking at him, she ran her hands back and forth under the cool water. "Because she seemed too young to afford anything else? I don't know, Judah. I said it was a guess. Don't bully me. Anyway, I can't tell you anything else. You've picked my brain clean. There's nothing left."

He moved away, paced. Then the sound of his footsteps circling behind her ceased. "Okay. I'm through, then. If you don't know anything, you don't. Tyree and I'll have to start with where she was found and work outward from there. See if anybody recognizes her."

She couldn't stop rubbing her hands under the faucet. Water sluiced down them, swirled away down the drain. "I don't see how anyone could."

"The forensic photographer's good."

"Even so...not in the condition she was in."

"Right now that's our best shot at identifying her, what with no purse or any kind of markers. Fingerprints will take a few days because of the holiday." He passed behind her, and the swirl of air following him carried the scent of his skin, a scent she'd know anywhere now. "I reckon the baby's identity is up for grabs, too. Until we find more information, anyway."

She pressed her wet hands against her bleary eyes. His statement had sucked all the tension and energy out of the room. "The baby," she said. "She was so quiet." Water dripped from her hands, her face, small sounds in the silence. "You'll find where she belongs?"

"It's a crap shoot. It's likely there's a connection with your vic. Either way, I want to know. The *Coast Herald* will run the story, have pictures. If she's lucky, we'll find her people." His steps moved to the door. "Or not." The screen door squeaked. "Sophie, somebody stuck that baby out in the rain on a cold night. Could be better for her if we don't find them."

"She needs a family."

"Not necessarily. And not the one that dropped her like an unwanted puppy in the first convenient spot."

"Or where they knew she'd be found and taken care of."

He made a rude noise. "Anything's possible, I guess."

Slowly Sophie turned to face him. "By the way, Judah, why didn't you ask me these questions at the hospital?"

He paused. "There wasn't time."

"Really?"

"You don't believe me?"

"I don't. Like you said, it's in the eyes."

"Then *you* tell *me,* Sophie. Why did I bike all the way out here?" He was a dark shape in the doorway. "What other motive would I have? Tell me."

"As I mentioned a few minutes earlier, I think you have reasons for everything you do. And they're not necessarily the obvious ones. So, detective, are you on duty, or off?"

"I already told you, I didn't plan what happened this morning." He shifted, a shadow in shadows. "Look, Sophie, this thing that happened—"

"No." She shook her head, couldn't stop shaking it. "No."

He sighed. His hand lifted, fell. "I had questions about the case. I didn't ask them earlier. I'm on my own time. Working the case. That's all."

"All right. Whatever you say." Sophie walked toward him. Sand gritted under her bare feet. "Any more questions? Are you through here?"

"No more questions." But he hesitated, still holding onto her door. "Not for the time being, anyway."

Sophie took the door from him, closed it gently. "Fine." The mesh of the screen patterned his face. "If you think of some more questions, Judah, find me at the hospital. Make time there. Don't come back here."

He studied her, his tired eyes like burned holes in a blue blanket.

"And for future reference, I don't like being called a fool. Don't do it again."

His expression never changed. She met him stare for stare, silently. She wanted him to give her some indication that he understood what she was talking about, to acknowledge at least that her viewpoint was as valid as his harsh one, that hers offered the possibility of hope while his saw only the certainty of evil.

Still expressionless, he shrugged once again and turned away. Midway down the steps he half-pivoted, his face in the gloom of the overhang. "You are a fool, you know. If you think people are more good than bad."

"Then I'm a fool. I'll live with it. Go home, Finnegan. Or go back to whatever dark cave you call home. Just go."

This time he walked out into the gray day, the watery light casting his shadow westward in front of him.

At the side of the road, his bike roared into action. The faint red taillight winked and disappeared down the south road to the bridge.

"Damn you, Finnegan," she whispered. Her hand curled against the screen. "You turn my life upside down and then walk away. How many times do I have to watch you vanish into the darkness?"

Behind her, her house was silent, waiting.

It had never felt empty before.

Now it did.

A window creaked with a gust of wind. A floorboard popped in one of the bedrooms. Sophie listened to the whispers coming from her empty house.

She leaned her cheek against the screen door. She'd loved this house from the first minute she'd seen it. She loved the way the sun flooded it and bleached its old floorboards. She even loved the salt-sticky feel of the walls. All its spaces had welcomed her the minute she'd walked in with the Realtor. She knew she'd come home.

When had it started feeling empty to her? It seemed to be holding its breath, waiting.

The wind rattled the palm fronds, sent dried brown branches

crashing to the ground. Pieces of cardboard and news-papers cartwheeled across the yard.

She'd have a real clean-up job after the storm finally blew out.

She went back into her kitchen and reheated water for tea in her orange microwave, waiting while it merrily ticked the seconds away.

Another year winding down.

Odd, Judah appearing in her life again, after a year. Their lives coming full circle in a way. Yet nothing was different.

Everything was different.

What had she done?

The microwave timer ticked down the final seconds.

She stared blindly at the bright reds and yellows of her kitchen. *What had she done?*

The bell dinged. She picked up the mug, swished a new tea bag up and down and headed for the bathroom.

With one hand she turned the shower faucet as hot as it would go. With the other, she set the mug on the sink edge. Shucking her clothes, she let the surfwear fall to the floor. A whimper escaped her as she stepped into the steam. Puffs of shampoo foam collected around her toes, floated around the drain. Rubbing the peach-soap-filled loofah over her body, she drew a quick breath and looked down.

Her skin bloomed with whisker rash. Near her belly, her breasts—*everywhere.* The pounding of the shower pebbled her nipples into hard, aching points. The long muscles of her thighs trembled with strain and remembering.

She smoothed the loofah down her body and gasped. The touch was unbearable. Head bent forward, she let the loofah fall.

Too much sensation. Too much…*everything.*

Her back against the tile, she slid to the shower floor and curved her arms protectively around her empty, aching body.

Shudders wracked her for a long time before the tears came. Head buried against her drawn-up knees, she surren-dered to the ugly, wrenching sobs.

She cried for the patient she'd lost, for the baby who had no one, and, finally, a little, she cried for herself and the emptiness within her.

When the water ran cold, she reached up and turned it off, then crawled out onto the bath mat and wrapped herself in one of her thick burgundy towels. Her skin was still too sensitized to dry with a towel, and her knees kept buckling.

Bracing herself against the toilet, she stayed there for a long time on the warm mat, drifting in and out of awareness. Awake but not. Not asleep, either.

Some burst of wind and rain startled her out of her sleep-that-wasn't, and she blinked, coming fully awake.

She rose clumsily to her feet, the towel trailing behind her. Looking down at herself, she examined again the trail of tiny marks, marks that Judah had left on her. She touched one and shivered, but not in pain.

In remembered pleasure.

In the bathroom mirror, her stunned eyes met her gaze. Uncombed dried hair coiled messily around her face. A faint discoloration showed at the base of her neck. But it was her eyes that fixed her attention.

Judah was right. It was all in the eyes.

With a shaking hand, she reached for her tea. It was cold, with a film topping it.

Still wrapped in the towel, she trudged to the bedroom. She slipped a soft, midriff-baring shirt over her running bra. And then a pale purple shirt over that. She couldn't seem to put enough layers of fabric between her skin and the air. The lightest brush along her skin sent shivers through her. She grabbed faded low-rider jeans and socks and shimmied into them.

Even the tips of her fingers tingled.

Did she need gloves?

A full body wrap?

She banged her head gently against her chest of drawers. She'd gone round some quaint Southern bend of thinking, that was it. She'd slipped into full Looney Tunes mode. It was time to move back north. Her brain had gone tropical.

In the kitchen, she made a fresh pot of tea, opened a package of lemon-cream ginger cookies, and carried everything on her grandmother's red-and-gold painted tray to the porch.

Folding herself into the rocker, she rested her elbows on her knees and watched the waves boom and crash toward her as she sipped her tea and nibbled the cookies.

And thought.

Sex changed everything.

Boy, did it ever.

Later, even though the weather hadn't cleared, she walked down the beach toward Sarasota. Socks stuffed in her pockets, she scanned the sand to see what the storm had washed up from the deep. Shiny pieces of sand-smoothed glass. Horseshoe crabs, wickedly ugly and perversely fascinating.

Starfish.

She picked them up and flung them back into the Gulf.

Pretty shells, their colors shimmering in her hand and sparkling in the air as they spun over the water.

One shell, all pearly and pink and perfectly formed stayed in her palm as she traced the whorls and crevasses glistening with salt water. The tip of a questing foot peeked out from its depths, tickled her hand.

Storms always dredged up something interesting.

You had to keep your eyes open.

You could never tell what you'd find right underfoot.

She sent the shell arcing and tumbling into the water, sending it home.

As it spun out, rising, falling, a sudden shaft of sunlight turned it into a tiny star, sparkling against the gray clouds.

Chapter 6

What had he done?

The rain was sporadic now, sudden gusts slashing against his sides as he gunned the Harley's engine and let it rip. Bent low, hands clenched on the handles, he had to concentrate to keep the bike riding straight against the buffets of the wind.

He'd lost control.

He'd never lost control in his life.

Never.

Not with anyone. Not with his father, not with George. Damn sure not with Sallie. He'd let her walk out of their marriage without a second thought. Leaning into the slope of a curve in the road, he tried to picture the tiny redhead who'd been in his life for three years. He couldn't get a clear memory of her face. But he'd loved Sallie, right? Sure he had.

He must have. After all, he'd married her. You don't marry someone if you don't love them. They'd been eighteen. Sallie was cute, sexy as all get-out. He'd been hotter than a two-peckered billy goat. So they'd gotten married.

Seemed like the reasonable thing to do at the time.

He reckoned a nineteen-year-old guy getting regular sex would consider that a good marriage by definition.

So why couldn't he remember the color of Sallie's eyes?

Because he hadn't cared enough to remember?

Or because he hadn't *wanted* to remember?

Two very different motives.

Gravel spat against his arm, nicked his chin. Hunching forward, he pushed the engine to its limit.

The bike slid greasily on the sharp turn to the bridge, and he fought to keep it upright as he sped onto the old wooden-planked bridge that shivered with the wind.

He'd never lost control with Sallie, not in any way. Not sexually. Not emotionally. They'd never argued. They'd never fought.

Not even when he'd come home and found her packing her collection of crystal animals. Walking slowly toward her, trying to make sense of what she was doing, he'd looked down to see shards of the steins she'd given him for Christmas. His shoes crunching over the glass, he'd said only, "If you're sure this is what you want." He'd helped her swaddle her crystals in bubble wrap and carried everything down to the sports car he'd bought her for their first anniversary.

Alone in the apartment, he'd swept up the glass and felt weirdly relieved. He should have felt sad. Lonesome. He should have felt *something*. He hadn't. He'd felt only relief.

Losing control was a sure ticket to disaster.

But he'd lost it with Sophie, no question about that.

Why?

Why now?

And why Sophie?

She'd stood there in her kitchen, her hair wild and salt-coiled, her eyes tired and pissed off, and it had been all he could do not to grab her and take her again right there on her kitchen floor.

Being Sophie, she would have argued. He'd have had to kiss her mouth quiet, show her that there were better things to do with it than talking all the time. She would have known what he was doing. She would have thought it was a great idea.

Or maybe not.

But whatever she decided, she would have been as involved as he was. She would have fumed at him, stormed around, or they would have been on the floor, together. No question about *that.*

Every time he'd looked at her in her funky kitchen, he'd lost the thread of his questions. He didn't think she'd noticed. Not until that last question before he left. Smart, that was Sophie. She'd seen right through him.

But she'd been doing a little dance of her own, Sophie had.

For all her can't-shock-me manner down on the beach, he'd surprised Dr. Sugar.

Remembering the tiny sounds she'd made as he'd entered her, he slowed as he took the left turn off the bridge.

Sophie hadn't been as cool and collected as she'd pretended, not when she was pulling him down toward her, urging him inside her, milking him dry.

And afterwards? Arms folded, caution signs posted all around her, she'd watched him with those wary eyes as he'd asked his questions, eyes that shaded from blue to gray the longer he talked. He'd kept wanting to ask her what she was thinking, but he'd felt stupid and off balance. Underneath the questions, there was another dialogue cracking back and forth.

He'd wanted to ask her if he'd hurt her, he'd needed to know that she was all right, that he hadn't—

But he had.

No curbs, no brakes. Full steam ahead and damn the torpedoes.

No protection, nothing. He still couldn't believe that detail. Him? Mr. Always Prepared? Hell and damnation. He wondered now if he could have stopped in that last moment. He'd told her he would, that he could, but—

She hadn't wanted him to stop.

That kind of attitude from a woman was a surefire turn-on.

With all the reasons to stay as far from Sophie Brennan as he could, he'd deliberately sought her out, rolled around on the beach with her—and wanted more.

And now? All he wanted was to turn his bike around and race back to her house. He'd give his last dime to see the expression on her face if he came strolling through her door.

He had enough sense not to.

Standing in the rain outside the first convenience store off the island, Judah held the phone receiver in his hand. He knew he was holding cold plastic, but what he felt was the hot silkiness of Sophie's skin.

Sex.

It changed everything.

He groaned.

What had he done?

"Judah?" Tyree's sleep-clogged voice rasped in his ear. "Why the hell you calling me at—" Metal clanged as something fell to the floor at the other end of the line. "—at 7:00 a.m., man? We're off duty."

"What's going on, honey?" Yvonna's husky voice mixed with the sounds of sheets rustling. "That's Judah on the phone? Why's he calling? And at this hour?"

Over the static-crackling line came Tyree's muffled, "Hush, baby. You stay right here. I'll be back before you know what's what."

More whispered sounds, then finally Tyree's voice slipped over the wires. "Man, you got some nerve, you know? After the week we've had and then last night?"

"Busy, I guess?" Judah wrapped the grimy cord around his fingers.

Tyree yawned. "Where are you?"

"Off the island bridge, this side of town."

"The island? Why? What's out there?"

Judah cleared his throat. "I wanted more info on the beating vic we found."

"Now that you have my attention, you better make it good, since I'm not on duty and you aren't either. What you got?"

"Not much new. More work. Slog work. Hitting-the-bricks kind of work. I'm curious about the vic, curious about the baby we found. You in?"

There was a long silence. "Damn. I'm jumping up and down and hoorahing with excitement."

"Like a hound dog on the scent. Can practically hear you baying, Tyree."

"Well, hey, man, I'm enjoying my time off. Maybe you should be, too, instead of waking me and Yvonna up on this fine, rainy morning?" Tyree sighed. "But you know how it is, Judah. You and me, we're getting to know each other. Like I said, I don't know who you are yet. It's bumpy right now. For you, too. Getting used to your first full-time partner since—"

"Yeah." Judah tightened the cord around his wrist. *Partner. George was his partner. Not Tyree.* "Yeah, since." He took a deep breath. "I'm a jerk, Tyree. You'll get no argument from me there. Don't read too much into it. We can work together. It's gone okay so far."

"Word was, you didn't want a partner."

"I didn't." Judah rested his forehead against the wet chill of the metal cubicle. "I don't. I like working alone. But it doesn't have anything to do with you."

"I see."

After a long silence, Tyree added, "So. You don't like anyone. Not just me, huh?"

Judah's laugh was rusty. "You got it. I'm not a people person."

"I picked that up right away. Due to my keen detecting skills."

"Can you live with that?"

A refrigerator door opened, shut. The sound of liquid pouring into a pot, a hiss as Tyree turned on a gas burner. "All right. You just don't like the human race in general. I can live with that."

"Good." He tapped the cubicle. "That's good."

"Hey, man, don't get all sloppy and emotional, hear? Folks'll start saying we're in love."

"Yeah. You and me. A couple." Judah snorted.

"Yep. Scandal in the department, huh?"

Judah laughed again. "Well, moving on from this love fest, what do you think about checking out the location where that beating victim—" He stopped, Sophie's words echoing in his head. "We should check out the woman who was beaten last night. While I was on the island, I interviewed…Dr. Brennan. She made some pertinent observations."

"Did she? The bodacious doctor babe had some—what did you call them? Observations? That why you're up and about, Finnegan? Because of the doctor and her observations? You mean you haven't crashed yet?"

"No." He looked out at the puddles shining in the gravel of the parking lot, stared at the orange Stop 'n Go sign. "I couldn't sleep, so I thought I'd run down a lead or two."

"That what you thought? That you'd run down a lead while I was sleeping?"

"Yeah, Tyree. That's exactly what I thought. Just trying to do some of that sharing you said you wanted. Thought you'd want to know. That's all."

Tyree covered the receiver, but Judah heard the muffled, "Hey, Yvonna, you gotta hear this!"

Judah kept his mouth shut.

Sometimes you had to let the other guy have the last word.

Later, finally surrendering to exhaustion, lying naked and clean on his bedspread, he folded his arms under his head and somberly regarded the dark beauty of the carefully measured-out inch of Lagavulin single malt in his glass. Oblivion. *Yes? No?* He looked away, staring at the ceiling where shadows moved and flowed in endless gray.

He couldn't sleep. He was past sleeping. He needed to sleep.

Oblivion, then. Half sitting, he reached out for the glass and sipped. He'd bought the whisky several years ago. At almost one hundred dollars a bottle, it had been a deliberate purchase. A thumb of the nose at the old man.

Now, savoring the smoky taste of the sea in the Lagavulin, he reckoned he'd gotten his money's worth. Even so, the whiskey hadn't done anything so far to shut down the racket in his brain.

Tipping the glass up, he downed the remainder. The alcohol burned with the taste of sea and smoke all the way down to his gut. He wiped the bottom of the glass and placed it back on the side table.

All the jangle in his head had gone smooth and quiet when he'd been with Sophie on the beach. She'd done what the Scotch couldn't. With her, he'd had that strange emptiness, that sense of being washed clean.

Peaceful.

Like what his daddy had talked about when he'd baptized his faithful flock. He'd used those words. *Washed clean.*

Bracing himself against the headboard, Judah sat up. He'd never let his daddy baptize him. The old man's mix of hellfire and damnation had sent him running as far and as fast as he could.

A peculiar satisfaction rippled through Judah as he thought about the way he'd found peacefulness today. Nothing like barreling down the road to hell fueled on expensive liquor and sex. His preacher daddy would have erupted in fury and red-faced screaming.

Playing with the devil had its own reward.

With a smile, Judah gulped the last of the amber liquid in

his glass and slid under the covers into sleep, his last conscious memory the compassion in Sophie's blue-gray eyes as he'd closed them and then lost himself in her.

It was two in the afternoon before Sophie walked into the Peds ward, a plump pink teddy bear tucked under her arm.

She hadn't allowed herself to think about Judah. She'd deliberately closed the door on the events of the morning. The slight soreness in her body, the marks he'd left on her, marks she'd welcomed, were invisible to the outside world. She'd opened a closet in her mind and locked the memories there.

Where they were safe.

She hoped that when she was sixty, she wouldn't open that closet and find nothing but dust.

She had no intention of living the rest of her life on memories and lost dreams.

She had plans.

A smart woman knew when it was time to reach out for what she wanted.

And Sophie knew what she wanted.

She walked over to the crib. The small, neatly lettered sign read Baby Doe. She traced the letters. "How's she doing?"

"Like a princess." The nurse on duty smiled and walked over, her white shoes shushing across the floor. "We fed her. She ate. Went to sleep. Woke up, ate again. She's quiet, but alert. All her signs are good."

Sophie traced the tiny ear, smiled as baby-brown eyes watched her. "Have they done a hearing test, too?"

"Not yet, but she's responsive to sounds. It's been slow up here today, so we've all been playing with her. It's been hard to resist her. She reacts to sounds, stimuli. She's been well taken care of, no abuse, no signs of dehydration. She's one of those quiet babies, that's all. An easy baby. Seriously, I don't think this cutie has a single thing wrong with her."

Sophie placed the teddy bear in the crib and lifted Baby

Doe out. "Except that she's here. And nameless." Cuddling the baby in her arms, she went over to the rocking chair that one of the doctor's wives had contributed to the Peds ward. Sophie glanced at the nurse. "Has anyone called about her? Any inquiries at all?"

"Nothing so far."

Unexpected relief flicked through her, embarrassing her. How could she be so selfish? She wanted the baby's family found. Truly, she did. But this baby felt so right in her arms. And she didn't want the beating victim, that poor, poor woman, to be this baby's mother. It would be too sad a history for an infant. The tiny mouth moving next to her breast made her yearn for something. But Baby Doe was someone else's little girl, not hers. Not hers to think about. Hers for these moments only, she reminded herself. Anything else was an illusion. "She'll be here a little longer then. Until someone claims her or Children and Families sets something up."

"Their offices have been closed because of the holiday. That will slow things down even more. We might not hear from them until tomorrow—oh, heck. Tomorrow's Sunday, isn't it?"

Sophie nodded.

"With all the shift changes up here, I lose track. We won't hear before Monday or possibly Tuesday. DCF is backed up."

"Not like the instant response TV shows suggest." Sophie smoothed back the cap of dark hair, twiddled her fingers in front of the baby's eyes. The baby's cheeks creased upward, and a pink tongue poked out of her dot of a mouth. "Oh, look. She's smiling. Yes, you are, aren't you? You're smiling at me, you little sweetie-pie." Sophie tapped the button nose.

Following the movement, brown eyes crossed. Sophie made her hand flap and float like a butterfly across the space between them.

Baby Doe gurgled.

"My goodness, you can talk, can't you?"

Baby Doe slid a gurgle into a goo-gah.

"You didn't have anything to say before. That was all, right?"

More gurgles and soft coos. And all the time the baby watched her with solemn attention.

"You are a clever little girl, aren't you?" Snugging her closer, Sophie bent her head and, nose to nose, nuzzled the baby. "Just the smartest little girl in the whole wide world."

From the corner of her eyes, she saw the grin on the nurse's face. "I know. I'm a pushover. But it's hard to resist this sweetheart." She sighed and stood up. "I suppose I should—"

And then she remembered that she had the whole day to herself. She could do anything she wanted.

What she wanted right this minute was to stay here in this padded, comfortable rocking chair and cuddle this baby.

"Lolly?"

"Yes, Dr. Brennan?"

"I'm going to stay a bit longer. I'll look after Baby Doe while I'm here."

"Sucker." Lolly grinned again and walked back to her station.

Sophie smirked and kissed the baby's sweet-smelling neck. "Not me. I'm a tough ER doc, remember?"

"Sure. No need to convince me. I know you made a point of being certified as a foster parent so you could baby these little guys. And that you used vacation time to do it. Yep, you're a softie." Lolly guffawed and shook her head.

"Short term. A week here, couple of days there. No biggie," Sophie said.

"Well, thanks. This will give me a chance to catch up on the paperwork. Yes, yes—" she nodded as Sophie lifted an eyebrow "—I'm a sucker, too. But she's so gosh-darned hard to put down. I figured the paperwork could wait. It did, but now you're here, it's back to work for me. No more yielding to temptation."

"Yielding to temptation's not all bad, you know." Sophie tried to hold back the tiny smile, but she couldn't.

"That's what I've heard." Lolly's sudden giggle had them both laughing.

Sophie set the chair rocking again with the tip of her toe. "Do you have children, Lolly?"

"Two." Lolly rustled papers, looked over. "But they're teenagers. Love 'em to death, I do, but, jeez Louise, they're hard to cuddle. And they don't have that nice baby smell." Green flashed on the computer as Lolly opened a file. "I miss that smell. There's nothing else like it. Stinky socks aren't the same."

"You have a boy?" Sophie rocked the chair gently back and forth, and the baby's eyes glazed over.

"Two. Seventeen and fifteen. And in my weak moments I think it might be nice to have another baby in the house."

"So you work Peds rotation instead?"

"Exactly." Lolly flashed a wicked grin. "Best of both worlds."

"But you have your babies. And the awful truth is they'll always be your babies even if they are hairy and tall and sweaty—"

"Don't forget horny! At this age, sex is all they think about. It's enough to make me want to run away from home sometimes. I swear, you can smell the testosterone in the air." Shaking her head, Lolly went back to her file.

Sophie laughed and wiggled deeper into the chair, her toe pushing the rocker in a steady, comforting rhythm.

Lifting one starfish hand to her lips, she pressed a kiss against the softness. "You need a name, don't you, angel baby?"

As if she understood every word, the baby watched Sophie with grave attention. From across the room, she heard the faint tapping of computer keys. Through the broad plate-glass windows, a splash of sunlight dappled the floor.

This was good. After the blood and death in the ER, rocking Baby Doe was very good. It soothed her hungry heart.

And filled her soul with an unexpected peacefulness.

"Angel." Sophie leaned her head against the tall back of the chair. "That's what you are. That's your name, baby girl. While you're here with me. Angel."

A hungry heart. That's what she had. Like the one Bruce Springsteen sang about. How long could a heart live with this aching hunger without shriveling up and dying? Oh, her heart was indeed hungry.

Holding Angel close to her breasts, Sophie drifted into a half sleep, a dream state where all things were possible, even this.

Chapter 7

Like a mole coming up from its tunnel, Judah blinked at the sudden shaft of sunlight.

"Nice." Tyree yawned and stretched out his hand, turned it in the warmth. "After the storm."

Judah was confused. His semiconscious dream had involved Sophie's mouth, her supple body and what she'd been doing with both. He echoed Tyree's yawn, blinked again to chase away those images. "I think I fell asleep."

"You did. Because of my smooth driving."

"Right. The smooth driving." He yawned again and peered at the neatly groomed lawns in front of the compact, old-time Florida concrete houses around them. "Odd place for the woman to be found, don't you think?"

"I do."

"Doesn't look like the kind of neighborhood where folks go around whomping on each other."

Tyree opened the unmarked squad's door. "You think that happens only on the wrong side of the tracks?"

"I know better. Cool your jets. I know we're in a shakedown phase, but we're going to be real uncomfortable if you keep calling me on everything I say. Cut me some slack, okay?''

"When I'm sure you've earned it, I will.''

"Fair enough.'' He leaned forward. "You know, Tyree, you called me on not opening up, but you put up walls, too. You act like the joker, but underneath, man, you hold up this measuring stick of yours to everything I say or do. Behind your easygoing mask you're pretty damned judgmental and untrusting yourself. You ever going to get past your suspicions of me being a white-bread Southern cop?''

Tyree waited a beat, then said, "Looks like that's something we'll both have to find out. Not going to be easy for either of us.''

"Anyway, I was thinking of something Sophie said.'' Feeling cranky with Tyree and tired in spite of the short sleep he'd had in the car, Judah climbed out the passenger side. "She said the woman took care of herself. Sophie thought she probably lived in a house or apartment. Not expensive, but nice. Well-kept. She could have been describing this neighborhood.''

Tyree said blandly, "Sophie would be the doctor you *happened* to talk to earlier this morning when you were running down the lead? And then decided we should be the primaries on the case? That doctor?''

"Yeah, that would be Sophie.'' Judah grunted irritably.

Tyree sent him a quick, measuring look. "Hands off?''

"Yeah. No. Hell, I don't know.'' Judah shrugged. "We're both running short of sleep.''

Tyree laughed. "There's the understatement of the month. And you decided we needed even more work, huh? Okay. Let's move on. You think our vic might have lived in this area?'' Scanning the quiet sidewalks, he frowned. "Worth a shot, like you said. Baker and Radar give you any grief about taking over their case?''

"Nope.''

Beside him, Tyree stepped around a deep puddle. "How'd you talk them into letting us have it?"

"Asked."

"Ask and ye shall receive?"

"Something like that, yeah." Judah halted and, like Tyree, scanned the area. "They hadn't had time to work it, weren't that interested, thought they'd sooner head down to Okeechobee for some post-Thanksgiving hunting and fishing. Didn't seem to care we're ass-deep in cases."

"And nobody's caught the kettle thieves. All that time wasted yesterday. So here you and me are, working on a Saturday when at least *one* of us has better things to do," Tyree muttered glumly. "I mean, I know everyone calls you St. Jude, patron saint of lost causes, behind your back, but still, I figure that makes both of us idiots."

"You could be right. St. Jude, huh? I didn't know that." A tiny movement caught Judah's attention. He narrowed his eyes, waiting for it to repeat. "There. Did you see that blind move?"

"In the white house?"

"The green one. With the lemon tree in front." Judah stared at the still house where nothing now moved. "Somebody's checking us out."

"Probably because we're such studs."

"Must be." Judah lengthened his stride. "C'mon, stud. Let's go to work."

"Want me to take the north side, you the south?"

"Let's stick together. See if we get the same impressions."

"Hoo, joined at the hip, it is then. Not gonna be too much togetherness for you, cowboy?"

Judah stifled a grin. "Probably, but you're growing on me, dude. But don't think this means we're in love or anything."

"Damn. And I had my hopes up."

They walked up the narrow sidewalk leading to the house closest to them. Yellow hibiscus bloomed brilliantly along the edges of the walk, and a freshly painted red door with a brass dragon knocker opened before they set foot on the stoop.

"Whoa." Judah stopped, Tyree close behind him. "Afternoon, sir. Wonder if we could ask some questions?" He flashed his badge. "We're with the police—"

The door slammed shut. The brass knocker banged hollowly against the strike plate.

Glancing down the block, Judah saw the same quick flicker at the green house again. "You know, either people in this neighborhood are scared of cops, or somebody knows something about our dead woman."

"You're about as good at this detecting stuff as I am," Tyree said. "Figuring that out so fast. I am impressed. Want me to buff up that shiny badge for you?"

"You're full of it, that's what you are." Judah scowled at the shiny red door. "I don't like having doors slammed in my face. How about you?"

"Nope. I don't like it either. Sort of gets my dander up." Tyree rested his hands casually on his hips. "Seems kinda unfriendly-like, don't you think?"

"Very unfriendly." Judah stomped up the concrete steps. He rapped the knocker twice.

No sounds came from behind the door. Somewhere in the distance he heard the tolling of a church bell and remembered there was a Catholic church a few blocks over. Saturday afternoon mass. Poinciana was a town of churches. And synagogues and temples now.

He waited, then rapped harder. "Open up. This is a police investigation."

Slippered footsteps approached the closed door. Eventually a crack appeared between the shiny door edge and the doorjamb. A brown hand gripped the door. An Asian man peered out, his manner guarded.

"Police," Judah repeated quietly. He could smell fear mingled with cilantro and lemon grass and the faint aroma of fish. "We have some questions, that's all. No problem, sir." Holding his badge to the crack, he stepped back a step, made his posture unthreatening.

From the sidewalk Tyree nodded toward the door. "A couple of questions, sir. Nothing to worry about."

The door opened. The man's hand still gripped it closely. He might have been afraid, but he wasn't intimidated. His wary eyes met Judah's. "Very well."

"An injured woman was found on the corner last night."

"Yes." The door never moved. The man's eyes never left Judah.

"We have a picture of her. Would you take a look at it? Making no sudden moves, Judah waited. Despite the man's slight, stooped frame, Judah could see he had once been tall, though still shorter than Judah's six feet. "We're wondering if you know her?"

"Why is that?" Shrewdness and sharp intelligence gleamed in the man's dark eyes. "I do not know her." He started to close the door.

"Take a closer look." Judah flipped the picture out and stepped up to the door so fast that the man, startled, stepped back, letting the door swing wide.

He didn't glance at the picture. "I tell you already I do not know her."

"Hey. Slow down a second, will you?" Judah blocked the door. "Take a good look. That's all we're asking. We'd appreciate any help you can give."

"I can give you no help." Almost as fast as Judah, the man reclaimed his door. "I do not know this young woman."

"Perhaps you've seen her, sir? In the neighborhood?"

"No, no. Goodbye. Large of luck in your job." He shut the door again.

Judah snatched the picture free as the door closed gently and with finality.

"Tough old bird, huh?" Tyree said.

"Absolutely. He knows something. But I don't know if he knew our woman." Judah moved swiftly down the steps. "He wouldn't look at the picture, but he knew she was young. So he has information. And if he does, someone else does, too. Let's hit some doors before the phones start ringing. You think this is a Vietnamese neighborhood, Tyree?''

"Could be.''

"The old man's English is good. Smooth, except right at the end. He understands better than he lets on. And he was getting nervous. He knew what I was asking. From the door I saw a watercolor map of Vietnam. New immigrants tend to live close to other immigrants. The woman who died was Asian. Nobody knows if she was Vietnamese, but she might be. She was found here. I'm betting there's some connection. I thought I knew Poinciana inside out. Didn't know about this block, though. I should have.''

"Lot of changes going on in this town. Anyway, like they say, you learn something new every day.''

"Guess you do at that.'' Judah thought of what he'd learned today about Sophie Brennan, and heat speared through him once more. He couldn't decide if that was a good thing or a bad thing.

It was definitely a disturbing thing.

And inconvenient. He adjusted his slacks inconspicuously.

He tapped Tyree's shoulder. "Let's go knock on some more doors.''

"Right behind you.'' Tyree matched him stride for stride. "Want to start with the green house?''

"No. I want whoever's behind that blind to watch us and get good and nervous first. I want him or her, and I'm guessing it's a woman, to wonder what's going on and when we're going to walk up that sidewalk by the lovely lemon tree. I want that person to be panting with anxiety and ready to talk.''

Judah was wrong.

The block wasn't a Vietnamese neighborhood at all. It was part of a neighborhood primarily made up of retired midwesterners, wintering in the Sunshine State. Like the man they'd first interviewed, these transplanted, tanned senior citizens said they didn't know anything about the excitement in the neighborhood. Unlike him, however, they wanted to talk. They knew where the best early-bird dinner specials were. They knew about the local golf course. They knew which grocery store gave double coupons.

And they were eager to relay it all to Judah and Tyree.

They were curious, sure, about the police activity the evening before, but with their windows closed—"We wouldn't dare leave our windows open at night!"—several of them hadn't known that a woman had been found beaten on their block.

After the eighth house, the buzzing in Judah's head was so painful he was ready to kneel down on the sidewalk and beg for aspirin.

"Officer, are we safe?" asked one woman with fluttering be-ringed hands and carefully styled bright-white hair. A set of expensive golf clubs leaned against the wall near the door. "This is dreadful. I'm here alone. I'm not going to be able to sleep a wink." She tapped her hand against the V-neck of her turquoise shirt. Cataract-dimmed blue eyes narrowed. "I need to get a gun."

"No, ma'am. You do not." Tyree beat Judah to the punch. "That's a really bad idea."

"But you have a gun," she said reasonably. "I'd feel a lot safer if I had one, too."

"But you wouldn't be," Judah said. "Poinciana's a safe town."

"I read the papers, young man." She shook her hand at him. Rings glittered in a blinding rainbow on twisted fingers. "I may be getting on in years, but I keep up with things. My girlfriends do, too. Don't underestimate us older folks."

"No, ma'am, I sure won't. I don't." When she closed the door behind them, Judah raked his hands through his hair and pulled. "That's just what we need. A gang of senior citizens armed with guns and golf clubs."

"You gotta admit they're a game bunch." Tyree laughed. "Damn. We should deputize them. I think it would cut down on crime. Wouldn't you freeze in your tracks if she came after you with a gun?''

Judah shuddered.

Taking a deep breath, he headed through the late-afternoon splashes of sun to the house with the lemon tree in front.

A cluster of small birds scattered with a rush of wings and chitterings as he pounded on the door. ''Open up! Police!''

A woman finally opened the door slowly. She was small, delicate, and middle-aged. Terror shone in her brown eyes. Her words spilled forth, the distress and fear rising with everything she said.

And Judah didn't understand a single word.

With his head pounding and Tyree shadowing him, Judah finally repeated, ''Okay, okay,'' in the most soothing voice he could manage.

The woman was so frightened, her head turning constantly to check the sidewalk, to look up and down the street as the incomprehensible flood continued, that Judah felt helpless to ease her distress. She flinched when he reached for his badge.

He felt like the bully of the Western world.

He didn't think he bullied people, but Sophie had accused him of doing so earlier.

Did it come with the cop territory?

He tried to dial down any threatening aspect so that the woman would relax.

But the whole situation got sillier and more frustrating as he tried to mime his questions, pointing to himself, to Tyree, their badges. Her terror, his inability to get through to her, the not-so-subtle clearing of Tyree's throat added up to a headache of bragging-rights proportion.

Finally, in desperation, he slowly reached for the grainy photo of the woman who'd been beaten to death.

Figuring a picture was worth the proverbial thousand words, not to mention the humiliation of miming the impossible, he held it out carefully. ''Do you—''

Her moan was soft, stricken.

Nobody needed a translator.

Here was grief and distress, raw and immediate.

He patted her arm. This time she didn't flinch. The picture in her hand shook violently. Touching the face in the picture, she kept saying something that sounded to him like she was asking about a bay and a duck.

He repeated his question in Spanish. Bewildered, she shook her head.

He turned to Tyree. "Know any French?"

"A little high school," Tyree said.

Hearing Tyree's comment, the woman said, *"Français? Non, non."*

Tyree continued in halting French, then turned to Judah. "She is Vietnamese. Her name is Hoang Lan Thoa. I didn't get much more, but I think she said our woman is Le Duc Nhu. And *bébé*. This is going to get ugly, man. I feel it in my bones. She's asking about a baby."

As the woman repeated *"bébé?"* hopefully, Judah felt a shiver down his back. He shook his head in a universal no. "Well, that didn't work. Since your French isn't much better than my Spanish."

As helpless as they, the woman continued to stare at them, the photograph held in her trembling hand.

Feeling like an idiot, Judah mimed holding a phone to his face and pointed to the car. The woman gestured down the block. He thought she pointed to the house with the hibiscus plants where they'd interviewed the man earlier. He reckoned she was indicating that the man could translate.

Judah considered trotting down to see if the man would help, but figuring the gentleman had made very clear his desire to stay uninvolved, Judah stayed where he was. He didn't trust the man to tell them exactly what the woman said.

They called from the car to see if the department had anyone who could translate. They did, but it would take a while for them to get there.

"Never fails, huh?" Tyree put down the mike. "Hurry and wait. And wait."

"Oh, the glamour, the glamour." Judah rested his head back against the seat. "Got any aspirin?"

"Nope."

"Well."

"Deep subject."

Judah shut his eyes.

Time passed in a dreamy haze as sunlight warmed the interior of the car. In those sleep-hazed moments he found himself on a sun-bleached beach, where white sand blazed and everything was clean and blue.

Peaceful.

Far out on the horizon, beyond the breakers, a small, bright figure endlessly beckoned to him.

Sophie.

Every time he tried to swim toward her, a huge wave came rearing up out of the tranquil sea and tossed him back onto the sand, where he watched hopelessly as she drifted farther and farther into the blinding sunlight and away from him in the darkness on shore.

A knock on the side of the car door shot him bolt upright. Sweat drenched his clothes. "Sheesh!"

Hoang Lan Thoa stood there. Gesturing them toward her house, she poured an imaginary drink, then used both hands to urge them out of the car. The edge of the photo peeked from the pocket of her dress.

Inside her neat home, they waited while she put a kettle on the gas range, assembled ingredients for tea, and kept up a constant stream of talk. Somehow it was all soothing— waiting for the water to boil, the small woman's low voice murmuring like a gentle river, the brush of sun against the red placemats on her table.

He almost dropped his head onto one of them and went back to sleep.

When the elderly translator arrived, the work began. Dressed in a suit and tie, slim and tall with carefully cut black hair, Mr. Dai introduced himself, shook hands, and sat down at the table with them. He sipped his tea and then, placing his cup gently and precisely on the table, he translated their questions.

Judah found himself watching Hoang Lan Thoa's face as she responded. It was clear to him that the woman was terrified and sick with worry. Tyree was right. It was going to be ugly.

And he and Tyree had to make it right.

As right as anything could be when death and violence were involved, anyway. They would do what they could.

It wouldn't stop the ugliness. It wouldn't change anything for the victim.

But they'd give her justice.

They could do that small thing.

His stomach tightened. He shoved his chair back from the table, folded his arms, and waited.

In a tremulous voice, the woman responded with questions of her own. *"Co Le Duc Nhu bay goi o dau? Chuyen gi da xay ra voi co ay? Con cua co ay o dau?"*

Back and forth the questions and responses went.

"Here's what she's telling me," Phan Dai finally said. "She's very frightened. Her friend has vanished. She wants to know why you have her picture. What has happened to her and to her baby? What you want I tell her?"

"The truth." Tyree looked at Judah. "Right?"

He nodded. "Mr. Dai. See if you can find out where the woman lived, if she had any relatives. You know the drill, I'm sure."

"Thank you. Yes, I know the drill very well."

Finally he inclined his head to Hoang Lan Thoa, folded his hands and reported to them. "Three young boys came to Le Duc Nhu's house. Three very bad boys, she say. Much noise. They run up and down the block. Loud boys. Perhaps not quite boys, maybe older. They disappear. Mrs. Thoa hasn't seen her friend since. Mrs. Thoa does not call the authorities. She is afraid. She does not speak English. She does not know what to do. She is worried about Le Duc Nhu's baby, very worried. She wants to know where is Le

Duc Nhu's baby?'' Mr. Dai lifted his hands. "Do you know?''

"No.''

Across the table, Tyree sent him a questioning look.

Phan Dai studied both of them. But he said only, "I see.''

In a fast series of words, he reported back to Hoang and continued his questions. With a small exhalation, he concluded. Rubbing his forehead, he said, "This woman was alone. She had no relatives in this country. She had a sister in Texas. This sister died. Le Duc Nhu had nothing except her job at the orange juice bottling factory, no one except her baby. Mrs. Thoa is very concerned about this baby, a girl. She wants to know who's taking care of her?''

Again Judah didn't answer. Directing his question to the translator, he said, "Find out where our victim lived. Did she live here with Mrs. Thoa?''

No, no, Hoang Lan Thoa waved her hands, rose from her chair and pointed out the kitchen window, her meaning clear.

They left her sitting at the kitchen table, her face tight with worry.

They went to the house she had shown them. Smaller than most of the houses on the block, it shared part of the back yard with Mrs. Thoa's house. Looking back, Judah could see that Mrs. Thoa wouldn't have seen anything that happened once the three boys had left the sidewalks of the block. A large hedge ran down the lot line. A huge magnolia tree in full leaf further obscured the view. She would have heard the noise of the three boys in the street. She would have been shaking with fear.

But she couldn't have seen or heard anything that might have happened in the house.

In the late-afternoon stillness, a chill danced along his skin. Pushing through the bushes, he and Tyree came upon a clothesline. A wooden pole supported one end of the rope. The other end, torn from the branch of an avocado tree, lay on the ground. Diapers trailed on the still-wet grass, mute and muddy testimony.

The back door was wide open, the screen door hanging drunkenly on one hinge.

"Oh, boy." Tyree took a deep breath and brought his Sig 9 to his side.

"Nobody's here."

"Huh. You sure about that?"

"Not positive. Pretty sure." Judah lifted his head, sniffing the air. "We're the garbage men, now, Tyree. Cleaning up the mess."

Tyree kept his pistol at his side. "You understand? Not that I don't exactly trust your judgment—"

"But you don't. And you're careful. So keep your weapon at the ready."

They edged up to the house, listening. "No." He motioned Tyree behind him. "I'll go first." Taking a deep breath, Judah entered the house and went into the kitchen.

It was bad.

The walls were sprayed with graffiti. A container of flour had been upended on the kitchen floor, flour tracked across the hall to the living room. The refrigerator door hung open. Jars of baby food were lined up neatly on one shelf.

On the wall, framed photos of a baby hung crookedly. On a table that rose higher than the other furniture in the living room a collection of other pictures were grouped on a gold silk cloth. In one, a laughing woman in a pink filmy dress held a chubby baby up to the camera.

He recognized the smooth, young face of the woman.

An immense sadness welled up in him before he could catch his breath, the weight of it pushing against him.

Drawn by the joy shining in the woman's face, he almost picked up the picture. Keeping his hands at his side, he didn't touch it.

All that joy, that love smiling at the camera.

Gone.

Tyree joined him, saw the picture. "Oh, man. I hate this job."

"I love it," Judah said, walking past the black-and-red spray-painted walls to the bedroom closest to the kitchen.

Like a capital letter *I,* the house was laid out with the kitchen at the back, two bedrooms separated by a bathroom off a hall, a large room on the other side of the hall, and then the living room at the front. The front door was partially open.

"How you figuring this?" Tyree stood in the hall. "They came in the back?"

Looking at the flour tracks, Judah nodded. "They must have busted down the back door, come through here, then into the living room." He stooped down to look at the two sets of tracks. "Something's odd, though. What do you think, Tyree?"

"Didn't our witness say there were three guys? I see two sets of footprints in the flour, least it looks like two different sizes."

"That's what I see, too." Judah stood. Every bone in his body ached. "Let's finish up the walk-through and call it in. Let the lab boys do their thing."

"But where's the third guy?" Hands on his hips, Tyree scowled at him. "Where's that damned third guy, Judah?"

An empty crib stood against one of the walls in the front bedroom. A mobile hung crookedly from its support at the head. A stuffed pink bunny was jammed head first through the crib slats.

There was no baby. Not in the closet, not under the heap of baby clothes strewn about the room.

No baby anywhere.

Judah inhaled.

"Make the call, Tyree."

Tyree stomped out to the front porch and pulled out his cell phone.

Judah turned in a circle, absorbing the destruction and the mess. Taking in the desecration of what had been cheerful orderliness.

He leaned his forehead against the doorjamb, the only graffiti-free spot in the room, and waited.

There was no small body waiting for him.

He took another deep breath.

There was that, at least.

He wanted to feel relief, to feel grateful.

But around him he felt only the rushing of a dark and terrible wind.

Chapter 8

Sophie stroked out with one leg. Her roller blades hissed against the asphalt. Working for speed now and half bent forward, she zipped past the low cement bunker toward the far end of the parking lot. This shady, deserted end of the hospital parking lot was her favorite cool-down area.

Who knew that one's life could turn around in the blink of an eye? In the touch of a baby's small hand?

Who'd-a thunk it? Laughing, she wiped the sweat from her forehead. From underneath the plastic helmet shell, sweat dripped down the back of her neck, down her nose. The late-afternoon sun had finally dried up most of the puddles and chased the chill from the air. She'd burned off a lot of confusion during an hour of steady blading. Still…

Swaying sideways, she made a wide loop.

Stroke and think. Stroke and think.

She'd hoped the hypnotic motion would free her mind so that she could figure out her strategy. She knew what she wanted. But not how to make it all happen.

It had all seemed so simple in the Peds ward.

Angel had fallen asleep as naturally as if she'd always slept in Sophie's arms.

Nice. Perfect.

Reluctantly, Sophie had finally put her back in her crib.

How could she let this baby go into the system? All babies were precious, but Angel? To let her disappear into that vast bureaucracy with its current abysmal follow-up?

She had no power to prevent it.

But perhaps...

Ideas rose in her head like gaily colored balloons, one after another, their bright colors luring her.

Anything could happen when a woman knew her own mind. A determined woman had powers that could shake the world. If she wanted them to.

And, oh, how she wanted...*everything!*

She came to the curb of the hospital parking lot, bent her knees, and jumped the curb in a flashy, show-off motion. Laughing, she whirled, jumped it again just for the heck of it. Everything!

From the shade of the huge banyan tree came the sound of slow clapping. "Bravo."

She stumbled. "Whoops!" Her legs lurching left, right, the rollers going out of her control, she crashed on her butt. Bracing her arms clumsily on the asphalt, she steadied herself and grimaced. "Finnegan. Like a bad penny, you keep showing up."

"And you keep wiping out." Strolling toward her, a scowl on his face, he leaned forward and held out a hand.

Ignoring his offer of help, she hunched forward on her knees and balanced herself on her hands.

"Oh, hell, Sophie." Cupping her elbows in his palms, he yanked her straight off the ground into a standing position. He kept his hands, warm and rough, on her until she was balanced. With the tip of one finger he traced a line of sweat down her throat, down to the edge of her scooped T-shirt. Studying the cling of her shirt at her ribs, under her breasts, he sighed. "How come you're always...wet when I run into you, Sophie?"

The heat roaring through her should have turned her desert-dry.

His fingers played at the neck of her shirt, tangled in the chain dangling there. His eyes were brooding, the blue filled with darkness.

"What do you want?"

"One of the nurses told me you were out here. We need to talk." The chain slipped like a rosary through his fingers.

"That's a line every woman loves to hear the morning after. Even though it's more the afternoon after for us." Wishing she weren't so thrown by seeing him, she wiped her hands down the sides of her shorts. "Yet you keep harping on it, don't you? I thought we'd settled this. We don't have anything to talk about, Finnegan. You're like a dog worrying a bone to bits."

"But you like to talk, Sophie."

"Not always."

"Oh, you have to choose the topic and set the agenda, is that it? Or give orders? Action, movement. Sparkle. That's you. But always on your terms. Under your control. You like being in control, I think. Ever really lost control, Sophie? Ever really wanted to?"

"It depends on the purpose." Still sliding through his fingers, the chain drifted like the lick of cool snow flakes against her breasts. "And, Judah, once again I don't know whether to be insulted or to say thanks."

"Good." Back and forth he moved the chain across her chest, shiny against her damp skin. "Because I'm not sure what I meant either."

"Why am I not surprised?" She puffed her hair out of her eyes irritably and unclipped her helmet. She didn't think she could go another round with him clarifying and discussing the aftermath of the morning's madness. No, not madness. After all, she'd known what she was doing. She'd let that lovely, wonderful oblivion take her where it would. So while it wasn't madness, she still didn't quite know how to label what had happened.

Even more disturbing than trying to skirt the several issues that lay between them, though, was the need to muster the energy to deal with his presence. Like water dripping steadily on a stone, he could wear her down and make her say things she didn't want to say, couldn't admit. Wasn't prepared to handle. His presence stole her certainty and made her doubt everything. She definitely didn't need the agitation of Judah's presence when she was trying to stay focused on this cloudy dream that seemed born of sea foam and shower steam. And now he was talking about losing control? Judah could fry a woman's brain with a glance. Short out all the circuits. Turn her into a gibbering mass of wanting.

She'd learned that. And loved every minute of scorching to a crisp.

But not now.

The tip of his finger caught against the edge of her top.

"Stop that." She batted his hand away from her neckline. She could hear the short, sharp sounds of her own breathing. My God, she thought, I'm panting. Two seconds around him, and he has me panting, for Pete's sake. "Why are you always touching me?"

"I like touching you, Sophie. That's why. Indulge me."

"Why should I?"

"Because. That's all." His gaze held hers. "Just…because."

She didn't say anything. She couldn't, not faced with the sadness in his eyes. She didn't have it in her to move away at that moment from the lost, damned look in Judah Finnegan's eyes. It was that glimpse into some dark corner of his soul that got her every blasted time.

Still holding her gaze, he played with the necklace, his fingers tightening around the chain. "What is this?"

"An heirloom. My great-grandmother's cross." Late-afternoon sun and birdsong cocooned her in a hazy stillness. If she backed up, she'd break the chain. She wished Judah would take one step back. One step would give her room to breathe.

"Doesn't look like any cross I ever saw." He lifted the pendant for a closer look. The backs of his knuckles skimmed her skin.

Heat, pleasure in the brief touch.

She wished he'd move his hand lower, dip underneath the satin-bound edge of her shirt.

"Russian Orthodox," she managed to say, her belly going liquid with want.

He frowned. "I don't understand." Blue enamel winked at the edge of her view as he twisted the cross, studying it.

"Slanted footrest, extra bar at the top. Different from the usual Christian crosses."

"Okay." He coiled the thin chain loosely around his thumb, drawing her closer. "Let's chat about your grandmother, then. Can we agree on that topic?"

She realized she was leaning in toward him and jerked back. The cross slipped out of his fingers and fell hot against her skin, all its snowflake coolness gone. She flattened her hand over the emblem. "Bushka brought it with her when she left Russia at fifteen. She's all I have left to call family now. The rest are…gone. But this cross? Not worth anything."

He let one hand stray to her shoulder, his fingers moving restlessly against her damp skin. "But you wear it?"

"Call me sentimental."

"Are you sentimental, Sophie? Soft-hearted, you tough little cookie, you? One more surprise."

"She gave it to me when I was twenty-one. She put it into my hands, cupped them around it, and told me the story of her mother, an illiterate Russian peasant, who'd escaped untold horrors. I wear it. For them. For me. To remind me."

"Of what?" Frowning, he stepped forward. "Explain. Please," he added as she sent him a look.

She closed her hand around the emblem. "To remind me that I come from a long line of strong women. To remind me that even when I think I can't take one more step, I always can." She tucked the cross safely under the edge of her shirt. "It reminds me that life is good. Not easy, but good."

"You think?" Brooding, he stared at her. "That life is good?"

She raised her shoulder, letting it push against his hand. "I do."

"In spite of what you see every day?"

"What I see is good nurses and doctors working their butts off to take care of people. I see people giving up vacation days to help when we're short-staffed. And, yes, I see the broken people, Judah. I see the pain, the suffering. Death. I don't understand why you keep coming back to this. But I told you this morning, I'm not a fool. I'm not blind."

"I think you are."

"As you've said already. Numerous times. Every time we talk about anything personal, Judah, we go around in circles, getting nowhere. That's not my style."

She knew why they did their little waltz. All the easy teasing, the sense of something growing between them had been stunted, like a bonsai tree, not allowed to grow and bloom naturally. In these last two days, all the chopped off feelings and emotions were sprouting every which way, like Kudzu along the highway, taking strange and frustrating directions. And she didn't have a clue how to regain her balance, to recover her self, that old, direct, supremely confident *self*.

His head bent toward her. His lost, dark-blue eyes looked into hers. "You're so blind, Sophie. You don't see what I see in the world."

She shook her head. "You remind me of the little kindergarten boy who colored all his pictures black. When his worried parents and teacher asked him about it, he said all he had was a black crayon. You need more crayons, Judah."

He rubbed his forehead. "Handing out free psychological advice with your medical treatment?"

"When it's needed." She skated past him, swirled and

returned to where he stood, half in sunlight, half in the shadows of the trees. "Is this part of the cop thing, Judah? This coming back again and again to a subject? Is this how you break down a suspect?"

"I don't know what you mean." Arms folded, he leaned against a live oak tree.

Sophie tripped over a bump in the asphalt, wobbled, waved her hands and steadied herself. "I don't understand you, Judah. You make me feel as if you're trying to make me confess to some unnamed, unknowable crime." Her stomach clenched as the words slipped out. She wondered if he'd use her carelessly spoken words to open up the topic of George's death. She hoped he would. Talking about George would lance the wound, let out the poison. Then, perhaps, they could stop their endless circling around each other.

Because they had never been able to air out what had happened with his partner, that poison had seeped into everything between them.

Except sex.

Sex between them was something else. Pure, clean. Glorious. Direct.

When the silence dragged on miserably and he hadn't moved, hadn't spoken, she gave a mental shrug. Evidently they were going to keep diverting the real topic onto her life view, a subject he couldn't seem to leave alone. "I hope you've noticed that although you say you want to talk, you keep returning to one topic, my so-called blindness. I don't see any place for this kind of conversation to go with us. Once, you weren't quite this negative. At least, that's not how I remember you." She gave him the opening, left the door cracked, but he ignored it. "Do you think you're going to wear me down until I agree with you? That I'm going to change my version? This isn't a story, Judah. It's who I am. You can't keep hounding me about this because it is what it is. It won't change. You can't keep picking at how I look at the world, hoping I'll trip up and reveal some inconsistency.

There isn't any inconsistency. What you see is what you get.''

Not a flicker of movement revealed his thoughts, his reactions.

Frustrated, she took a breath, making one final effort to make him see what was happening. "Are you trying to make me say, 'Yeah, life sucks. It's awful'? Is that why you keep insisting that I'm a fool, I'm blind, I'm wrong to see life and people the way I do?'' She waited in the afternoon silence for him to answer.

He shrugged.

"Fine. Don't answer. Because the bottom line is, you aren't going to persuade me of your point of view. I'm not going to change yours. We're at a standoff. So retreat into your impassive cop mode.'' She wanted to thump on his hard chest, shake him up, do something to get a reaction from him that wasn't calculated and programmed. "By the way, as the TV doc says, 'How's that working for you?'''

He was as silent as the tree he leaned against.

"I hope it is. Because the truth is, I don't care. Really. I don't.''

"I'm not trying to convince you of anything. I like my life exactly as it is, thank you very much.'' His chin jutted forward.

"Then I'm happy for you. I don't believe you, but if you want to believe it's fine, terrific.''

The other truth, the one she couldn't admit to him, was that she didn't want to care. She couldn't afford to care about this man whose torment plucked at her heart.

When they'd first met, she'd been immediately drawn to his stillness and gravitas, so different from herself. But, since she'd first known him, those qualities had changed. He'd gone to some darker place in this last year. Going up country, the Vietnam vets had called their physical venture. It seemed to her that in an odd way the Judah she'd first met had made a similar trip, vanishing into some unknowable and killing landscape. While she didn't begin to understand what had made Judah the way he was, her instincts told her that more than his partner's death was involved. He was more complicated than the old cliché about still waters running deep.

And, like some guerrilla of the emotions, he kept slipping under her guard. She doubted he realized how easily he held her feelings hostage.

There was no future for them. She understood that. Maybe there never had been. All the qualities she thought she'd sensed in him—the kindness, the passion for his job—all those seemed changed now in the wreckage of what he saw as her involvement in his partner's death.

Even so, she wished she had the power to go back a year.

Maybe things would have been different if they'd had more time. Maybe Judah could have trusted her then. If they'd had that time.

But they hadn't.

All this bristly bumpitty-bump-bump of words had its roots in the past, but in the here and now, there was still the pull of this *something* between them. She hoped it was only chemistry. Because caring, like talking, was a one-way ticket to nowhere.

When the silence and tension between them at last became unbearable, she gave up and went down the road he'd laid out. "So why *are* you here, Judah? What's going on?"

"I figured you'd want to know the follow-up."

"What?" Without thinking, she laid her hand on his arm.

"We identified your beating victim. Le Duc Nhu, a Vietnamese woman. We did a neighborhood sweep. Found the crime scene. Not far from where she was discovered."

"She'd left her house?" *Angel,* Sophie thought. *Angel.*

"Yeah. But we don't know the chronology. She had a child. A baby. We didn't find it. The place was trashed. Graffiti on every wall. You know. The kind of thing we've been seeing around town."

"Bad?"

"Lousy."

"Oh, Judah. I'm so sorry." She felt an enormous weight

of sorrow for the poor woman she'd treated. This suffering, deep and soul-killing, was what she'd seen in Judah's eyes, was the reason for the darkness around him. The urge to comfort was so strong, she reached up and touched his cheek even as a strange dread coiled inside her. "Tell me about it?"

He shook his head.

"It would help."

"It wouldn't."

She didn't know why she'd bothered asking.

He shifted his weight, a whole paragraph of body language saying *don't push.*

She didn't. But she left her hand cupping his face. She could speak body language, too.

"Anyway, I figured you'd want to know. And since Tyree and I had to come to the hospital to tie up loose ends—"

"Killing two birds with one stone? Very efficient, Judah." She smoothed the lines at the edges of his eyes. She didn't want to comfort him, didn't want to get pulled into the no-win situation that was Judah Finnegan. A really, really smart woman wouldn't. But he was too thin, too tired, too strung out. And maybe she really *was* a fool and not as smart as she thought because she found herself asking, "When did you eat last, Judah?"

He shook his head. "I ate. I'm not hungry."

For food. Unspoken, the words were there in the burn of his eyes, the flush along his cheekbones every time he looked at her. Seductive. Dangerous. There was always that between them, even if they couldn't manage to find the right words to bridge an abyss as wide as the universe.

She laid the back of her hand against his face again. The skin was dry, the circles under his eyes dark. Dehydration. She should have caught those signs earlier, but he'd pushed her hot button so fast, and she'd gone off like a rocket. "You look like something the cat dragged in. Am I finally getting the lingo right?"

"Sure. Or you could tell me I look like I been rode hard

and put away wet.'' Even in his exhaustion, he raised an eyebrow slyly.

She rolled her eyes. ''You look like hell, that's what, and like you're incubating a category-5 headache.''

''Yeah. I've got a headache.''

''You're an idiot, Finnegan.''

''So say they all.''

''You need food, you dope.'' As if he were one of the patients coming into the ER who might go down in a heap, she put her arm around his waist to support him. ''And I'd bet a monkey's uncle you've been drinking during the last twenty-four hours.''

''But only really, really good Scotch.''

''That makes a difference?''

''Oh, yeah, Dr. Sugar. Trust me on that.''

She made a face. *Men.* ''Come on, let's go to the cafeteria and feed you. And how much sleep have you had since you played undercover Santa at the charity kettles and got knifed in the process? Not much in the last forty-eight hours, right?''

His hand on her shoulder stopped her, spun her around. ''I'm not your patient, Sophie. Don't make that mistake.''

''I won't.'' Her breast softened against the hard muscles along his ribs. Oh, she knew exactly what he was. Six feet of trouble and heartache she couldn't deal with. ''But I'm not letting you leave here until I've gotten some food and liquid—and I'm not talking about expensive whisky—into you. You may not be my patient, but I wouldn't let my worst enemy leave here in the shape you're in.'' She skated forward.

''Am I your worst enemy, Sophie?''

She shrugged, took a stroke away from him. ''No.''

''I see. Must be your sentimental nature.''

''Probably.'' She skated forward.

His long strides kept up with her, his palm open against the bare skin of her back. Right at the dip of her spine into the waistband of her shorts, his fingers teased the sweat-soaked edge.

She wanted him to stop.

She would have paid him a hundred dollars to let those restless fingers stray just a bit lower.

She glared at him.

"What's the matter?"

"Quit doing that stuff."

"What stuff?" A five-year-old with his hand caught in the cookie jar couldn't have looked more blandly innocent than Judah Finnegan as he paced beside her, his hip bumping hers companionably, his hand moving in easy, lazy strokes on her back.

"You know. *That* stuff."

"You could skate faster," he offered helpfully. "And then I couldn't do…stuff. If you wanted to."

"I could."

"But you don't want to."

"Maybe I feel sorry for you."

"Or maybe you like this stuff." He traced a slow, tantalizing arc that finished under her ribs, a hand's span from her belly button.

"Nope. Don't seem to."

"Liar." His thumb brushed under the edge of her waistband. "But notice that we're talking, Sophie."

"Talking? You think this is *talking?*" She skewed around to face him, dislodging his hand and throwing up hers. "You make me crazy, is what you make me!"

"I make myself crazy. If that's any consolation."

She flung both hands up again. "I give up." She started to skate off.

Judah tugged at the back of her shirt. "Slow down a sec, firecracker. I should let Tyree know where I'm going to be. He's in the hospital morgue with the neighbor woman who knew your patient. They have one more stop to make."

Exasperated with him, with herself, she plunked her hands on her hips. "All right. You said you were tying up loose ends. What other loose end is there?"

He rubbed the silky material of her shirt, tethering her to

him. "I told you your woman had an infant child. Tyree's taking the neighbor to see the baby we found at the church last night."

In front of them the Poinciana River curved wide and lazily to the west, toward the gulf. One lone sailboat tacked silently across the purple-and-pink blueness.

Sophie knew what was coming. She'd tried to keep the door closed, but here came reality. Her heart started a slow, sick tumble. "Angel."

"What?"

"The baby you and your partner found last night. I've been calling her Angel. You're pretty sure Angel is the child of my beating victim, aren't you?"

He nodded. "We're hoping the neighbor can give a positive ID of the baby as well as the woman."

"What about the woman's family? The baby's father?"

. "I don't know all the details. Hoang Lan Thoa said Le Duc Nhu no longer had relatives in America. She'd had a sister in Texas who died. I didn't hear anything mentioned about the baby's father. He could be in Texas, too. Anyway, Tyree, the woman and the interpreter are sorting all that out. If the baby is hers, we'll know soon, and we'll take it from there until we find out where the baby belongs."

Sophie gazed into the distance as Finnegan made his call. Of course Angel would be Le Duc Nhu's. Nothing else made sense. She'd expected that from the beginning. This was good news. Angel wouldn't be thrown into the maw of foster and state care. Somewhere she probably had a father, a family. They would be sick with worry about her. Of course Judah's information was the best news possible.

This sense of emptiness was nothing more than—than what?

And how silly of her to feel that anything had been lost. How selfish.

But she remembered the tight grip of Angel's hand on hers and something broke loose inside her, an almost physical tearing apart. Clenching her grandmother's cross, she closed her eyes against unanticipated and wholly self-centered pain.

Her plan had been only a dream, nothing more.

An impulse of the moment.

Angel was going to be with her family. That was what was important, she kept reminding herself.

The wrenching pain would vanish.

Pain always did.

And if the loss of her scarcely articulated dream left a forever phantom pain, the way a lost limb did?

She clutched the necklace tightly.

"Done. Tyree's going to catch up with me in the cafeteria." Frowning, Judah looked at her for a minute.

She was terrified that he'd start hammering her with questions.

She could have wept with relief when he didn't. This rawness was too humiliating. Too self-indulgent. But she felt as if the entire protective layer of her skin had been peeled away.

Even a strong woman needed a dream.

Silently, side by side, his hand resting on her hip, they made their way back into the hospital.

There was an odd comfort in the touch of Judah's hand against her. No future in that touch, but sometimes a woman could be forgiven for seizing the moment.

Chapter 9

Judah couldn't take his eyes off Sophie's narrow shoulders and tidy butt as she waited in the cafeteria food line. She'd told him to save seats and skated off to snatch a tray and get in line. He'd watched her every move, from the quick efficiency of her moves through the crowd to the way her wrist bent as she pulled at the material of her shorts. Crazy, this inability to ignore her. He could tell himself it was merely professional observation of his surroundings. Except for the fact that the only surroundings he seemed to study were Sophie's.

A man in the grip of a sexual compulsion ought to be locked up until he got his sense back, he thought sourly as he noticed her conversation with the sallow-faced, ponytailed man in his twenties. Judah frowned, trying to recollect where he'd seen the man before. He knew he had. He just needed a context to put the memory in. And then he had it. Mr. Ponytail was the face that had kept hovering in the background of the ER last night. Satisfied, Judah let his gaze drift around the noisy room.

There, he could concentrate on something other than Sophie's long legs and the glimpse of curved buttock as she leaned over the counter.

Footsteps snapped his attention away from her. Tyree. But without the interpreter and the neighbor. Grateful for the diversion, Judah leapt to his feet before Tyree arrived at the table. From the corner of his eye, Judah caught a glimpse of a blue-shirted back and a stringy ponytail disappearing through the swinging doors leading to the service area of the cafeteria.

Sophie met them both in the aisle.

"Mrs. Thoa and Mr. Dai, the interpreter, are headed home as soon as I go back upstairs and get them. I came down to give you a quick update. Mrs. Thoa identified the woman. And the baby," Tyree added in acknowledgment of Judah's lifted eyebrow. "She recognized the baby blanket, too. She showed us the corner where she'd embroidered the Vietnamese word for good fortune for Le Duc Nhu's baby."

A tiny sound came from Sophie.

Judah sent a swift glance in her direction. She'd recovered her game face so fast that he didn't think anyone else had seen the stricken look in her eyes. But he had.

Before Tyree could say anything, Judah asked, "Did she have any kin? Anybody we need to get hold of?"

"Nah. Mrs. Thoa clarified through the interpreter that she'd checked and found an old telephone number for the sister she'd mentioned in Texas. According to what Mrs. Thoa was told, Le Duc Nhu, her younger sister, and an uncle and aunt came here in the seventies. Le Duc Nhu was around eight or nine at that time, so she must have been around thirty when she was murdered. Mrs. Thoa also explained that Le Duc Nhu's husband had been killed in a fishing-boat accident before the baby was born. He'd hired on as part-time labor over in Cortez. That's it on the information front. Judah, I'll be back to collect you as soon as they're ready. Mrs. Thoa wanted to spend some time with the baby. She used to babysit for her while the mother worked, I guess." Tyree shrugged and left, slapping his way through the cafeteria doors.

Behind him, Judah heard the slide of Sophie's skates, the clatter of the tray on the table, the rustle of her shorts against the plastic chair. Breathed in the light scent that was pure Sophie.

Silently he turned and joined her.

She plunked the tray down and folded herself into a chair. "There. Eat."

"You do like to give orders, don't you?"

"I'm a doctor. It's what I do."

Judah picked up the overcooked hamburger Sophie sent sailing down the cafeteria table. He took a bite, chewed. "This is going to cure what ails me?"

"Sure. Grease and white bread. Southern haute cuisine, right?" Her smile was a pale reflection of its earlier sparkle and sass.

"But we have our standards, especially for our finer things." He swallowed a dry chunk of burger. "Sorry, Doctor Sugar, but the *Coast Herald* won't give this five forks."

"Tell it to the hospital board. They're on an economy kick." She rested her forehead on her folded hands. "It's better than letting your glucose whack out."

Taking another bite, he chewed steadily as he studied her and thought about that tiny sound she'd made at Tyree's news. "I've had worse hamburgers, I reckon."

"Haven't we all?"

"Yeah, but you're not eating. Playing it safe, I reckon?" But he couldn't get her to react.

Out in the parking lot she'd glowed with exercise, with that inner light that fascinated him. Then, suddenly, the light had switched off, and everybody left the building, so to speak. This quiet Sophie disturbed him. He missed that Sophie glow.

"Med-school food sucks, huh?" He took a swig of Dr. Pepper and managed to wash down the wad of bread and meat. Studying her over the rim of the paper cup, he waited to see how she'd react to his choice of 'sucks,' her earlier word. He didn't have to wait long.

Her head whipped toward him so fast it was a wonder she didn't give herself whiplash.

He almost grinned.

A bit of color washed over her face as she squinted in his direction. "I'm beginning to get your pattern, Finnegan. I'll bet when you were a kid and went to the zoo, you couldn't resist rattling the grizzly's cage just to see what it would do."

"You'd bet actual money?" He swatted a clot of ketchup onto the meat patty. Ketchup ought to make the godawful burger slide down his throat without choking him.

"Yep." Her smile wavered, but it was back. "A hundred dollars at least."

"Whoa. Quite the high roller, aren't you, cookie? You'd win. I was a difficult kid." He offered her a French fry dripping with ketchup.

Still resting her chin on her hands, she cocked her head. "And you can be a difficult man. All that pushing, needling—it's exhausting." She wrinkled her nose, and her rumpled, tired face suddenly looked like a cranky five-year-old's. "But I suppose you know that, don't you?"

He concentrated on his hamburger.

"Why are you always pushing, Judah? Is that how you are with everyone? Or only with me? Seriously, I want to know."

He swirled another fry in ketchup, plopped it in his mouth. Possibly because she looked so unexpectedly forlorn, he found himself saying, "I don't like surprises. I don't like turning a dark corner and not knowing what's around it. So I reckon I pick at things until I'm sure I won't be ambushed."

"And yet you chose a job filled with the unforeseen, where every day you turn a corner, not knowing what's there. Why is that, do you imagine?" Her question was surprisingly gentle, her wariness momentarily absent.

"Well, I have a gun. That evens out the odds."

"It gives you control of the situation at any rate. But you

won't always have that gun. What are you going to do then? When you go around some dark corner you hadn't planned on?''

He knew she wasn't talking about his 9mm. But he didn't have an answer.

"You like control."

"I do. And you do, too."

"But you gotta learn to ride the wave, Finnegan. Go with the flow. Mellow out, dude." She closed her eyes and yawned, let her chin drop again onto her propped-up hands.

"Good surfer-girl philosophy?"

"Oh yeah." Her face blurred into soft lines of exhaustion and weariness as she closed her eyes.

Nothing he'd done had brought back that inner spark. He knew he should get up, find Tyree, get back to work.

"Want another?" He poked another loaded fry at the edge of her mouth. Ketchup dotted her lower lip, and he had a sudden hunger for Sophie-flavored ketchup.

Not opening her eyes, she shook her head.

An instinct he had no intention of analyzing compelled him to ask, "What's wrong, Sophie?"

Big and soft and sad, her eyes aroused some protective instinct he wasn't prepared for as she said, "Angel. Angel's what's wrong."

"Things happen." He shook his head. "You can't fix everything."

"I've been on a losing streak lately. One or two would be nice." She crisscrossed the cold fries on his plate until she had a log pile. "She won't leave my head, you know. I keep thinking about that little baby, about what's ahead for her, and my brain goes into weird places. Round and round and where it stops—" Sophie dismantled the logs and began rearranging the salt and pepper shakers on the table. "I went up to see her earlier today."

"Why?" He handed her his Dr. Pepper.

"Does it matter?" She took the lid off the paper cup and

swirled the ice cubes before taking a sip. "Ugh. How do you drink this stuff?"

"It's one of those Southern things you keep complaining about, Yankee Girl." He snapped the lid back on. "You like kids? Is that why you went to see her?"

"I'm crazy about kids."

"And?" He ripped open the plastic-wrapped Sno-balls, scattering flakes of coconut across the table. He pushed his plate away. "Where'd all the fizz go, Sophie? What's going on here? You have dark corners of your own, don't you?"

She placed her hands flat on the table, started to stand up, sank back down into the chair. Bending over, she fiddled with the bindings of her skates until she'd loosened them and could remove the boots. Still bent over, she paused until, as if she'd reached some kind of decision or couldn't help herself, she said in a voice so whispery and melancholy that he had to strain to hear, "I can't have babies, Judah. That was what I meant earlier…when I said you didn't have to worry about anything on that front."

He felt as if she'd sucker-punched him.

He remembered the look of Angel in Sophie's arms and how Sophie had held her, the soft smile on Sophie's face. "Aw, Sophie, I'm sorry." And, stunned, he realized his sympathy was genuine.

"Me, too."

Only the top of her shining hair was visible, and the urge to smooth his hand against that gleaming cap, to offer the comfort of touch, was frightening in its intensity. He leaned back and tucked his hands into his pockets.

"Don't look so glum, Finnegan. It's not the end of the world."

"No?" He thought she slid over that part way too easily.

"Hey, it happens to women all the time. I'm not special. That's my gramma's mantra. 'You're not special, kiddo, so deal.' My gramma's the really tough one. I'm a wuss in comparison." She smiled, Sophie at her coolest and most in control, Sophie not letting anyone see behind the brightness.

He knew she had no idea how much her face revealed. "So you deal?"

"I deal." Her chin lifted. "See? It's lousy, but it's not a tragedy. Tragedy is an infant with a brain tumor."

"But it's still a loss. For you."

She waggled her hand back and forth, swallowed, and kept smiling. But the smile wobbled at the edges, and her eyes went bright with the shine of tears she wouldn't let fall.

In that moment he remembered how much he'd liked her when they'd first met. He'd forgotten that sweetness, and now, remembering, he liked her again.

And fought that simple reaction with everything in him.

Lust was simple. Liking was dangerous.

Earlier, he'd heard what she'd said about pregnancy not being a problem. Why hadn't he picked up on it? Because he'd been bullheaded, totally focused on his own worries about what he'd allowed to happen, that's why. Because he was an idiot like everybody kept saying, that's why.

She pressed her hands against her eyes, swallowed. "Do you want kids, Finnegan?"

Before he could answer, she dropped her hands and looked at him, startled. "Oh, rats. You mentioned once you'd been married when you were nineteen. And divorced. I forgot. I'm sorry. You probably have children, don't you?"

"No. And, no, I didn't want kids. Absolutely not. No way. Not now. Not ever."

"Gosh, you sound so wishy-washy." Her melancholy voice held a faint teasing note.

"Look, I don't like kids, don't want one, never felt any need to pass on the Finnegan genes."

"That's emphatic."

"Damn right." Because she looked at him as though she didn't believe him, he added, "I have no ego investment in little Judah clones, Sophie. I like being a dead-end DNA street, if you want to know the truth. It ends with me."

"Really?" She wrinkled her face. "I suppose the whole biological tick-tock is different for men."

"I don't know about other men." He didn't want this conversation. "I know about me."

"It's good to know what works for you." She shrugged. "As for me, I kept having this crazy idea that I could adopt Angel. Silly, huh? But there's some connection I couldn't explain in a million years. Angel feels like mine even though she isn't. Even though I know now that was her mother I treated yesterday." Covering her face, she slumped in her seat. "That I lost her mother."

"You were ready to adopt her? That fast? Without even thinking about it?" Her ability to open up her life, no holds barred, sent shivers down his spine. "Impulsive."

"It felt *right*. As if it were meant to be. A risk? I suppose. Oh, heck, I don't know what I'm thinking." She beat her forehead lightly against the table. French fries bounced off his plate onto the tray. "It's all such a mess."

"Damn right it's a risk. Didn't you even consider all the trouble you'd be bringing on yourself? Hell, Sophie. What if her mother was attacked because she'd been involved with criminal elements, and then they came after you? Came after that baby for some reason?"

"Then Angel really would need someone, wouldn't she? And I would be there for her."

"Sheesh, Sophie." He couldn't pull his thoughts together, not faced with her ability to dart down a path that was riddled with potholes and potential disaster. And so impetuously. That's what took his breath away. That impulsive, quicksilver streak. He shuddered and then realized she was still talking, earnestly, softly.

"Anyway, I know that's why you kept pushing to talk this morning."

"What? What?"

"You may be difficult, Judah, but you're a responsible man. If I know anything at all about you, I know that much. You were worried I might get pregnant. You said you don't like surprises. An unexpected pregnancy would be the ace of all surprises. I get that. But what happened between us was a one-time thing."

"That what you think?"

Startled, she glanced up, frowned. "It's what I know. We both understand this morning didn't mean anything." She sent a careful look his way. "It was a momentary…impulse. Two people reaching out for comfort, I think. For connection after a crummy day. Nothing more."

He agreed with her. Sure, he did. He would have said the same thing if she hadn't beaten him to it. So why was her calm dismissal of the greatest sex he'd had in this life starting to piss him off again? But, afraid of what he might let slip, he kept his mouth shut.

"I gave you the information you needed, but I didn't think we needed to get into my medical history. The details weren't your business. Anyway, I didn't want to talk about them. It was personal."

"And screwing our brains out wasn't personal?"

Stubbornly she continued. "You didn't need to know. But you wouldn't leave it alone." She lifted her head and then bent down again, concentrated on her boots. "By the way, Judah, I should compliment you on your technique. You managed to get a confession out of me after all, didn't you?"

He heard the world of hurt in her admission and felt like the lowest snake in the grass. Irritation drained away as he watched the play of expressions across her face. "Did you want kids?"

"I always knew that scenario wasn't possible. I love my career. I concentrated on it. I didn't think about children. I knew what I had to do. I did it. I didn't dwell on what wasn't in the cards for me. Life was good. It still is. I'm a lucky, lucky woman. And I appreciate that."

"But?"

"But my wonderful, lucky life has begun feeling…empty in a way I'd never imagined it could. I thought I'd come to terms with the way things were." She wouldn't look at him as she worked her feet free of her boots.

"And then Angel showed up on your doorstep."

"Ah, Angel." Sophie tucked her feet in their white socks behind the rung of her chair, looped her hair behind her ears, settling in. "There she was. After that long, lousy day. I don't know how she fits into all these crazy thoughts I'm having. Well, not exactly. It's difficult. Judah, she looks at me with that tiny, trusting face, almost as though she's trying to tell me something, as if she *knows* me. Oh, I can't explain it." Sophie wrapped her arms around herself. Laughed. "I'm such an idiot."

It was the shaky laugh, its gallantry, that broke him. He brought his hands out of his pockets and gestured. "Give me your foot, Dr. Sugar."

"What?"

"Give me your foot."

"Here? In public?"

"Nobody's paying attention to us." He gestured to her to lift her foot to him.

Bemused, even a little amused, he wasn't sure, she swung one foot up, rested it on his knee. He peeled off the thick sock and pressed his thumbs against the ball of her foot and along the slim arch while he sorted out his impressions.

He liked Sophie's foot, its elegant curve, the unexpected bright-red polish on her toenails, the delicate skin over its bones. He liked the tiny hiss of pleasure she made as he worked his fingers against the sole. "You had a fantasy. About Angel."

She nodded. Her eyes locked with his. "A fantasy. Yes. That's all it was. But it started me thinking about things. About my life. Then this afternoon when I saw her again, everything snapped into focus, just like those slide shows. Pictures, one after another. I could see this…" She hesitated. "…this *future* ahead. All these possibilities. And I wanted them. As much as I've ever wanted anything. Somehow it was all linked to Angel. Silly, huh?" She pulled her foot away and rolled her sock back on. "That was nice, Judah. Thank you."

"I'm not finished." He gestured for her to lift her other foot and was entertained by her surreptitious glance around the cafeteria. He figured she was more vulnerable than he'd realized since she wasn't giving him major grief about the foot massage. "You thought since Angel was abandoned that—?"

"I didn't think anything through."

"No big shock there." He wiggled her little-piggy toe.

"It was those pictures in my head. And they all made such good sense. Speaking of things that make good sense, here's one that doesn't. Why are you rubbing my feet, Judah?"

"I told you. I like touching you. Or because you look miserable. Or because I can't help myself. Choose one. Or go for D, all of the above."

"And why am I letting you?" She sighed and tried to tug her foot free.

"That's an entirely different matter. I've been mulling that one over myself." He crumpled her toes forward, flexing out the kinks. "Because you needed something I could give you, Sophie? That I wanted to give you?"

She went completely still. Then, leaning forward, she peered into his face as he traced tiny circles on the curve of her knee. He left his hand on her knee in spite of a sudden urge to hightail it out of the cafeteria.

"Sympathy, Judah?" She curled her fingers around his hand, stopping his restless movements. "For me? I don't want charity, you know."

"Not charity." The words came reluctantly, and he didn't understand why he said them. From the moment she'd parted the curtains and walked into the examining room the night before, she'd stirred up a killer brew of emotions in him. He didn't like them. He didn't want them. But they were there.

"Then what?" Her clear eyes met his, and this time he saw the vulnerability behind their straightforward gaze. This time he saw the wounded woman behind her cleverness and self-confidence.

"I don't know." Understanding settled heavily on him, a

solid weight in his belly. Earlier he'd thought he wanted to chip away at her bossiness, her damned utter self-assurance, thought he'd wanted to see her taken down a peg or two. It hadn't turned out the way he'd expected. He hadn't seen past the white coat to the fragile woman. Arrogance of his own had blinded him.

He saw now that he had the power to hurt her.

And he finally understood that she could destroy him.

Abruptly she bent even closer toward him, her eyes narrowing as if she were reading a streaming video of his thoughts scrolling by on his forehead. "You're afraid of me, aren't you, Judah?"

He felt as if she'd turned over a rock and found a nasty little something he hadn't wanted to see the light of day.

"Truthfully?"

With her hard nod, a faint scent of her, delicate, delicious, came to him over the hospital and cafeteria odors.

"You scare the hell out of me, Sophie. And I don't know what to do about it. That's the God's honest truth."

Sophie raised one eyebrow and then tipped her head, almost as if she was examining him under a microscope.

And Judah wanted to slide under the table and crawl out of the cafeteria like a dog with his tail between his legs. With that damned admission echoing between them, he felt like he'd given her some kind of hold over him. He'd give a good year's pay to have the damn words back, unsaid. But there the suckers were, laying out there as if he'd carved off a piece of himself and offered it up to her on a silver tray.

Sophie, being Sophie, wouldn't let it go without a comment.

But Tyree interrupted, and Judah took a deep breath. Ambling up to the table, Tyree nodded in Sophie's direction before leaning over the table and snagging a fistful of fries from Judah. "What kind of partner are you, Finnegan? You didn't save me much."

"You want to stay away from hospital food, Tyree. No lie. What's up?"

Giving him a sharp look, as if he knew that the word *partner* would stick in Judah's throat, Tyree returned the remaining fries, uneaten, to the plate. "I sent the witness and our interpreter home in a cab. That's done, at least." He rested one foot on the rung of the chair next to Judah.

Exhaustion grayed Tyree's brown skin, but Tyree would never admit he was tired. Judah had learned that much about him in the months they'd worked together. Tyree would fall down dead in a heap before he'd admit to any weakness.

Pride. It afflicted them all.

Made them do stupid things.

Tyree rocked the chair with his foot. "Has anyone checked in with Department of Children and Families? I been wondering what's going to happen to her. Looks like that bitty girl's going to have to go somewhere. Damned shame."

Sophie's tray made a shushing sound as she slid it to the side. Very carefully she gathered up the debris of their meal, fingers moving efficiently through the mess. Too carefully for Judah's mind.

But then her skates clanked against the floor as she shifted, and he realized she wasn't as calm as she appeared. At least Tyree had directed her focus elsewhere. Sort of like the cavalry coming to the rescue. Not that he could put it that way to Tyree. But sure as grits and gravy, he felt like Tyree had saved his bacon. The cafeteria ambiance, so to speak, had his thoughts running in food comparisons. He nudged his tray away.

"I'll make sure that everyone's notified," Sophie said

Her voice was so professionally friendly and so carefully helpful that Judah squinted hard at her, his cop nature making him automatically suspicious.

"I was going back upstairs anyway before I headed for home. No problem."

Of course she wouldn't leave the hospital without going up to Peds to see the baby who'd hijacked her heart. He knew that. He could almost see the wheels turning in her head. She'd make the call, but he figured she wouldn't be in any hurry to turn the baby over to Children and Families, and she didn't want to show her cards to him and Tyree.

He kept his mouth shut. The baby wasn't his concern. What Sophie did or didn't do wasn't his concern either.

"I got babies of my own, and that little scrap upstairs? Shoot. She's got a hard road ahead of her. Let us know what happens with her, okay?" Tyree's foot jiggled the chair again.

"Of course, Detective. I'll leave a message for you." Her weary smile was as insubstantial as wispy smoke at twilight. "As soon as I know anything." Her fingers twisted around a straw, let it drop onto the tray.

Judah's pager vibrated against his waist. Tyree looked down at his own belt at the same time.

"We're done here, Judah?" Tyree checked his pager. "'Cause it looks like we're up again. This one's on the clock. So much for a day off. Let me go phone and see what's going on."

"Sure." Judah avoided Sophie's eyes.

He didn't need to look at her. He was preternaturally aware of her every move.

Five minutes ago, those words had blurted out of him, and now, even with the reprieve Tyree had bought him, the words hung like knives suspended over him. One wrong move and they'd tumble down in a lethal rain.

He heard the crinkle of plastic against plastic as she consolidated the trash, saw the stringy-haired guy edge into the cafeteria again, do an about-face and leave, and he sensed Sophie's tilt of her head in his direction.

He managed to look at everything in the room except her.

"So we're finished here, Judah?" Tyree repeated as he glanced uncertainly from Sophie to Judah. "Because we got a problem over at the A.M.E. Church."

Judah wasn't finished, not by a long shot. One way or another he had to rebalance the scales.

Like Tyree, though, he knew when it was time to retreat. "The African Methodist Episcopal?"

Tyree nodded. His long frame vibrated with impatience.

"Yeah. I'm done." Judah slid out of the chair so fast it tipped toward the floor. Grabbing it with one hand, he risked a look at Sophie.

Too much knowledge, too much understanding in her clear-eyed gaze. Every time, damn it, she managed to *see* him.

He ran.

Sure, it was more of a well-organized, purposeful, business-like lope, a man-on-a-mission kind of lope, his movements all full of cop rhythm, a lope meant to tell her he really hadn't meant those last words, that he'd been having fun with her. Yanking her chain one more time.

As he turned, not for any reason except to be polite and toss off a farewell wave, he knew by the quirk of her lips that she wasn't buying his playacting.

His face burned as he followed Tyree to the exit doors.

Halfway through the sliding doors at the far end of the cafeteria, he turned again, compelled by some instinct.

He didn't want to think it was a need to have one last look at Sophie.

The why of it didn't matter.

The mistake was in the hesitating. Because he did.

And like Lot's wife turned to a pillar of salt, he froze.

For him there was no one else in the room, only Sophie seated once more, her head down on the cafeteria table, her arms wrapped around the back of her head, her feet curled tightly under her chair.

At the edge of the swirl of noise and color in that chaotic room, she was the loneliest sight he'd ever seen.

Chapter 10

Judah didn't even realize he'd stepped back into the cafeteria until Tyree grabbed him by the arm.

"C'mon, man. We got work to do. And nasty work by the sound of it."

"Yeah. Right." Judah dragged his attention away from the small figure. He didn't like the fact that he'd almost gone back inside. Weakness. Shrugging into the tattered remnants of his old anger, he forced himself to remember the bill of charges against her and was dismayed to discover that anger was no longer a comfortable fit.

He wanted the anger back.

But he was stuck with this baffling need to comfort Sophie Brennan. No good could come from this.

He preferred Doctor Tough Cookie, not this woman whose pain plucked at him and sneaked in under his radar screen.

Torn between the impulse to go back to her and the urgent desire to get the hell out of Dodge, Judah found himself following Tyree's quick steps into the cool early evening where the sighing of the wind in the palm trees echoed his own confused sigh.

In a flat-out run, he caught up with Tyree, who'd already fired the engine and had the car rolling forward. Tyree leaned across the seat and wrenched the door open without slowing down. "Get your butt in here! Come on, man!"

Holding onto the roof with one hand, Judah crawled into the passenger seat and snapped his seat belt in place as Tyree slammed the accelerator to the floor. "Sheesh, what're you doing? Payback for the fries? Low blow. I warned you, remember."

"You warned me." The car barreled forward, jolting Judah's head back against the seat.

The gleaming white of the hospital with its sparkles of holiday red and green grew smaller and smaller in the side mirror. And then winked into darkness.

Hospital food and holidays sucked. Big time.

The fire from five bags of burning dog crap was almost out by the time they wheeled into the parking lot. They would list it, of course, as 'canine fecal material' in the report, but crap was what it was, and it stank. The fire truck was still there, but several of the firefighters were winding up the hoses. "False alarm," the chief said. "No damage done."

At the chief's words, Tyree strode over to the charred remnants and glared at the mess. "This—*mess* on the front steps of my church, and you say there's no damage done?"

One of the firemen edged away from the heat in Tyree's face and voice, sidled back to the truck and climbed in.

The chief turned to Judah. "You know what I mean, right?"

Ignoring Tyree, Judah said, "Nope, Hank, can't say's I do. Looks like damage to me. I'm thinking it needs the full report. Been way too much of this kind of junk going on in Poinciana. Now me and Tyree here, we're going to do the full run-through. You and your boys need to do the same."

"Hell, Finnegan. When did you turn into such a hard-nose?'' Hank Bonniface swung back to the truck and growled out orders. ''We've been running like ten cats scratching litter since I don't know when. This was a nothing deal. A fat waste of time.''

Tyree's whole body bunched up, an arrow ready to fly.

Judah grabbed Tyree's arm, felt the tight muscle, the fury. Judah looked back at the men shooting surreptitious looks at him and Tyree. ''Cool it,'' Judah murmured. ''They don't mean anything. They were just trying to make a short night. They're good guys. They work hard. You know how it's been with all these fires being set lately. Everybody's strung out. Bonniface's men are simply relieved that nobody got hurt. And they're making stupid jokes, nothing more.''

''Just a few good ol' boys, huh, Judah? All of 'em just so damned glad it wasn't a five-alarm burner. But it's a *church*. *My* church. Damage *was* done, man.''

Judah held on. ''Hey, I didn't know this was your church, Tyree.''

''Why would you?'' Tyree's face went shiny-tight with barely contained violence. ''You don't know *nothing* about me, Judah. You don't know the names of my kids, you don't even know I drink tea, but you don't ever ask why I throw out all that lousy damned coffee you keep shoving in my face. You never even been to my damn house. Why in hell would you know what *church* I go to?''

''Don't lay it all on me, Tyree. You keep your distance, too, you know.'' His anger flared to meet Tyree's, a crackling of heat and flames as destructive in its own way as any of the recent fires in Poinciana.

''Judah. Step back.'' Tyree's flat voice held none of his usual teasing. ''You don't want to jumble with me right now.''

That fast, the facade of their partnership crumbled. It was all out in the open now, the doubts, the wondering, the effort it took Tyree to be a cop in Poinciana. All laid out for Judah to see. He couldn't walk on by this time. Like it or not, and he was pretty damned sure he *didn't*, he was involved.

Taking the two steps forward that no man took without being prepared for the consequences, Judah stepped right into Tyree's space.

"Back off, man. I won't tell you again."

"I hear you, but take a good look, Tyree." Judah jutted his chin toward Tyree. "See me standing here? You see me moving anywhere? Because I'm not taking a step back. Got that? Me and you got to make this right. You're my partner, and by damn, we're going to settle things. You want to bring it on, go right ahead. Right now and right here's as good a time and place as any. All this, this *garbage* that floats underneath everything you say, under what I say, all this damned history that hovers between us is going to end tonight."

"Garbage?" Tyree's eyes narrowed into hard slits. "You don't know what you're talking about. You're not the affirmative-action detective in the department, the guy promoted because, funny thing, Poinciana didn't even have one single black detective until me. Plenty of my brothers on patrol, but not one detective or sergeant. Lots of promises and excuses about budget and department size and seniority. But no action. Until me. You're not the guy they're all watching and expecting to screw up. Hoping I will? You bet they are. And my people are watching, too. I got this weight on me, man, and you don't have a clue. So take your big talk about settling stuff elsewhere. Over to those guys on the truck, for instance." The muscle along Tyree's jaw bulged.

"This is between us, Tyree." Judah struggled to find the right words, one clear word that would make the other man see that he was trying to reach out, trying to get it right for the two of them, at least, if not for the whole wide world, the world neither could control nor fix. "Everything you say is true. I get it. Sure, you make an effort to be one of the guys. You bring Yvonna's potato salad to the station. But you don't let anybody see who you are behind all your jokes. It's like you're playing a part or something."

Tyree's shoulders rolled forward, and a dull flush shone on his dark skin. "Yeah?"

Judah took a deep breath. "So if you want me to know who in hell you are, *partner*—invite me over for some of your damn beer and barbecue."

Nose-to-nose, they glared at each other, anger and frustration steaming off them.

"Yeah?"

"Yeah."

Tyree gave him one of the longest, fiercest stares Judah had ever received. Fury and frustration and a pain so deep Judah had no understanding of it burned at him from Tyree's dark eyes.

Neither of them moved.

A century passed between them in the parking lot of the A.M.E. Church. The cool night air of Poinciana eddied around them as they stared at each other, not speaking, each standing his ground. So close their breath mingled, they could see each other's dilated pupils, yet they were separated by a chasm so deep and so wide it might not be crossed.

Judah understood there were words that could never be said, things that could never be explained between men like them. Their profession shaped them and made them wary. Their natures rendered them inarticulate.

Still, something beyond words kept him, kept Tyree, rooted there in the night.

Suddenly, the big old-fashioned bell in the church rolled its heavy sound through the night and the silence, the deep tolling reverberating through them, wrapping them in that majestic sound until the very air shook with its power.

In that moment Judah felt as though someone had reached into his soul and wrapped a fist around the darkness and loneliness and misery there before moving away, leaving him bereft.

The bell shuddered to silence again.

Even in the quiet, Judah still felt the sonorous reverbera-

tions echo inside him, tolling, calling him to account for all
that he'd done, for all that he'd left undone.

In that instant something shifted in Tyree's face. "All right
then. But it's not barbecue. It's shrimp. Sunday night. After
evening services." Tyree glowered at him.

"What do I bring?" Judah glowered right back.

"Nothing but your own sorry damned self." Tyree
stomped away toward the still-smoking piles on the church
steps. "Now I got work to do. By God, somebody's going
to pay for messing with my church."

Later, showered and changed, Sophie rested her head
against the back of the chair. Angel's warm cheek lay against
Sophie's as she rocked back and forth. Through the tipped
shades of the Peds Ward, Sophie watched the heavy night
settle in. Chicago nights had never had the deep black of
Florida nights. In the distance she watched the twinkling
Christmas lights maintenance had hung on Friday shimmer
and move in the night breeze. A reminder of another world,
their brightness seemed to keep the darkness outside the hospital at bay.

A snuffle and a baby snort tickled Sophie's nose. She stifled the sneeze that would have jostled the baby awake. Sophie marveled again at Angel's easy nature. She'd been a
well-loved baby, and now, poor dumpling, she was set adrift
on an uncharted sea.

"Ah, sweetie, it's going to be okay." With an aching
heart, Sophie nuzzled Angel's fluff of black hair. "I'm on
your side. There's love out there for you. We'll work out
what has to be done. You are not alone in this big old world.
Trust me," she whispered into the soft ear so close to her
heart. "I'll figure something out." She touched her grandmother's cross to Angel's cheek. "I promise. Trust me" she
repeated. "Can you do that? In spite of everything that's
happened to you? Trust me a little?"

Easing up from the chair, she tucked Angel into her crib
and covered her. Since Sophie had last seen the baby, some-

one in the ward had washed the blanket Angel had been found in, and Sophie tucked the silky edge of it into the baby's fist. As Angel's fingers curled around the edge and brought it to her mouth, Sophie murmured, "Sleep tight, baby girl. Sweet dreams. May angels watch over you through the night."

Lolly had gone home some time ago. As Sophie walked to the door and past the nurses' station, she nodded to the nurse on duty. She gestured casually back at Angel. "I'll make the calls to set things in motion for Baby Doe, save you the trouble, since she was my patient originally. Tell Lolly when you see her that I've taken care of the paperwork."

"Thanks, Doctor Brennan." The nurse flipped her hair back. "I'm backlogged on charts. I sure do appreciate it, you taking care of the calls. I'll miss the little love-bug, though."

"I know what you mean." Sophie squished into silence the voice that whimpered that what she was doing wasn't exactly kosher, that she wasn't adhering to hospital policy. She smiled and headed for the elevator. Even though she'd never pulled rank before, she had to admit that there were some advantages to seniority and hospital hierarchy. To do what she was planning, she would need every single advantage.

When she reached her car, she realized that she didn't want to go home, not to the silence.

Not to the emptiness.

Yielding to impulse, she zipped back over the bridge and skidded to a stop in a sandy parking area at the east end of the island. Music vibrated in the air, a low bass thumpa-thump that whomped right down to her bones, a beat that had her two-stepping straight through the front door and to a table.

She'd found Catfish Charlie's not long after moving to the island. On Saturday nights Charlie opened the place to local bands. Overlooking the water, loud, and off the tourist beat, Charlie's was her place, her version of her Chicago neighborhood hangouts. Charlie, who was really Gordon Moskal from the southside of Chicago in another life, understood and watched out for her, made her feel safe. So Catfish Charlie's was where she went after a day of surfing, where she went when she wanted easy company.

She needed people and noise tonight.

Not these unwelcome and haunting thoughts.

An hour later with a light beer buzz making her silly and giddy, she laughed at the young man in the cowboy hat who insisted he could cure whatever ailed her, "ma'am," with a fast waltz around the dance floor. Ten years or more her junior, "Cutter's my name, ma'am," had the relaxed charm of Southern men. He looked so hopeful, the music was irresistible, and his lanky body reminded her of Judah Finnegan in some perverse way, and so she let the boy lead her onto the dance floor and through the steps of some complicated movements set to a zydeco beat.

He was good. His energy and, yes, the glances from his appreciative eyes rollicked through her buzzing body.

"You're right!" she gasped, finally collapsing back into her seat after five numbers, her melancholy thoughts sent a-spinning in the heat and movement.

Standing spread-legged, Cutter tipped his cowboy hat back with a forefinger and drawled in what had to be his best Chris Isaak imitation. "So, little darlin', why don't you and me do a little more than dance?"

"Well, Cutter, sweetpea," she said as a giggle bubbled up, "I'm old enough—"

"Naw, darlin', don't you dare say you're old enough to be my mama." He stepped close and his lanky frame had all the tensile strength of the very young. "You can't be my *mama*'s age, honey."

If she'd been twenty-two instead of thirty-four, Sophie might have been tempted. "Cutter—ma'am" was cute and awkwardly sweet. His smile held the promise of the charmer he would become once he outgrew his puppy-dog eagerness and into his shoes, so to speak. But he was a boy, and he wasn't Judah and—

She slammed the door shut on that errant thought.

Still, his flirting tickled her, reminded her of better times, and he was adorable, and she didn't want to hurt his feelings, so she smiled as she answered, "No, really—"

"You maybe could be my very, very *young* aunt, darlin', but never my mama."

His smile slid from hopeful to rueful as she continued to shake her head decisively and said, "Thanks, but…no, thanks."

"Not my night, I guess. But, honey, you sure are one fine woman. My bad luck." With a wave of his hand, he vanished into the smoke and music.

Humming to herself, Sophie collected her purse and asked for a cup of coffee to go.

"Cutter give you any trouble?" Gordon handed her the coffee carefully. "Because I can kick him out of my establishment, you know." Gordon's broad Polish shoulders hunkered over the bar.

Sophie had a moment of concern for the blissfully ignorant Cutter. "Nope. He was just doing that Southern thang," she drawled, "making a woman feel like a girl again. Nice, after a couple of really lousy days. Thanks, though."

Inhaling the coffee scent, she headed to the back door and the sand at the water's edge to clear the smoke and alcohol fumes from her head.

Fun and games were over. No way to avoid the inevitable now. Nowhere to go except home.

To that very empty house.

The feelings that had sent her to the hospital earlier in the day drifted in through the open door with the mist and fog off the Gulf. That sense of emptiness, of the house waiting for something, seemed to be a permanent awareness now.

Standing in the shadows at the entrance to Catfish Charlie's, Judah hadn't been able to take his eyes off her. Swing-

ing in wide circles, her gauzy pink skirt flipped against her
bare legs and tangled around her calves. Head thrown back,
she danced with abandon, her body a fluid, shifting shape
under the honky-tonk lights. He could hear the peals of her
laughter as the wannabe stud twirled her around the floor,
one arm glued around her waist, the other clamped to her
hand. Her hair had gone all frizzy and wild, and her eyes
glittered. Her legs flashed and scissored to the beat of the
song.

The woman he'd left head down on the table in the cafeteria hours ago was groovin' and movin' to Charlie's band
for the night, the music a throbbing invitation to low-down
sex and wickedness.

He didn't exactly understand why that pissed him off.

The music did its own beat inside him, through him, a
smoky, rhythmic invitation, and all he could think about was
the way Sophie had felt under him, around him, and he
wanted her there again. Wanted her with such intensity he
couldn't take a deep breath, couldn't think.

Skin to skin, stuck together by salt water and passion—
that had happened this morning. Not even twenty-four hours
ago. Layers on layers of images blurring in kaleidoscopes of
colors. This was how the dead must feel, lost souls hovering
in a disembodied state where longing and need had no outlet,
with all the color and richness of life out of reach. Caught
between memory and desire, he believed those dawn moments must have happened in another lifetime.

To a different man.

Yet his skin remembered the touch of her. His mouth remembered her taste. Everything.

With an ache he didn't understand, he remembered most
of all the fragile curve of her neck hours earlier as she'd laid
her head down on that cafeteria table.

But now in the hazy yellow lights of Catfish Charlie's, she
whirled in this dream-like dance, luminescent, with some
other man touching her, breathing in the scent of her.

With a guy in a cheap cowboy hat who didn't have the right to... Judah stirred against the wall.

Why was Sophie letting this, this *kid* wrap himself around her?

The baby stud's hand slipped to the curve of her butt. He looked like he'd died and gone straight to heaven.

Judah blinked. The urge to punch the stud's straight-toothed shiny smile to kingdom come and back galloped through him in a red haze.

But he stayed where he was, watching Sophie, absorbing her delight while the raw sting of...something flicked inside him.

She dipped backward, holding onto the guy in the cowboy hat but laughing so hard she lost her grip. But he caught her under the arms and lifted her up until her toes were clear of the floor. Laughing, too, he steadied her as he hip-bumped her over to a table where a slim red purse claimed her place. She collapsed into the chair he held for her and fanned herself rapidly with her hand.

Judah couldn't see her face, but he knew what the kid was asking, what he wanted from Sophie. The angle of his body toward her, the way her arm moved on the table, the jiggle of her foot as she listened—all told a story.

Judah knew he shouldn't care how the story ended. Sophie wasn't *his*. She could do whatever, whomever, she wanted. But... He didn't understand why it mattered so much to him whether or not she left with the guy.

But since it did, and since he'd already gone way past any comprehension of his behavior on this strange day winding down into late night, he waited in the shadows while that prickling heat ran over his skin and through his gut.

When Sophie rose and walked to the back door alone, Judah followed her. He didn't allow himself to think. He simply followed the flicker and shine that was Sophie.

And relished the rush of a righteous, pissed-off anger.

Perched on the edge of the rocks that formed a breakwater against the moonlight-iced gulf, she held a cup in one hand.

She'd dropped her sandals on top of her purse. Red on darker red and the drift of her pink skirt in the breeze.

Sophie.

How could a man not be drawn to the life in Sophie's every movement, the vibrancy in that mobile face?

No wonder the moth banged its wings madly against the flame, yearned to plunge into the heat that destroyed.

What other choice was there?

She didn't even turn around as he stepped onto the breakwater behind her. "How did you know I was here, Judah?"

"I spotted your car."

"Liar, liar."

"All right." He wanted to yell at her for dancing with the kid, he wanted to…

"Where's your partner?" She gazed out to the thin horizon where dark met darker.

Judah took a careful, small step toward her. "He went home after the call." He didn't want to think about the incident at the church. He was still unsettled by what had happened. "A prank." He raised one shoulder dismissively. "When Tyree and I finished, I ran your plates. One of the island cops spotted your car."

"You ran my plates?" There was little curiosity in her voice, almost as if she'd expected him. Tipping her cup back, she drank deeply. "And so here you are."

"Yeah." Her calmness ratcheted up the pissed-off factor one more notch.

"Why?"

Not answering, he took another step and caught her wrist. "How much have you had to drink, Sophie?"

"I'm not drunk, Judah." She rose and faced him. In the night wind her skirt lifted and floated around her, offering him a glimpse of skin-colored lace over smooth belly, and then the umbrella of her skirt collapsed around her. "See?" Tossing off his grasp, she flung her arms to the side and slowly, precisely touched the tip of each index finger to her nose. The foam cup slopped coffee onto the ground with her movements. ''I can walk a straight line, too.'' She took one long step off the breakwater and lurched into him, laughing. ''Whoops!''

His arms, with a will of their own, closed around her.

The cup whispered against the rocks as it fell from her hand. The scent of coffee rose from her skin, tantalizing him. Her mouth would taste of that dark, rich brew.

And all he could think of was the look of her all tangled up in that kid's arms. The way she'd smiled at the boy, the way she'd laughed and tilted her head, opening up the line of her slim throat for the boy's touch, maybe even his kiss.

Wrapped against her now as close as the boy had been, Judah didn't kiss her, not even with his mind hazing over with a self-righteous and welcome blind fury. ''Why were you practically screwing that kid on the dance floor, Sophie?''

''Because it felt good?'' She laughed again, and the wind tossed her fog-damp hair against him.

''Oh, excellent reason.'' Judah ran the back of his hand deliberately down the length of her neck and watched her eyes turn slumberous.

She pulled against his grasp. ''It's as good as any.'' Her laughter held an edge. ''We were dancing. Having fun. Not that it's any of your business. Do you even know what having fun means, Judah? Did you ever know?'' She pulled harder and he tightened his grasp.

''Fun?'' Holding her wrists together between the two of them, Judah leaned forward. ''He was sniffing you like a dog in heat.''

''A puppy.''

''A puppy with a hard-on and not enough good sense to keep his distance.''

''Maybe I didn't want him to.'' In the changing light of the mist, her smile taunted him. ''And don't be crude.''

''But cops *are* crude. Remember? That's what you said about George. That he was a fat, crude cop.'' Judah wanted her uncomfortable, but her chin slanted higher.

Waves slopped against the breakwater.

"But you're not George, are you?" Her eyes were wide and knowing.

"Maybe I am."

"I know you better than that." She shifted restlessly. "You're not like him. You've never been like George."

"You think you know me that well?"

"Well enough." Again she moved, fabric shimmered, and like tiny whips, her misty hair snapped against his wrists.

"You should have left the boy alone, Sophie."

"But I didn't want to. What's going on here, Judah? Are you jealous?" she asked, and pushed him right over the edge into some territory he didn't recognize.

He reached behind him, grabbed his handcuffs off his belt and clamped them onto her wrists.

"What on earth are you doing?" She glanced down at her hands. Mist sparkled against the metal of the cuffs. The links clanked together as she lifted her hands. Her eyes were huge and disbelieving as she stared at him. "You're arresting me for felony flirting?" A grin touched her lips.

"For once in your life, just shut up, Sophie. Let me think." With his index finger jammed through the links, Judah pulled her toward him even as he wondered what in the hell he was doing.

Sophie laughed at the serious expression on Judah's face. She had an idea of what he was thinking, and the thought made her breathless. "This is crazy, Judah!"

"For damned sure."

"I don't understand. Are *you* drunk?"

Huge and stunned, her gaze never left his face while the night wind murmured around them.

Judah stooped, and so fast he didn't even realize what he was doing, he hoisted her over his shoulder. He thought he was taking her to her car. He meant to, it was the only thing that made sense, but she wriggled and thumped his back with her cuffed hands until he stopped abruptly, letting her slide to her feet.

They were at the far corner of Catfish Charlie's, away from the back door. Not even thinking, he turned her toward the wall. Pine trees and the overhang of the building sheltered them from the skim-milk moon and pitched them into darkness, a darkness that grew more intimate and private with each rasping breath, each graze of skin as he braced her face forward against the wall.

The music thumped through the walls and into the palms of his hands, an insistent beat.

He felt as if he'd stepped into some alien world where nothing made sense, where all the rules he lived by had disappeared into silent mist and fog.

She was warm, soft. He bent his knees, fitting himself closer to her, to the illusive warmth of her body.

"What are you doing, Judah?" she whispered, and the faint sound slipped across his mouth, lingered.

Cupped against her back with his mouth against her ear, he placed his palms on the cypress walls of Catfish Charlie's, and then, precisely and in great detail, he told her exactly what he was going to do. And made her breathless all over again.

"Here," he said. And taking one palm from the wall, he slid his hand slowly down over her breasts and the gentle slope of her belly, past the curve of her hip and under the gauzy pink that shimmered ghost-like in the darkness. Bit by bit, brushing against secret skin, he edged her skirt up until he touched the thin line of lace he could no longer see but remembered. Bit by bit, he tugged until lace gave way completely to skin, warm, silky. And then, compulsively, he flattened the heel of his hand against her, stroking.

A shiver rippled over her skin. Twisting, she stared at him over her shoulder. "In public? Like this?"

"Yes," he said. With one long stroke of his finger, he pressed upward, parting smooth folds. "Exactly like this."

Chapter Eleven

Sophie was aware of the weight of the handcuffs on her wrists, aware of the vibrating wood boards against her cheek. Aware of Judah, so close against her that she could feel the shape of his buckle, the shape of *him*. So much heat surrounding her. Off in the distance the Gulf breathed against shore, took the night-pale sands into it and out on a long, sibilant sigh.

In front of her the hard lumps of the metal handcuffs were caught between her stomach and the wall of Catfish Charlie's. Up against a wall, captive to his touch, she felt like one of Judah's perps, all power gone. She swallowed. "You're... different Judah. You're in some mood—"

"What mood am I in, Sophie?" He tilted her head back toward him.

"I don't know. But you're not acting like yourself," she clarified, aware that even as she spoke, her body quivered to his touch.

"No?" His fingers separated her, sent heat and dampness rushing where he touched and stroked. "Are you sure?" He touched his mouth to the pulse fluttering in her neck. "You don't seem one-hundred-percent positive, Sophie. Persuade me," he whispered and ran his thumb over her most sensitive spot.

For a moment she wanted to turn around, to try and regain some control. But then she realized she didn't want that control. She *wanted* this wildness, this feeling of no responsibility, no thought, this sense of going completely into the wilderness. Of letting *him* take control.

She shook as night mist and fog whispered against her nipple. Insane, this pleasure he was giving her, this yielding to her darkest fantasy.

"We're having sex, Sophie. That's all. Remember? That's what you said earlier. Nothing more than sex. Sex didn't mean anything between us. We were scratching an itch, that's all."

"That's not what I said," she murmured, tingling at his soft touch.

"No, you weren't that crude."

"You know that wasn't what I meant." She understood now that she'd trivialized what she'd felt on the beach with Judah. "But this is different."

"We can stop if you want, Sophie." He cradled her with his bent legs and belly, bracing her against the wall. "If you want to. Think you can?" he teased and took one step closer, one leg coming between hers.

She inhaled, a shaky rasp of sound. She thought she felt him smile against her shoulder where his tongue left a warm, damp trail. The throb of the bass inside Catfish Charlie's vibrated through the wall and into her breasts and belly. Against her fanny, his knee tight against her, Judah moved, a silent echo of the throbbing music.

Pressure and touch and all this *sensation.* Trapped between hard wood planks and hard, aroused male. Helpless. Unable to control the pace of his movements, or hers.

And yet—

She moaned as he clasped her with his whole hand, pushing hard, his body and hand working her so insistently that everything was movement, heat and sensation, that pulsing rhythm driving through her body, taking over.

She must have whimpered or murmured something because she heard Judah mutter, "Oh, Sophie," against her ear.

Some dim space of her brain registered the clatter of a door opening. Heard the click of a lighter. Saw the small red dot of a cigarette and understood that she was concealed by nothing more than darkness and the weight of Judah's body. Then, faintly, she heard the faint snick of his zipper. With each second, everything except Judah's touch and scent drifted away and vanished down the intense tunnel of her pleasure.

Her skirt was bunched around her waist, her panties somewhere around her knees, and her bottom bare to the slide of Judah's hand there, too. She gasped as his jeans scraped against her flesh, sensitized it to a different kind of touch even as he held her there in the most intimate of embraces.

Helpless to do anything except *feel*.

"You're not running home?" he whispered.

"No."

How had she never realized the power of surrender? Of yielding everything—her body, her control, her emotions—to someone else?

She'd never wanted to.

Each deliberate movement Judah made, each slow teasing slide down her spine and lower, owned her, dictated her response. Pure male, he held her, joined his body with hers in an act that was primal mating.

He was big, strong, his muscles clamping her so close that, held open to his touch, she moved in concert with him. Smaller, more fragile, used to being in control of herself and others, she should have been terrified.

But he seduced her with his determination. Seduced her with his intoxicating, raw desire. She knew she welcomed the hunger and desire in him, that it called to her soul in the most elemental way.

Sinking further into pleasure, she thought there was something else, too, something she couldn't analyze in the sensations swamping her. She would have to figure it out. Later. But not right now. Because it was seductive beyond anything she'd ever known to be wanted this passionately, this… recklessly.

This uncontrollably. Because he was as out of control as he was making her feel.

There were no limits.

He twisted, moved and touched her in the deepest core of her femininity, holding the tension for long seconds, hours, for eternity, everything tightening unbearably. And then he gave one definitive, hard stroke.

She lost control over her muscles, over everything, subject to his will, his touch.

"Judah!"

"Sophie," he grunted. And then he thrust into her, stretching her and filling her completely.

Like the string of a bow pulled by the hunter, she tightened, shook with the strength of his touch against her womb. "Ah!" Her head fell back into his shoulder. Her body cramped, convulsed and the world disappeared.

When she opened her eyes, she wondered if she'd lost consciousness. Her forehead rested against the wall of Catfish Charlie's where the thrumming, booming still sang through the boards. Judah's hand was splayed against the wall, his wrist on her cheek. He shuddered against her back where they were joined, and her body answered with a last, astonishing flutter.

There was an odd sheltering in the cover of his body around hers, in the clasp of hers to him, a sense of rightness to the feel of him inside her.

In that moment she understood that no matter with whom she ever made love again, Judah Finnegan had imprinted her with himself. He had claimed her with his body, claimed her by triggering the most deeply felt instincts of her femininity.

In darkness he had taken her.

Taken her.

And with that act, he'd rattled her to the core. Sex up against Catfish Charlie's back wall? Where anybody could have walked and seen them?

Joyful sex, mutual pleasure—that she'd always understood and reveled in. But this? This aggressive desire mixed strangely with pleasure? It was basic male-to-female bonding; something in his DNA speaking to hers and recognizing her at some level beyond words, beyond her understanding.

In taking her, and, really, there was no other word, he had revealed to her something about her own nature that she could never have imagined.

What she accepted, though, was that he had claimed her as his mate, turned what she thought she knew about herself upside down, and changed her forever.

He had blurred the lines between her self and that of another.

She didn't know how she felt about that blurring, that sense that she'd given away a part of her most private self, that Judah had penetrated not only her body but her soul.

She knew, though, that she had been cut loose from all her moorings and set adrift on some uncharted sea not of her choosing. She'd lost control. And loved every thrilling second of it.

Against her back, she could hear his labored breathing. Speech was impossible. After all, what was there to say? Careless words, wrong words would be dangerous. In silence and darkness something had been communicated, acknowledged between them.

Sophie turned to face Judah. A heavy, immovable weight, he'd collapsed against her, one hand against the wall bracing them, one hand supporting her.

She was surprised by how easy it was to free herself and face him.

Her body still quaking in the aftermath of pleasure so intense she had no word for it, she raised her handcuffed wrists, stood on tiptoe with her back to the wall and slipped her cuffed hands over his head.

His eyes were dark and brooding, their color gone dark with pain. "Why did you play games with the boy? How could you?"

"It doesn't matter," she whispered against his lips, moving until her hips and pelvis were tight against him, female to male.

"It does."

"No." She had no sense of the passing of time as she held him within the circle of her cuffed arms. Long, quiet moments while the world went still and she sorted out her confused thoughts.

Tentatively, she lifted her leg, curling it around his waist until her body teased the tip of his. Holding her gaze, his eyes studying hers, he clasped her fanny and lifted her until she could wrap both legs tightly around him, sink onto him. That easily, he was inside her again, moving slowly, gently. He ran his hands under her skirt, warming her skin, holding her. His pupils were dark, pulling her into their depths. Watching each other, never looking away, they moved together in a languorous joining of murmurs and soft, sliding touches. A silky, luxurious pleasuring that was like the afterquake of a major temblor.

A miracle, this ability of touch to give such pleasure, to provide this transport to another realm. A gift from God to humans caught in a world of sadness and loss and pain, this joining.

As the delicious coiling inside her spiraled ever higher, tighter and tighter, Sophie felt her eyelids flicker. Focusing on Judah, drawing him even deeper, she saw the slash of his mouth tighten, witnessed the control he exerted to keep his eyes fixed on hers.

And in that final paroxysm, Sophie watched over Judah's shoulder as the Gulf moved in swells gone silver with night and mist.

"Home?"

"Yes," she said.

He nodded, adjusted his jeans, and then, not speaking, he swung her up into his arms and carried her to his car, her handcuffed wrists still circling his neck.

In the car, he unsnapped the cuffs and flung them into the back of his car. During the short ride to her house, Judah touched her constantly, his palm smoothing her bare thigh, edging up to the juncture of thigh and belly, lingering.

And entranced by his silky length, she touched him, too, her hands inside his jeans as busy as his. A slow fever pulsed through her blood, heavy and insistent, powerful. She was mindless, caught in the exquisite pleasure of touching and being touched.

At some point before leaving the beach, she must have picked up her purse because now he took the keys from it and opened her front door with an impatient twist of the key. She'd scarcely shut the door behind them when he crowded her against it and pulled her to him in the familiar darkness of her house.

She slid away and pulled him toward her bedroom. "Come with me."

"Wait." He unbuttoned the rest of her blouse, slipped it from her shoulders, trailing the light fabric against her breasts and ribs. With a pinch of his fingers, he unfastened her skirt, letting it fall in a shadowy pink heap.

Unexpectedly shy, she hesitated, crossing her arms around her waist. The shadowy recesses of her house were no protection for the surprising vulnerability she was experiencing.

Not moving, Judah stared at her for a long time. "You have no idea how beautiful you are, do you?" He unfolded her arms and slicked his palms over her hips, up her rib cage. "Aw, Sophie, you almost make me believe in...something." Stooping, he covered her trembling nipple with his mouth and lifted her into his arms. Following her murmured directions, he stumbled blindly toward her bedroom. Her head bumped the doorjamb of the hall. His elbow knocked over a vase on a low table. The vase shattered as it smacked the floor. Glass crackled under his shoes. "I'm going to wreck your home, Sophie."

"Too late. You already have."

"What?" Startled, he careered off her hall bookcase. Paperbacks and hardbacks thudded to the floor. "What?"

"In there."

He stepped across the threshold into her bedroom. "Where's your bed?"

A laugh escaped. "No inclination to go find a sandy, public spot? The mall, perhaps?"

"Not this time." Placing her across her bed, he followed her down into her uplifted arms. "Your skin gleams, Sophie, even in the dark. How can that be possible? It's like you have a candle inside you, glowing through your skin." He circled her ankle with his thumb and forefinger.

His palm rested on her arch and the bottom of her foot, shooting tingles straight to her belly. To her forever-empty womb.

Sliding his hand over her calf, he limned the muscles, praised their shape with his touch. "Such strength. Like silk-covered steel. Beautiful." He spread her arms wide to the edge of her narrow bed and ran his open hands over her, butterfly touches that tickled and spritzed along her skin. "You leave me breathless, you know."

"It's complicated, isn't it, Judah? Between us?"

"No kidding." His laugh was shaky as his lips tickled the inner skin of her thigh and moved up. "*Complicated* doesn't even begin to cover it." Slipping his thumb along the crease between her thigh and belly, he added reluctantly, "You know, I never intended what happened at Charlie's."

"Then why?"

"I saw you with that boy. You were like a campfire, glowing, sparking up into a black night. I'd never imagined you so lighthearted, I reckon."

"You didn't want me to enjoy myself?"

"No. Yes." He shook his head again in frustration. "Seeing you dancing with that kid shouldn't have mattered. It shouldn't have been important. But it was.''

"I won't apologize.''

"I don't want you to." Elbows on the bed, he stared down at her, broodingly. "You didn't do anything wrong."

"But you—"

"I didn't like seeing you in that twerp's arms."

"Don't call Cutter a twerp. And he wasn't that young."

He buried his face in the crook of her shoulder and neck, nipped. "Don't defend him."

"I told you Cutter doesn't matter."

"Lousy name. He should sue his mama and daddy. But he matters, Sophie. Because he made me—"

"Jealous?"

"Maybe. I've never been jealous before."

"Never? But you were married. Weren't you ever jealous then?"

His eyebrow lifted. "No." Nibbling at the cord of her neck and down, he said, "Maybe that was the problem. One of them, anyway. Hell, who knows? I messed up with Sallie." He jerked his head up. "Redheaded Sallie with the brown eyes." He paused, his focus somewhere else. "I'm glad I remembered what color her eyes are."

Sophie thought Sallie might be a perfectly acceptable name, but at the moment she hated the sound of it. "I don't know how to handle what's happening, Judah."

His fingers lingered intimately, sending sparkles of fire to her core. "I don't either."

"Two rudderless ships?" All of them—she, Angel, Judah—all adrift with no safe port. She twisted restlessly, her body and her emotions chaotic. "Neither of us knowing how the voyage will end? So why are we doing this?" She linked her fingers with his, touched him, urged him up over her.

"Damned if I know. I do know I feel clean and clear when I'm inside you. Inside you, Sophie, is where everything makes sense, where I feel that anything is possible." He paused. "I wanted to hate you." He shook his head and the whisk of his hair across her breasts made her gasp. "I still do."

"I know."

"I need to hate you." He hovered above her, frowning. "But I can't."

"I understand," she whispered forlornly. "It's—"

"Complicated," he finished for her. "Like you said." He entered her slowly on a long-drawn-out sigh of movement. "Aw, Doctor Sugar, none of this makes sense. I made up my mind I was going to stay as far away from you as I could. I meant to." He groaned as she lifted her hips. "Like a man with an addiction, I can't leave you alone. I thought it was nothing but hot sex, that I could walk away afterwards. And yet here I am. What am I going to do about you?"

"You're doing all right at the moment." She smiled up at him and brought his face back to hers.

"Yeah, well, this part I understand. I'm good at this part," he said ruefully and then groaned as she sidled closer, letting her nipples brush over him.

"Guys always brag." Even as her body moved with him, she grinned. "You're not bad."

"Thank you. But this—" he drove forward, a small smile on his face, too "—is the simple part."

"Ah!" she gasped. "Not always."

"For me it is. But you unman me, Sophie."

"Doesn't feel like that from where I am." She reached down and enclosed him in her palm, warmed him as he was warming her. "Stay for a while, Judah." She leaned forward, sliding her bent knees past his hips. "We'll see what happens next."

"You know what's going to happen next, Sophie. You know what I want. That part's as clear as Weekiwachee Springs."

She sighed and let the tide of sensation wash over her, gave herself utterly to its intoxication. "Afterwards. We'll sort things out then."

The room seemed to tremble around her with the sounds

of skin sliding along skin, of hushed breaths, sharp cries. Her bedding rustled to the floor as Judah kicked free of it. Abruptly, he rolled over and pulled her on top of him. The painted iron headboard wobbled and slapped the Chinese-red wall, leaving white streaks.

She didn't care. Head thrown back, she entered a world of sensation so overwhelming that nothing mattered. What they were doing together, creating together, went beyond the blurring she'd been worried about earlier. In this world of touch, one and one didn't add up to two. Here, one and one made one.

They slept, woke, touched again as moonlight moved across her ceiling, striping her walls with pale lines. He moved his hand down the line of her scar, lingering on each stitch mark, learning its shape and texture. "I'm sorry, Sophie. I wish—"

"Me, too." Her throat closed.

"Don't cry."

"I'm not."

But he took the tears seeping from her eyes with his tongue, bathed her scar with them in a slow, lingering kiss.

"What happened, Sophie?"

"Nothing," she said and tasted her own salty tears. "Nothing."

"Something." His mouth moved over the skin of her belly, and her womb fluttered as his lips passed.

"I was pregnant."

"And?" His lips moved back to the corners of her eyes and she tried to turn her head away from his searching gaze. "Tell me."

"Why?" She went still within his hold. "Why do you want to know the details, Judah?"

"I don't know. I just do, that's all."

"I was pregnant. Stupid. I should have known better. I was on birth control. I didn't mention it to the dentist when I went to have my wisdom tooth removed. Now, that's one of the automatic questions a doctor asks, of course. But not then. I thought I was protected. I wasn't. Nineteen and pregnant. A walking cliché. And things went wrong.'' Needing the privacy of her own thoughts, she tried once more to turn away, but Judah lowered himself until she could see nothing except his lean, intense face. "I thought I'd dealt with it.''

He took the corner of the pillowcase and tried to stem the slow seepage of tears. "But you haven't.''

"Guess not.''

He dabbed at her eyes again. "Hell, Sophie, this pillowcase isn't worth a damn.''

"I don't know why I'm crying.'' Rubbing the backs of her hands over her eyes, she gave a helpless sniff. "So dumb. I'm not a crier, and I've bawled more in the last few days than I have in years.'' Tears were burning her cheeks and she couldn't stop them.

"What happened?''

"A double ectopic pregnancy, that's what. Surgery to save my life. No more fallopian tubes. So, no more babies. For years I thought I didn't care. I don't believe in dwelling on the sad stuff, the stuff you can't change. I told you earlier. I had a full life, one I loved. *Do* love.''

"But you care.'' His thumbs rested at the corners of her eyes.

For a long time she couldn't answer. Didn't want to answer. Didn't want to give him that final, most secret part of her soul. But he continued to hold her gaze, patiently, totally focused on her and whatever she would say.

"I care.''

She waited for him to give her the usual facile answers. Her friends had. Surrogacy, in vitro. Modern medicine could create miracles. But not for her. Those weren't choices for her.

Instead of speaking, though, he gathered her closer, wrapping her tightly within his body. Then, her body still enclosing his, still joined with him in a miracle as old as creation, he made love with her until she fell asleep.

Sometime before dawn, she awoke briefly to find him

spooned around her, his chest moving slowly in sleep. It was
in that quiet, still moment that the rightness of her impulse
filled her. During the hours since she'd left the hospital and
been with Judah, her heart had sorted things out. She could
see her path clearly, all the separate bricks of it. All she had
to do was take one step forward, and her life would change
forever. Easing away from Judah, she crept out of bed and
took the portable phone into the bathroom.

"Jeannette?" Sophie stared at the walls. "I have a huge
favor to ask. You're my friend. But you're also head of Children and Family Services. I'm sorry to wake you at this hour,
but I need your help. You're the only one who can. If you
will—please?" Wrapping her finger into the towel lying on
the tub, she continued. "You know I'm licensed to be a foster
parent, right? And that I've briefly fostered some of the
babies before? Here's the situation. There's a baby we ad-
mitted Friday night to the hospital. Her mother was murdered. She has no family. Ordinarily, she'd go straight into
the system, but I want her. I want to foster her now and start
the adoption process. I know, I know. But it can be done.
You know how messed up the system is right now, Jeannette.
Everybody's overworked and underpaid. Remember the case
of the little girl recently who completely vanished? No trace
of her in anybody's records? If this baby goes into the system, it will be a drawn-out legal mess. I want to get the
paperwork moving as fast as we can." She took a deep
breath. "Because I want to adopt her. Help me?"

She made one more phone call after hanging up with Jeannette.

Setting the phone gently on the table, Sophie edged back
into bed. Judah hadn't moved. She walked her fingers up his
arm, delighting in the strength of his muscles, the shape of
his bones, and brought his arm around her waist, needing the
touch of him, the connection to him even in her sleep.

When she awoke again, Judah was dressed and standing
at the foot of her bed, frowning.

"Do you know how seldom you smile, Judah?"

"I'm not a smiley kind of guy."

"No kidding." She gathered her white sheets close to her. "You have me at a disadvantage here, you know."

"That would be a change." His frown deepened as she scooched back up against the headboard. He cupped her foot where it dangled over the side of the bed. "I have to go."

"So go. I'm not keeping you."

"If you only knew."

She waved her arms airily above her head. "I haven't handcuffed you to the bed, Judah."

"Smart aleck." A ghost of a smile touched his face. "Might be fun."

Sophie couldn't help the blush that rose from the top of her chest and burned the tips of her ears. She raised the sheet to her chin until her eyes barely peeped over it. "Not that you'll ever know."

For a second she thought he was considering the idea, and the blush burned hotter on her face.

Then he shifted restlessly. He checked his watch and grimaced. "I really have to go." He still hadn't moved from the foot of her bed.

She wanted to beg him to stay. Lifting her chin, she said, "Then why are you still here?"

"Yeah. That's the big question, isn't it?" He shook his head.

"I don't have an answer."

"Neither do I." He came to sit on the bed beside her and pulled at the sheet until it drooped at the top of her breasts. "All I know is that I want to stay."

"And you still hate me." She gripped the sheet tightly.

"Want to," he corrected. "Need to. Can't."

"Somehow that doesn't make me feel a whole lot better."

"Didn't mean for it to. I'm being straight with you."

"That's decent of you."

"I'm a decent guy, remember, one of Poinciana's knights in blue? Except that you don't like cops."

"I don't like some cops."

"And that leaves us where we always wind up, doesn't it?" Abruptly he stood. The bed jounced. "I don't know how this has happened, Sophie. You're a drug in my system, making me feel things, do things that—" He rubbed the back of his head. "I don't understand it. I don't like it."

"If anyone ever tries to convince you that you're a silver-tongued devil, Judah, seriously, don't believe a word they say," she said politely.

He sat down again. "I'm trying to explain—"

"Maybe you shouldn't."

"Yeah." Placing one arm on each side of her curled body, he leaned close. "You're right. I'm not good with words. I'm better at showing instead of telling. And you have no idea, Sophie, the things I want to show you, do to you. With you."

Her stomach lurched. And, that fast, she wanted him in bed with her, needed to have him wrap himself around her. In bed, the tiny pinpricks of words wouldn't matter. "Easy talk, buster."

This time a real smile danced over his drawn face. "By the way, what's with all this sudden modesty?" He plucked once more at the sheet.

"You make me shy?"

"Not likely." He dipped forward and closed his mouth around her nipple, dampening the sheet and making her groan.

But the truth was that he did make her shy, and she didn't know why.

Pulling the damp sheet down her body, he paused. "I heard you on the phone this morning. I wasn't asleep."

She grabbed the sheet from him and moved away from the heat of his lips. "I started the paperwork to foster-parent Angel."

"At four in the morning?"

"Jeannette's my friend. She's head of Children and Family Services. She can make it happen. I'm not asking her to do anything illegal. I'm asking her to take a shortcut. I'm qualified to be a foster parent. I've fostered babies from the hospital before for short periods.''

He didn't move for long seconds. ''You're serious about doing this.'' It wasn't a question. Then he shrugged. ''Well.'' He circled her damp nipple slowly, reluctantly, with his forefinger. And before she could gather her thoughts to tell him the rest, he sent them spinning. ''Come with me to Tyree's barbecue later today.''

She sat bolt upright. ''What?''

''Tyree and his wife have a monthly barbecue at their home. After church services. Come with me.''

''Like a date?''

''No, not *like* a date. It would *be* a date.''

''A date.'' She blinked. ''This is weird, Judah. After everything that's happened between us, to go out on a real date— Don't you think that's a little bit strange?''

''At least you won't have to worry about whether or not I'm going to try and jump your bones on a first date.'' He traced the line of her hipbone. ''By the way, I like your bones, Sophie.''

''You made a joke.''

''I might have.''

''A date?''

''Now you're making me nervous. I'm having second thoughts.''

''Wouldn't you be uncomfortable?''

''I'm going to be uncomfortable anyway.'' The frown returned and he stood up.

''Why? Won't all your cop buddies be there? The guys you hang out with?''

His face closed up in that way that made her crazy. He stuffed his hands into his pockets.

''Oh. I get it. You don't hang out, do you?''

''I've never been to Tyree's before.''

''You're afraid to go alone?'' She wrapped the sheet around her and stood up next to him. ''Is that why you're asking me to go with you? You need protection, that's it. Awww, poor baby," she cooed.

"I told Tyree I'd come. You might enjoy it. I don't know who'll be there. But I don't think there'll be many cops."

Tilting her head, she studied him. "What's going on, Judah? What's the hidden agenda?"

"Damn it, there's no agenda, and I'm not 'afraid' to go to Tyree's by myself." He glared at her. "Sheesh, I'm not that socially inept, Sophie."

"You couldn't prove it by me." Biting her lip to keep from giggling, she added, "But all right. I'll go. And I'll protect you."

"Okay, then."

"Well, okay yourself, hotshot." She anchored the sheet under her arms and started past him. "Tell me when and where."

He caught her arm. "Your car's at Charlie's. I'll pick you up. We'll get your car after the barbecue."

"No. I'll get my car and meet you at Tyree's house."

"Sophie, don't be stubborn."

She twitched the end of the sheet free of her feet. "I'm not always stubborn."

"Really?"

She nodded vigorously. His hand rested between her underarm and the swell of her breast, and she wanted to turn toward it, let her breast fill his palm. "But I don't want to be stranded here all day without my car."

"Fine. Give me your car keys. I'll get someone to drive it back here." Moving away from her, he lifted the heap of bedspread and clothes.

Without his touch, her skin felt cold.

"Where's your purse?"

"I can get my car. Nobody has to drive it back here." She suppressed a strong urge to stamp her foot. Not her style, and she'd probably trip over the sheet. "Lord, you're a pushy man."

"And you're a hardheaded woman." He didn't move an inch.

"Probably why we get along so well. No arguments and all that."

He threw up both hands. "All right. We'll do it your way. Go take your shower, Sophie. I'll call you with the address."

"You have to find out Tyree's address? You don't even know where your partner lives? For someone who notices every detail, how could you not know that one?"

"I'll see you at Tyree's around eight." He wheeled on his heel and barreled out of her bedroom.

"What shall I bring?" Tripping and stumbling after him, she clutched the sheet to her. "Judah!"

Her front door slammed behind him. She winced.

And then she giggled as she caught a glimpse of her tousled, red-faced, sheet-wrapped reflection. She did a little dance step and curtseyed to the mirror, flinging the sheet open and closed in a parody of a strip tease. "Sophie Brennan, you've been a bad, bad girl, haven't you?"

In the mirror the woman with the wicked smile and flushed body danced in circles as sunlight blazed across the floor of the bedroom.

Chapter 12

When Sophie drove up, Judah was waiting with his bike at the end of Tyree's driveway. She braked her small red car in a rattle of oyster shells. As she climbed out, the breeze caught the ends of the red scarf she'd tied around her waist and blew them up against her sweater.

"Nice," he said, his glance following the lick of red against cream.

"My outfit?"

"Sure, that, too." His glance lingered where red and cream smoothed against her breasts.

As aware of his gaze as if he were touching her, she tossed him a casual wave as she went to the rear of her car. She was relieved he stayed with the bike while she popped open the trunk. Seeing him under the streetlight next to the driveway had taken her breath away. A cliché, all that black leather stretched over a flat belly and wide shoulders, rockstar mufti, but her mouth had gone dry as he'd straightened from his slouch against the black bike.

Even in the space of hours, she'd forgotten the impact he

had on her senses. Judah Finnegan had her number, that was for sure. Breathing carefully, she took out a food carrier. "Pirozki," she said and turned as his footsteps came up behind her.

"You didn't have to bring anything."

She shrugged. "It's my Bushka's recipe. Remember I told you about my grandmother who gave me the cross? She taught me how to make these. Pirozki are Russian, but almost every country has its own version." She poked his arm as he wrinkled his nose. "Wuss. Where's your spirit of adventure, country boy? It's nothing weird. See? Comfort food." She lifted the lid to show him the small pastry packets. "These have meat and cabbage inside." She held one to his mouth. "Taste."

He took the offering in one bite. "Good. But not precisely what I'm hungry for." He tugged at a scarf end and touched her mouth. "I told you, Sophie. You're in my blood. I see you, and I want you. Right that moment. I heard a line in a song once, and I never understood it before I met you. 'Every little thing you do fills me with desire.' It's that simple. And, yes, like you said earlier, that complicated. I keep thinking this is some kind of madness that will leave me. I want it to. I *need* it to. It doesn't."

"I know." Her hands trembled slightly as she held the food container. Stunned, she glanced down at them. "But, Judah, do me a favor? Don't ever come into an operating room when I'm holding sharp instruments. It wouldn't be safe." She held the carrier in front of her and watched her shaking hands. "I can't believe this. What have you done to me?"

"Exactly what you've done to me. And I'm not any more comfortable with your effect on me than you are with mine on you. But it is what it is." He touched her trembling fingers, stilling them.

"Why didn't you go inside? Why were you waiting out here?"

He slung the grocery sack he carried over his shoulder and took the food from her. "I wasn't sure you'd come."

She matched his strides. "I said I would." She was still troubled that he could affect her so easily.

"Folks change their minds." He motioned her toward the walk leading up to the front door. "I figured I'd wait and see. Something might have come up."

"I would have called." Catching his elbow, she stopped him. "I may be impulsive, Judah, but I'm not careless with people."

He studied her face slowly, as if he were seeking answers to the unspoken questions that lay between them.

As reluctant to disturb the equilibrium between them as he, she poked the plastic bag over his shoulder and peered inside. "Soft drinks? Not beer? Or wine?" She shook her head in a mock scold. "What a cheapskate."

"It's Sunday. Knew better than to bring alcohol to a church-going bunch."

She shot him a glance.

He sighed. "All right, Sophie, in the interest of full disclosure and you and me getting along, you need to know. My daddy was a preacher."

"I don't get the connection, but I'm all in favor of full disclosure. It's a way of getting to know a person."

"You think you don't already know me?"

"You think I *do?*"

"Reckon not." He shrugged. "Biblically, maybe."

"Another joke? This is a whole new side of you, Judah. So. Where's your father now? Are you in touch with him?"

"No."

"Oh?"

"He died a few years ago."

"I'm sorry."

"Don't be. The world's better off without that old man."

"That's harsh."

"Hell, Sophie, don't give me that look. There was no love

lost between me and my old man. He and his God aren't on my visiting list, okay?''

''Whatever you say. But what does that have to do with bringing colas to Tyree's?'' In the lamplit shadows of the sidewalk, Sophie waited patiently. What Judah was struggling to tell her was important. She hoped it would shine a light on some of the dark corners in this difficult man.

The sound of voices came faintly from inside the house.

He fidgeted, shifted. ''Okay. Okay. Here's the deal. Calvin Finnegan was one of the meanest sons of bitches alive. He clubbed me over the head with God and religion from the time I was born until the day he slapped me upside the head with his Bible for the last time, and I walked out. He used the stick of his religion to beat out the darkness and evil in my soul. I'm talking literally here, sugar. On me. And he used that stick and Bible on my pretty mama until all her joy and prettiness dried up and died and took her with it. His God was a God of damnation and hellfire. A God with no pity. No forgiveness. That's the God he preached and the God who ruled everything Preacher Calvin did. Everything he thought or felt. Hell? Nobody around Calvin Finnegan had to wait for an afterlife to find out about Hell. He made every living, breathing moment on this earth hell.''

Sophie took a slow breath and remained silent, absorbing his words. His tone was matter-of-fact. His lack of emotion disturbed her the most. Talking about an ugliness that had to have been soul-searing, he recited the details with complete detachment. She could only imagine the details he omitted.

Distancing. That was what she'd done each time she had to do a morbidity report. She separated herself from the emotions of losing a patient because if she didn't, she couldn't have gone on. That was what Judah was doing. Distancing himself exactly as she had. In order to survive. There were all kinds of ways to distance oneself. They'd talked earlier about how their respective jobs used language to achieve distance, to provide objectivity. But how much more destructive for a child to have to create distance in order to be *safe*. *Oh, Judah,* she longed to say. But didn't.

"No forgiveness? Not even for a small, scared boy?"

"He saw evil in me. His job—as he saw it—was to clean out my soul one way or another. And he tried. With every ounce of determination in him, he tried."

"That's a hard way to grow up."

"Don't feel sorry for me, Sophie. I was never scared."

"Really? Gave as good as you got, did you?"

She could picture the young, fierce-eyed Judah staring down a father filled with wrath and righteousness. No, he wouldn't have yielded. Not ever. Seeking the love and forgiveness denied him, he would have fought his father every inch of the way. A child denied love and forgiveness would have sought attention through the only tools available to him: defiance, indifference, numbness. Instinct made her take a risk and leap right off the high dive. "That's why you became a cop, isn't it? In a way, Judah, you're like your father. You mete out justice. Punishment. And like him, you don't offer redemption or forgiveness to those you arrest. You judge them."

"Like *him?* I'm nothing like him. We shared nothing except a batch of DNA." Judah's voice suddenly turned venomous. "That old preacher man is nothing to me. *Was* nothing."

"And yet he lives in your head, doesn't he?" She touched his cheek.

"Don't kid yourself. If he was alive and I saw him lying in the street bleeding to death, I wouldn't cross the street to help him. Okay? Got it?"

So much passion, she thought. Her heart ached for the child he'd been, the lonely, scared boy hungry for love and finding it nowhere.

"I get it, Judah," she said and stood on tiptoes, kissing him softly on his open, surprised mouth. "But that whole forgiveness thing? Think about it. Because not forgiving can become a canker on the soul. Now, let's go inside and have dinner.''

For a long moment he simply stared at her, and then he stooped and pressed his mouth against her forehead. Not a kiss, exactly—she couldn't put a name to that brush of his lips against her. But whatever it was, there was a tenderness in that lingering touch that made her eyes burn. "Dinner? It's suppertime down here, Yankee Girl. Don't you know anything?''

"Pish." Tweaking his nose, she tugged him forward. "Come on. This Yankee girl is hungry.''

"You're always hungry.''

"And you're still not talking about food, are you?''

"Nope.''

"Complaining?''

"Grateful.''

"You should be.''

The door opened before they could knock.

"Hey there, y'all." Breathless, a tall, slim woman beckoned them in. A toddler had both arms clamped around the woman's leg. "It's a madhouse in here, but come on in. If you dare." Stooping, she gathered the child up into her arms. "This is Taylor Bell, our middle child. She's—''

Sophie smiled. "Hi, Taylor Bell.''

The little girl buried her face in her mother's neck.

"Clingy?''

"You don't know the half of it." Smiling ruefully, the woman shifted Taylor Bell onto a hip. She extended her hand. "Hi, I'm Yvonna, Tyree's better half. You must be Judah's friend.''

Sophie realized her face must have registered astonishment because Yvonna gave a tiny smile. "Oh, like that, is it?''

Judah cleared his throat. "Hey, Yvonna, Taylor Bell.''

Friend? Sophie didn't know how to respond. Friendship required a level of trust. Judah didn't trust her. She thought perhaps he didn't trust anyone except himself. But he'd talked to her about his father. Coming from Judah, that revelation meant something.

But did she trust him? She thought on some level she must. And that was a realization that could cause her a sleepless night or two.

But friends?

No.

Definitely not…friends.

An hour later, balancing a plate of grilled shrimp, homemade cornbread, and a glass of iced tea, Sophie surveyed her surroundings. It was quieter here in a shrub-shrouded corner of the candlelit patio. Not far from her, Tyree and Judah stood beside the grill, their murmurs a counterpoint to the clamor and singing inside.

She'd been awash in noise and conversation since Yvonna had introduced herself. The children had brought food to her. The Joneses' friends had, singly and in groups, come over to introduce themselves and to solicit her opinions about the hospital, the people she'd met, and the town. One or two had alluded to an incident at the church late Saturday but hadn't gone into details.

When Judah had walked outside, she'd gone with him, welcoming the chance to take a step back from the chaos and sort out her impressions.

Sipping her tea, she saw Tyree shove a plate of grilled shrimp at Judah.

There was something going on between the two men, a twitchiness that confirmed her original suspicion. Judah *was* uncomfortable about this whole ''going to Tyree's barbecue'' invitation. In the two and a half hours she'd been here, she'd met only three other Poinciana cops, all three African-American. At first she'd been relieved, not having been sure how Judah's fellow cops would react to her presence. Once she'd made the round of introductions, though, she'd wondered about the absence of those fellow cops, concluding at first that it was a church gathering.

But there were those three cops. There were the teachers from the local high school where Yvonna taught, and they'd indicated they weren't members of the Joneses' church. And then there was Judah.

Considering the current tension in Poinciana, it wasn't too hard to figure out the situation. The boys in blue evidently still saw things in black and white.

Still, why the edginess between Tyree and Judah? She nibbled thoughtfully on a piece of the best cornbread she'd ever eaten in her life. Judah and Tyree knew she was in the corner of the patio, but their conversation had become uncomfortably intense. She wasn't sure if they realized she could hear them.

A less curious woman would have walked away.

She wasn't eavesdropping. Of course she wasn't. She probably wasn't.

But she was very curious.

As she watched, Judah unscrewed the lid of a plastic bottle of ginger ale and poured some into one of the paper cups on the picnic table. "You and Yvonna put on a nice party."

Tyree nodded stiffly.

Both men shifted awkwardly in that way that men did when they were forced to talk with each other and didn't want to.

Finally she heard Judah speak again. "You mind that I brought Sophie?"

"Sophie, is it? How long you two been on a cozy first-name basis?"

"I met her over a year ago. We had a couple of dates. Sort of."

"Sort of?" Tyree dabbed sauce onto the grill.

Shrimp hissed, and Sophie's mouth watered. Curious to hear Judah's answer, she leaned forward. She remembered those "sort of dates" all too well. Her remembering had been part of the turmoil of the past year.

"Nothing came of it."

"Nothing?"

"That's right, Tyree."

Tyree lifted his glass of iced tea, saluted Judah with it. "Looks to me like *nothing*'s becoming *something*."

"We're not real compatible."

"Not how it looks to me."

"You're wrong."

"Don't think I am. Remember? I'm one of Poinciana's mighty fine *po*-licemen. A *dee*-tective, in fact. I see what I see," Tyree drawled.

In spite of the apparent light tone, Sophie detected an undercurrent of tension, of things left unspoken.

As footsteps came up behind her, she turned. Minus Taylor Bell, Yvonna stopped beside Sophie. Like Sophie, she watched the two men. "They seem awfully serious. Do you think we should interrupt them?"

Sophie crumpled her paper plate with the shrimp tails in it. Cornbread crumbs dribbled onto her skirt. "It would probably be a good idea since I seem to be the subject of the conversation. And you know how it goes, right? Eavesdroppers never hear anything good about themselves. Not that, technically, I'm eavesdropping, you understand." She looked around for a trash can.

"Here, I'll take that." Yvonna took the plate and walked over to a plastic container near the back door. As she walked slowly back, her expression indicated that she'd made up her mind about something. "I was surprised Judah came tonight. Don't misunderstand me, Sophie. I'm glad he did. And I'm really pleased he brought you. It's a good thing, this breaking down of barriers. He and my Tyree need to move past some stuff."

"I did think it was strange that Judah had never been to your house."

Yvonna shrugged. "It was well understood in the department that Judah didn't want another partner. But you probably knew that?"

"No."

"These last four months have been a shakedown period for Tyree and Judah both. With the emphasis on shaky."

"That explains a lot." Sophie met Yvonna's gaze. "I wasn't sure I'd be welcome here. You know I'm the doctor who treated Judah's partner?"

"Uh, that could be a bit awkward for you, I'd imagine, if some of the oldtimers from the department were here?"

Sophie laughed. From the corner of her eye, she saw Judah turn his head toward her. "Wow. So if I'm not the reason, why are only three of Poinciana's finest in attendance? Oops," she added as Yvonna's face froze, confirming Sophie's earlier suspicion. "Oh."

"Not your problem. It's simply the way things are in this town at the moment." Yvonna shrugged. "You didn't cause it."

"Wow," Sophie repeated, wishing she could replay the last two minutes, "there's a whole lot of subtext going on at this party. And I've just come down with a galloping case of foot-in-the-mouth disease, haven't I?"

"You didn't know how things are. Some lines still aren't easily crossed here."

"I'm sorry." An awkwardness had been entered into the conversation, and neither one knew quite how to proceed. "Anyway," Sophie plunged ahead, "I thought either Judah or Tyree must have told you that I was the doctor on call the night Roberts was brought in. That I was the one who insisted on the test for his blood alcohol level? The test that would have resulted in his suspension?" Sophie didn't feel like adding the rest of the story. Either Yvonna knew that Judah blamed her for his partner's suicide, or she didn't.

"Tyree would have said something if he'd known. I'm sure Judah never mentioned it to him."

"Oh?" Opting for discretion this time, Sophie clamped her mouth shut. Why hadn't Judah told Tyree about what he saw as her role in George Roberts's death? "I'm surprised," she said finally.

"Judah and Tyree don't talk much. Or at least they didn't

used to. But, yes, I know about George's suicide. I've been told he and Judah were close and that Judah was really annoyed about being forced into taking a new partner. I don't imagine Judah was thinking clearly. Why on earth would the man want to work alone when the situation in Poinciana has gotten so dicey that even the suits in charge don't want the men going out on solitary duty? I also think that Tyree—well, that the brass were trying to make a point with Tyree once he had his detective ranking. As for how he and Judah are doing right now? Who knows? I think things are changing. I hope so. Because I want my man safe. And if things aren't right between him and his partner when they're out on the street—'' Yvonna hesitated, glanced over at the men. ''Look, I don't mean to pry or poke my nose into your business, but their partnership hasn't been easy for Tyree, you know?''

''And you want me to do what?''

''Whatever you can.''

''Yvonna, I don't have any influence with Judah. He blames me for George Roberts's death.''

Yvonna made a face. ''But he brought you here. When he's never been here before himself. That must mean something.''

''Not with Judah. I still haven't figured out why he invited me, in fact. I wish I could help you, Yvonna, but I don't see that there's any way I can. I understand your concern. Poinciana's a keg of dynamite right now, isn't it?''

''Everything's unsettled. Too many guns, too many angry folks, too many people looking for jobs and not finding anything. Add into that mix the changing ethnic population. A little tolerance and patience would help, but those seem in short supply in this town right now. Bad times and scared folks. That's a mighty volatile combination. Especially for cops manning the barricades. Or should I say manning and womaning?'' Yvonna touched Sophie's arm. ''Do what you can. I'd like my Tyree with us come Christmas.''

Sophie expected her to walk over to the men, but Yvonna

regarded them pensively before pressing her hands over her eyes and walking back inside, her back straight, her head up.

Cops' wives. Sophie had seen their strength before. Women who married cops had their own kind of courage. Or they didn't last.

She felt a hand on her back, low, near her left hip, and knew instantly it was Judah's. When she turned to face him, he was right inside her bubble of personal space, that one step that sent a clear signal to any woman.

She didn't step back.

Instead, she took a deliberate step forward, let her hip bump up against him. It could have been a friendly bump. But she made sure the nudge wasn't anywhere in the neighborhood of friendly. That hip bump took a detour right around friendly straight to desire. She smiled slowly up at him, liking the way he frowned back, liking that she could throw him off balance for a minute.

"You know what you're doing, don't you, sugar?"

"You betcha, big guy." She tugged at the edge of his collar. "Want to make something of it?"

"Yeah," he said slowly. He twined his fingers with hers, raising them to her shoulder level, their palms flat against one another. He moved his palm sideways, slowly, against hers. "Reckon I do."

"Then what's keeping you, slowpoke?" she whispered, not moving an inch, simply letting the words drift like dust in sunlight.

Judah looked over his shoulder, scoped out the patio. "Not one damn thing."

All her senses were concentrated in those few square inches of contact. She could never have imagined the sensory power of a man's hand pressing against hers.

Not any man's hand.

Judah's.

He let his hand drift to her fanny, gave her a tiny slap that sent tingles down to her toes. "Your place or mine, Sophie? And how fast?"

"Which is closer?" She pulled his head down to hers, skimmed his mouth with hers.

She meant to tantalize him, to tease with a hint, a promise.

But teasing went both ways, she discovered breathlessly.

"Mine," he said, and his eyes had gone dark with intent. "Definitely mine. Follow me."

Walking side by side back to the house, they said their goodbyes, keeping a distance between them, a distance bridged by the almost-brush of his little finger against hers, by a whisper of skirt against pants. Sophie understood why he didn't touch her once they were on the sidewalk with the clamor of the Joneses' party behind them.

One touch wouldn't have been enough.

Three minutes later, Judah held her car door open for her to slide inside. Sophie hesitated, but because of what Yvonna had asked her to do, she asked, "Why are you and Tyree so edgy with each other?"

Judah shut the door. "Because Tyree thinks I'm a white cop."

She ran the back of her hand down his throat and smiled as his eyes grew sleepy. "You could have fooled me."

"I'm a cop, Sophie. Period. Tyree's going to believe what he wants to."

As Sophie followed the red flicker of his bike's taillight, she wondered if some day she would look back on these December days and conclude that she'd been in a fever.

She'd never craved anyone's touch the way she did Judah's.

She was almost sick with wanting to be near him.

In a million breaths, she couldn't have explained to anyone the way he made her feel. What she felt when she was with Judah Finnegan was outside her experience and imagination. She'd never expected to feel this way, never known it was possible.

As the tidy neighborhood lots gave way to the open country of cattle and scrub pines, she followed the steady light from his bike. Into the deepening blackness of Florida country she let him lead her, and as she did, she sent up a tiny prayer to whatever female spirits protected a risk-taking woman like herself.

When this ended, and it would, it had to, please, she prayed, let it not end with ugliness.

This—what was it? An *affair?* Somehow the word didn't begin to cover the situation, but whatever she called it, she accepted that it would burn itself out. How could it not? Impossible for this kind of heat to last. Too fierce, too intense. These days with Judah were like a supernova flaring brilliantly in its final hours.

Turning a corner behind him, she resolved that she wouldn't waste these moments anticipating an ending. It would come when it came. Not for the first time since she'd met Judah, she promised herself that for now she would seize every moment. Go for the adventure, the wild ride of fate.

That was what she'd always done, reached out and grabbed hold of life, let it take her where it would. There was no reason to change her *modus operandi.*

Except a broken heart? She dimmed her bright lights in the face of an oncoming car. The physician in her reminded her that broken hearts might not mend but they went on beating. Willy-nilly, the earth whirled on through cold and dark space.

She would deal with whatever lay ahead, with the pain that might rise up and slam into her.

As for that old snake in the grass, pain?

A risk? Sure. Worse, much worse never to have had these moments. To have lived her life and never known Judah. Never to have known that there were places in the human heart and soul that were just as wild and exhilarating as the biggest wave she'd ever ridden.

Sophie parked her car under a cabbage palm near the porte cochere next to Judah and his bike. Getting out, she locked it and leaned against the door, waiting. Judah had braked, but the engine continued to rumble. Still straddling the bike, feet planted on the sandy ground, he threw her a long stare over his shoulder.

She straightened. "I'm not going to change my mind."

"You could have. Any time."

"I know." She walked across the sand toward him.

He gunned the engine once, turned it off. The cooling tick of metal counterpointed the chirping of tree frogs in the background.

He touched her elbow, pointed to a door of the porte cochere. "Come inside, Sophie."

She waited while he opened the door and led her through the small rooms to the back. His house was what she might have expected if she'd thought about it. Spare, plain, it was a cracker house as she'd heard Poincianians describe the pine-board frame homes on stilts with tin roofs. The stilts allowed air to circulate and cool these old-style Florida houses. Long, floor-to-ceiling windows broke the weathered gray of the boards. It was a house for another time, for a time when people didn't lock their doors in fear and hide inside air-conditioned isolation, didn't hide behind barred windows. A house for a time long gone, one not likely to come again.

In its simplicity and austerity, the rooms of the house whispered to her of Judah. No television, no clutter, no life. A board-and-brick bookcase. Empty.

Like an anchorite's cell, Judah's house told her that here was a man punishing himself.

In his bedroom, she turned in a circle, registering in one look the white-and-gray striped duvet over the bed, the ancient bureau against one wall. No mirror, no rug. No softness anywhere.

His house made her ache with sympathy for him, made her see him in a new light. It didn't detract from his strength, his hard edges. But it gave her a glimpse of what lay underneath the tough shell of the man. And she remembered the loneliness of the boy.

"Wait," he said as she tugged at the scarf around her waist. "Let me."

He undressed her slowly in the moonlight of his small, austere bedroom, his hands sliding and caressing until she felt as though she wore him, as if his hands clothed her. He spread his thumbs under the thin straps of her rib-length camisole, lowering them inch by inch down her arms, his thumbs brushing her breasts like a summer breeze.

"I like this." He touched the pale-gray chiffon of her camisole. "But I'm sure glad I didn't know you had these bits of nothing underneath your Sunday-go-to-meeting dress, Sophie." He plucked at the thin line at the bottom of the camisole, slid his palm underneath the soft illusion. "I'll bet it was expensive."

She leaned into his palm, welcoming the roughness of his callused hand against her. "And worth every dollar."

He traced the darker gray, embroidered roses that covered her breasts, palmed the single rose on her panties. "It's like smoke on clear water, but all you see is you, the gleam of your skin. You're a mystery, Sophie." He spread his hands flat on her fanny, slipped them under the illusion of fabric that pretended to be panties, tugged at the narrow waistband. Like a sigh, wispy gray roses drifted to the floor.

She undressed him with the same careful attention to detail, the same deliberate slowness. It was an appreciation of the physical, of the marvel of bone and sinew and skin. She had thought there was nothing about the human body that could surprise her any more.

But Judah's body delighted her. She touched the scar she'd stitched only days earlier, smoothed her hands over the muscles of his ribs and marveled. The texture of his skin, the scent of his neck. The taste of his mouth, the slide of his tongue with hers.

It was the slowness that destroyed her.

She hadn't expected this slowness, this gentleness. She'd expected the heat. The fire. After the way they'd left the barbecue, she'd wondered if he might not even pull over to the side of the road and take her then in the closeness of her car.

But what he gave her and asked of her now was tenderness.

Moonlight silvered his skin, hers. She watched his hands move over her, touching her, learning her responses and then retracing their way exquisitely across the geography of her body.

She remembered a song she'd heard years ago, something about a woman wanting a man with slow hands. She'd been too young to understand the song.

Judah had slow hands.

Wonderful hands.

Bittersweet in the silvered light, moments slipped into hours.

With the memory of her two pre-dawn phone calls, she made her touch achingly tender, too, as something in her recognized that this might be the last time she ever lay with him on silver sheets in a silver room.

Chapter 13

Morning tiptoed into the room, sly streaks of gold curling around the edges of night. Sophie opened her eyes to find Judah watching her. Facing her, he held her close with one leg thrown over her hip. She must have murmured because he placed one hand on each side of her face, eased himself over her and stayed there, resting on his elbows, his body slick against hers. But he made no other move, seemingly content to lie there with her in the morning sunshine.

Loving the early-morning look of him, she rubbed the back of her hand against his cheek stubble. "What do you want, Judah?"

"Nothing. Everything." His hands framing her face, he kept his eyes locked on hers. "I see you, Sophie. Believe me, I see you." And then he eased inside her so slowly and carefully that tears welled in her eyes.

She felt as if he were worshipping her with each touch, each stroke, every kiss.

Not hesitating for a second, not giving a damn for the

consequences, she enclosed him in her arms and took him, lonely child and stubborn man, straight into her heart.

Later, with sunlight advancing across the bare floor, she pressed her fingertips against his beautiful mouth, his clever mouth, and finally said, "Judah, I'm leaving." Not looking at him, she edged to the side of the bed away from him.

He caught her before she slid free of the sheet. "Early shift?" He wound her hair around his fingers, tugged.

"Poinciana. I'm going home. To Chicago."

Curled around her, his body went still. "When?"

"This afternoon." *Stay, stay,* she wanted him to urge her. She knew he wouldn't. "My flight's at two."

He withdrew. "All right." He tucked her hair behind her ears and levered himself away from her. He sat up, his back to her. "You flying out of Tampa or Sarasota?"

"Sarasota." Chilled, she gathered the edges of the sheet close.

There were so many questions he could have asked, should have asked. *When are you coming back? Where will you be staying? Will you call me? Can I call you? Will you miss me? Don't you know I'll miss you?*

Instead, he said pleasantly, "This afternoon? All right then. I hope it all works out for you. Merry Christmas. And Happy New Year, too, I reckon."

Then, caught by a note in his voice, she paused with one foot on the floor. The narrow line of his naked spine was a shade too straight. In her head, she replayed her words, his, and smiled. She didn't think he'd like knowing how well she was learning to read him. "Oh, I'll be back before then," she tossed off nonchalantly. "I'm not moving, for heaven's sake. I like Poinciana. I like my job, my house."

"Do you, now?"

"I'll only be in Chicago three days. I needed a few days off to take care of some things before I bring Angel home. And I need to see my Bushka."

"Your grandmother?" He turned in one fluid motion. "Of course. And Angel. I forgot." He caught her shoulders suddenly and tumbled her back onto the bed with him. The sheet tangled between their legs, and he stripped it off, leaving her bare in the sunlight. "You don't leave until two, huh? Looks like we have time."

"For what?"

He scooped her red scarf up from the floor. "For anything we can think of."

She laughed. "You have this thing about handcuffs, don't you?"

"Just doing my job, ma'am," he murmured as he slipped the scarf over her eyes.

It was amazing what two people could think of, Sophie decided. Imagination was everything. And Judah was very imaginative.

She lost track of the time.

When the phone rang, interrupting them, he held her in the circle of his arms for a moment before rolling over and sitting up. Late-morning sunlight splashed across his shoulders. Her scarf lay between his shoulder and chin. Half turned toward her, he took her hand and spread it over his chest, weaving silken patterns as he trailed the scarf back and forth over her breasts and stomach while he talked in the phone.

She'd never be able to wear that particular scarf again without blushing.

"All right, Tyree. Got it. Wait for me. I'll meet you there in fifteen minutes. Don't go by yourself. Hear? Wait."

He dropped the receiver into the phone cradle. "There's something going on at a trailer park off the Tamiami Trail. Tyree thinks it might be related to the graffiti and other incidents around town. A helpful citizen called it in."

"You have to go."

"I do. Tyree and I asked to work both cases because we thought there might be a link." He cupped the calf of her leg, stroked down to her toes. "And you have to do what you have to." He stood up abruptly. "About Angel. And your grandmother."

But he still wouldn't ask the questions.

Not even when he walked her to her car and waited with the door open, swinging it back and forth before finally shutting it with a quiet, decisive click.

This time she drove away, leaving him behind.

It should have satisfied something in her, some trace of pride. Something. It didn't. Leaving him. His leaving her. Both felt lousy.

During the entire flight to Chicago, she thought about how her life seemed more complete when she was with him and how bereft it seemed without him. Even without their history, there were other issues that made anything long-term impossible. She understood that with unwavering clarity. There was no solution, no fairy godmother around to wave a wand and make everything perfect.

Only her Bushka waiting for her as they deplaned at O'Hare in a swirling snowfall that coated the bare limbs of trees and bushes with blinding white.

Enveloped in her grandmother's embrace and the familiar fragrance of Tzigane, her Bushka's signature scent, Sophie was home at last.

So why was she homesick for palm trees and white sand?

Judah kept one hand on the wheel while he adjusted the seat belt. Action was good. That way he and Tyree wouldn't have to rehash the Sunday night barbecue. Action, hot and heavy, would keep him from thinking about the way his gut had tightened when Sophie had blithely informed him she was blowing out of town and back to Chicago. He'd been cool, though. He gave himself points for that.

"Okay," he said to Tyree. "What do we know about this situation?"

"The caller said, and I'm quoting the dispatcher, 'the bad boys are at The Palms Trailer Park and they're planning to be mean.' No other information. We don't know if they're armed, or if it's misinformation."

"In other words, the usual?"

"Guess so." Tyree tapped at the computer on the dashboard. "Nope. Nothing else comes up. Here, Judah, hang a left here. The Palms is down this dirt road. We're almost there." Tyree sat back in his seat. "Something feels wrong about this."

"Yeah." The car bumped over the washboard road and Judah spun the steering wheel, keeping the car under control as they approached the trailers sprawled like stranded hump-backed whales beneath the trees of The Palms.

Tyree leaned forward, frowned. "You ever get a bad case of the willies, Judah?"

"Once or twice."

"Well, I got a case of them right now. My skin feels like red ants are crawling all over me. I don't like this."

"I get your point. Stay sharp."

They spun to a stop near the first row of banged-up trailers.

Sandspurs and periwinkles peppered the sand around them. Whoever had laid out the trailer hookups of The Palms had done so with no discernible plan that Judah could see. That same whoever had been either hopeful or sarcastic in naming the park because as far as Judah could tell, there weren't any palm trees, not even a homely cabbage palm. He estimated there were seventy to a hundred trailers filling the acre and a half of scrub pine and live oak. He figured some folks might have called the rusting Silverstreams and camper wag-ons vintage Americana. He reckoned they were three steps up from a cardboard box. Slogans spray-painted on the Laun-dromat shed were more desperate and angry than patriotic. Overfilled garbage cans melted onto the ground like candle wax.

A smell of rotting garbage lay over the quiet afternoon.

It was too quiet.

No music. No barking dogs. No birdsong.

Not good.

Judah felt the back of his neck prickle as he scanned the weedy parking lot of The Palms and the woods in back.

Even drunks and drug dealers should be up and about by

this time. And back here in the piney woods almost everyone had a dog or two.

With a hand movement, he sent Tyree to the right of the first trailers while he crept to the left. Even as he did, he saw from his angle a flicker of white behind a trio of trailers fifty yards in front of Tyree. Nothing more than a fleck of white against the dusty gray of a trailer. Could have been a bit of paper. Could have been anything.

Judah froze. He pointed emphatically toward the gray trailer, but Tyree, intent on slipping from trailer edge to trailer edge, kept moving ahead, oblivious to Judah's warning.

"Hell," Judah muttered under his breath and dropped to crawl across the prickly ground.

From his vantage point, he saw the legs. Dingy white sneakers. Big ones. Two men were standing there, blocked from Tyree's view. They should have called out, asked what Tyree and Judah wanted. That would have been the obvious behavior. But they hadn't. They'd stayed sheltered in the lee of the big Silverstream. Judah had seen the almost imperceptible shift of one of the sneakers as the men had moved into position.

If Tyree kept moving in the direction he was, he'd walk right up to the men lurking there, and they'd have the drop on him.

Assuming, of course, that they were armed. And dangerous.

But as fast as he crawled, he knew he wasn't going to be able to intercept Tyree.

Judah kept moving. He didn't have a whole bunch of options here. He wanted these guys. He didn't want to spook them, sending them scattering out into the woods where they could disappear. But Tyree kept slipping silently and efficiently from trailer to trailer, the men just out of his vision range. He was so intent on the territory in front of him, his head moving left, right, that he never looked back toward Judah.

So that was that. No more options. Not unless he wanted to send Tyree home to Yvonna in a body bag.

Judah gathered himself into a crouching position, held his Sig Sauer steady and leapt sideways and in front of Tyree with a war whoop. "Down! Down!" He shoved Tyree hard in the back and kept running forward, hell bent for leather and yelling like a banshee, "Hit the ground! Damn it, hit the ground! Now!"

Tyree stumbled and then was running, too, side by side with Judah like racers at a finish line. Judah hadn't reckoned on that. He'd calculated on the element of surprise to startle the men, slow them down, and give him a chance to haul ass after them. It never occurred to him that Tyree would instantly figure out what was happening and react so damned fast.

George, older and fatter, slower all around, would have gone down.

"Damn it," Judah grunted. "I told you. Hit the dirt!"

"Going to. Any minute now," Tyree panted, "you first."

Judah knew he'd screwed up. He should have known Tyree could react so intuitively and swiftly. But he'd kept that wall between them because he hadn't wanted a partner, because Tyree wasn't George, because Judah had been so damned angry at everyone and everything, including himself.

He had to be very lucky in the next few minutes or his mistake was going to cost them. At the moment, Tyree was the target du jour.

Tyree had stumbled when Judah slammed into him, leaving Judah half a step faster. He used that half step to shove ahead of Tyree when the first man came out from the trailer, shooting.

Of course it was a big gun, the kind cops joked about. "Overcompensating," they'd snort whenever they saw some wannabe tough guy with one.

As Judah angled in front of Tyree, that big old gun made a hell of a noise. Revved on adrenaline, he didn't even check his rush forward.

The first shot burned across Judah's right arm. The second went wild, both men running toward the woods now, Tyree after them, screaming, "Halt! Police!" doing the stance, doing everything by the books, and Judah's arm dripping blood all over his shirt, but he was almost keeping stride with Tyree.

Thrashing into the shadows of the woods, they sent a cloud of crows winging up into the sky. Saw palmetto caught at their pants legs, slowed them both. Blinded by sweat, Judah lurched into a thick net of kudzu. Swinging his arms in a circle, he realized he was caught. Neither of them could see a way to shove through the carpet of vines.

Only yards ahead, the men whipped left, right, and then vanished under the kudzu-choked trees and into the wildness.

Judah tripped on a thick vine, caught his ankle in the tangles and crashed to the ground.

Taking a step back and struggling for breath too, Tyree looked down at him. "Didn't know white guys could run."

"Yeah, go figure, huh?" Judah looked off into the now-quiet woods. "But we didn't get the bad guys."

Tyree's face was stony with anger. He extended a hand to help Judah in the entanglement of vines. "Here. We're not likely to get them now. They're gone." He yanked Judah free.

Judah winced.

"You didn't have to play hero, you know." Hands on his hips, Tyree glared at Judah. "I knew what I was doing."

"You did everything by the book. But did you see them? At the trailer?"

Tyree's frown deepened. "No. Guess I didn't."

"Guess I had to do what I did, then."

"You had my back, Judah."

"I said I would."

"So you did. I won't doubt you again."

"That road runs both ways." His chest expanded as if he were taking a deep breath after a long time, something easing the constant tightness that seemed to have been there forever.

"If we're going to be partners." Judah plucked at the bloody fabric of his sleeve. "And it looks like we are."

"Yeah. Reckon I am." Change jingled in Tyree's pocket as he rocked back and forth. "Your arm okay?"

They exchanged a look.

Judah laughed. "We're going to have to fill out another set of papers. Discharge of weapons, officer wounded. Hospital incident report. I've lost count of the forms in the last four days."

"All that paperwork's a killer, isn't it? Wish I'd known you were so accident-prone. I might have taken a pass on riding with you."

"The brass probably didn't give you a choice." Judah wiped his shirt sleeve across the seeping blood.

"Actually, they did." Tyree peered into the wound field. "Now that you ask."

"Glutton for punishment?"

"Liked your style. Didn't like George's. Figured I'd see how things went."

Back creaking, Judah straightened. With the ebb of adrenaline, his body let him know it had been abused. He felt the sting on his arm, the ache of places that would blossom into purples and blues by tomorrow. "And now?"

"Think I'll stick around. Partner."

They headed back to the car, called in the report, and gunned the unit once more to Poinciana County Hospital.

Judah figured it was a sign.

He just wasn't sure what the sign meant.

The hospital seemed quieter and flatter without Sophie.

Cammie, the nurse he'd met on Friday, burbled greetings when he and Tyree walked into the ER. "You like us here, eh? You're welcome any time. But you don't need to get yourself all shot up or knifed if you want to come visit." Bustling them into an examining room, she waved a hand toward a table spread with cookies and carafes. "Have a cup of hot chocolate when you're all through."

Tyree stayed until Judah had been checked over and his wound, a minor one, cleaned and bandaged.

Afterwards, Judah told him to head home. "We'll do the paperwork tomorrow. If the suits don't like it, well, what are they going to do? Put us back on patrol?" Sharing his irritation over the bureaucracy that leg-shackled them at every turn, he lifted an eyebrow.

"In a pig's eye." Tyree rolled his eyes in agreement and laughed. "They aren't that stupid. We've been busting our butts this whole week on one thing or another. Don't know about you, but I can almost smell an end to this case and it feels good. I want to catch the creeps who beat that poor woman. And I want to be the one locking them up. It'll feel real good."

"It's that helpful caller again. Too coincidental for my taste. Somebody out there is Johnny-on-the-spot every time. But why won't he come in to the station and give us what we really need to know? Names? Addresses? I figure he's involved and working off a load of guilt."

"That's not my take," Tyree disagreed. "Assuming this caller is the same guy who called in about the baby—and dispatch center sure seems to think so—he comes across as protective too, you know?"

"Protective or not, I'd like to grab him by the scruff of his neck and shake him up one side of the barn and down the other until he gives us names. Information. Damn, Tyree, this afternoon was one hair away from ugly."

"It was." Tyree shrugged, twirled the car keys. "You want me to go then? Because I can stay as long as you want."

"Nah, go on. Be with your kids and Yvonna for a while. I'll get a ride. Call a taxi."

"If you're sure?" Tyree was clearly ready to bolt.

Judah didn't blame him. A gunfight did that to you. Made you antsy, ready to be with your woman. Messed big time with your head.

By now Sophie was in Chicago. He'd checked the weather

report while he was waiting for the nurse. Snow predicted all week for Chicago. Doctor Sugar was going to have herself a Currier and Ives kind of Christmas. She'd said she was coming back, but he wouldn't bet gas money on it.

People changed. He'd be pure-grade stupid to make anything of her blithe assurance that she had responsibilities here in Poinciana. Sophie was a creature of impulse, of the moment, and once she was in Chicago, with everything all postcard-beautiful and her right in the middle of it, she'd have second thoughts.

She'd be out shopping or skiing. In a red cap, he'd bet. Her hair would shine with snow flakes. Sophie in snowflakes would be a treat to see. Her cheeks would be cherry-red from the cold.

She'd be laughing. Sophie laughed a lot. Giggled, too. That had surprised him the first time the musical ripple of laughter had erupted. Doctors didn't giggle. But Sophie did.

He couldn't recall when her laughter and sunniness had become necessary to him.

Now they were.

He didn't know what he was going to do about it.

He couldn't stop wondering what she was doing. Whatever it was, she'd be enjoying herself, full steam ahead, throwing all her energy and enthusiasm into whatever she was doing.

He missed her with a longing that made him stop and catch his breath, easing the tightness in his chest.

Only hours without her, and in spite of the bright Florida-blue sky, his world was darker, colder. This past year had left him feeling beat up. Lonelier. Older and tired.

He didn't like feeling like an old man.

On an impulse, he took the elevator up to the Peds ward. Showing his badge to the nurse on duty, he headed toward the baby Sophie called Angel.

From the corner of his eye, he glimpsed the guy who'd been hanging around it seemed every time Judah was at the hospital. Billy something.

He looked down at the baby he'd found in the rainy night

and wondered what Sophie had found so irresistible. Babies were…an encumbrance.

Hostages to fate, they were hopelessly dependent on the adults in their lives.

Flawed, selfish adults. Impatient, driven, tormented adults. Hell, a person had to have a license to operate a vehicle. Nothing required to operate a baby or to make one. So where did Sophie find the grit to dive head-first into the idea of parenting this baby she knew nothing about? How could Sophie think she could raise this child? There was no way Sophie could make such an impulse work. You played the cards you were dealt. This abandoned child had a crummy hand. Bad luck for the kid, but that was life.

The baby's brown eyes met his.

Her quiet, still gaze was adult in its wariness. She wasn't a gurgly kind of kid. Observant, but not cuddly, as if she were holding herself safe, simply waiting for him to make the first move, like she knew exactly how her world had been destroyed in a moment of violence.

Her unwavering gaze made him profoundly uneasy.

The longer he watched, the more he had the strangest sense that Sophie's Angel was studying him and trying to make up her mind about him.

He couldn't speak, couldn't take his eyes from her.

No help from heaven, none from earth.

The ever-familiar rage stirred in him.

This kid's bad luck was one more tick in the column of Calvin Finnegan's all-knowing, all-powerful, perfect-in-judgment God's mistakes.

Judah knew he damned well didn't want to be on speaking terms with a God who couldn't do any better than this.

The awareness of the world's cruelty that he carried always with him seemed more burdensome than ever as he watched Sophie's Angel in the quiet Peds ward.

Confused and not sure why he'd sought out the baby, he turned to go.

And then Sophie's Angel waved one closed fist and

grabbed her toe, pulling it to her small mouth. She smiled in his direction, a quick rearrangement of minute features. The smile killed, no question.

He crossed his arms over his chest. "Look, let's get this straight, right up front. I don't like babies. I don't like kids. And I sure as hell don't like teenagers. I'm not a sucker, kid, so don't flirt with me. I'm not one of those wusses who go all goo-goo over kids. You're wasting your time. Got it?"

It might have been the sound of his male voice in the silence of the ward, a difference in her environment that startled her.

Because she whimpered once, the small sound of one tiny human being reaching out for comfort, for connection with another human being, her loneliness mirroring his. Only that one, forlorn whimper.

Silence.

Judah picked her up before he realized he'd even reached into her crib. "This doesn't mean anything, you know. Don't think it does."

Her baby palm swatted his face, offering him the very comfort she had sought from him.

He took a deep breath, and it was hard to suck in air. "Kid, I can't help you. There's damn all I can do. Don't look to me for help. I'm nobody's hero." He jiggled her gently, helplessly, while she kept her gaze fixed on him.

He couldn't change anything for her. He knew he couldn't make the past go away. There would be no happy ever after for this baby, no matter what Sophie believed. Nothing Sophie could do. Nothing he could fix. Life was hard, ugly, and this poor munchkin had been caught in the maw of evil.

All he could do was find her mother's killer. That much he could do.

Would do.

Chapter 14

Outside the Peds ward, a shadow moved. A flicker, nothing more. Furtive in this very public arena.

Judah went still. In his arms, Angel folded in on herself, a tiny, blanket-wrapped silent mouse. Looking down at her, he mouthed, "Shh," as if she could understand and heed his warning.

The on-duty nurse was attending to another infant in the far corner of the room. Something in Judah's posture must have caught her attention because she glanced at him, her eyebrows drawn together in a question.

Before she could speak out loud, he gave a minute shrug, *all cool here, nothing wrong,* and she resumed changing the IV tubing snaking from the baby in the crib.

In a remote corner of Judah's brain, he understood that he was behaving irrationally. There was no reason to be on guard, not here. No threat in a room full of babies.

But the animal brain whispered its warning, and he listened, all senses quivering.

Nothing happened.

No more movement.

Yet still there was that disturbance in the air.

Carefully he eased Angel back into her crib. Moving noiselessly to the wall separating him and that sense of wrongness coming from the hall, Judah stopped, muscles tensed, at the doorjamb next to the privacy panel for the ward.

And waited once more as he'd done for so many years, waiting for evil to step out and show itself.

As silent and as unmoving as a stalking lion, he could have waited forever. Within seconds, though, a muffled clank came from the hall.

The stringy-haired head that poked around the edge of the door was familiar.

"Hey, there, Billy Ray." Judah stepped out from the concealing panel. "Looking for something?"

Billy Ray's face went a pastier shade of pale. "No. Yes! I mean—"

Judah closed in on him, walking Billy Ray backwards into the hall, the sun-bleached blue of Billy Ray's eyes dilating into darkness as he stuttered and stumbled and never loosened his death grip on the mop he held in one shaking hand.

"Yes? No? What's it going to be, Billy Ray? What's that?" Judah asked softly, punctuating each word with a hard thump of his flat hand against the other man's sunken chest. The thump sent the man reeling backwards, Judah right in his face, murmuring, "Speak up, guy. I can't hear you. You really, really want to make sure I hear you, Billy Ray."

"I know!" Sliding the mop back and forth, Billy Ray backed into the wall. "I didn't do nothing, I didn't! I didn't hurt that baby!"

Once in a while you got lucky. Judah felt lucky. "Baby? What baby is that?"

"You know!" Billy Ray gestured wildly. "That baby!"

"Going to have to be more specific." Judah patted him hard on the chest. "There's a room full of babies in back of me. What did you plan to do with one of those babies, huh, Billy Ray?" With two fingers, Judah tapped him softly on the neck. "Going to steal one? Sneak it out of the hospital? Maybe you were thinking of doing that. Yeah, makes sense to me. Sneak some baby out and sell it. Make a bundle."

"No, no, no," he moaned.

"No?" Judah flicked the back of his hand against the man's cheek. "You on drugs, Billy Ray? You thinking of making a quick buck by stealing a baby to pay for some fine white powder to ease you through the day?"

"No! I work. My job is here. I do a good job! Every day, Billy Ray does a good job! I didn't hurt that baby!" His retreat cut off by the wall, the man crumpled into a heap at Judah's feet. One of his long, thin hands continued to twitch the mop back and forth off to Judah's left. Billy Ray's other hand picked at his upper lip, worrying the skin until a drop of bright red dotted it.

Billy Ray's fear rose like a cloud of mosquito spray off the man, toxic and suffocating. Underneath the fear, though, was confusion.

And distress. A distress that intensified with each shift of Billy Ray's glance to the door of the Peds ward.

Oh, hell. Judah finally got it, finally saw what he should have recognized the first time he'd seen the man. Judah felt his blood pressure drop as his icy rage drained away.

He'd been blinded by his fury that someone could threaten those babies. Holding Angel, he'd seen nothing else except one more threat to her.

He'd been stupid.

That's what happened when emotions sneaked in.

He still needed answers. Billy Ray would give some, lead him to the rest.

Eventually.

Then they'd know who'd killed Le Duc Nhu. Know, too, why her baby had been found in the manger.

Lowering his voice to a confiding tone, Judah squatted beside Billy Ray, hunkering down in a guy-to-guy posture. He let the tension ease from his muscles, let Billy Ray pick up on the change. He thought about taking Billy Ray down to the cafeteria, but decided it was better to stay casual, keep talking in the hall. That way he wouldn't spook Billy Ray any more than he had already. Eventually, as if he had all the time in the world, Judah pointed to the mop. "Hey, man. My bad. Sorry I came on so strong. You surprised me, that's all. Listen, I can see you're a hard worker. By the way," Judah stretched out his hand, "that's a mighty fine mop you're using."

Billy Ray drew the mop closer. "My mop. Nobody uses it but Billy Ray. I keep the floors real clean. That's my job."

"You do a swell job," Judah said.

"You the cop what brought in the baby. I seen you that day."

Judah let a beat of silence rest between them, let Billy Ray take a deep breath before Judah added conversationally, "And every time I've been at the hospital, I've seen you. You're a really busy guy."

The man jerked his head several times. But his glance once more went to the magnet of the Peds ward, and beads of sweat popped out along his hairline.

"I've seen how you keep to a schedule, stick to your routine—"

Billy Ray's bobbing nods increased frantically.

"But there's some other reason why you show up whenever I'm around, isn't there?"

The head bobs slowed, the smell of fear rose even stronger, and Billy Ray's hand on the mop resumed its twitching.

"You need to tell my why that happens, Billy Ray. Why you showed up in the cafeteria, for instance, when I was there."

"I keep busy. I go everywhere."

"And that's why I think you can help me." Judah placed one hand on the mop handle. He could feel the vibration of the man's twitches through the handle. He could feel the vibration of the man's twitches through the handle. "You want to help me, don't you, Billy Ray?" Judah saw the last name embroidered on the man's shirt. "Or you want me to call you Mr. Watley? You like that better?"

The man inhaled. "Everybody calls me Billy Ray."

"Okay." Judah nodded. "That's real friendly of you, Billy Ray. But that's why you've been following me around, right? To help the baby?"

Billy Ray's other hand finally ceased picking at his lip. "I help a lot."

Through the windows of the Peds ward, Judah watched puffy clouds move across the late-afternoon brilliant blue and rose-tinged sky. Stretching northward, blanketing Sophie, the sky there would be gray and snowfilled. If she'd been here, she could have explained Billy Ray. He wouldn't have been so stupid as to bully Billy Ray and scare him mindless. Sophie would have understood what Judah hadn't.

He'd called Sophie a fool for believing in people. Yet he'd been the fool for going off half-cocked when he'd seen Billy Ray sneaking around. He'd been pure cop in those moments, sure, reacting fast and aggressively, but he'd been a cop who wasn't seeing what was in front of him.

Sophie might have kept him from making such a fool of himself—

But she'd cheerfully turned her back on Poinciana and flown into the cold and snow, abandoning them. She should have been here, he thought.

He recognized his own pigheadedness.

Sophie had a right to be wherever she wanted to be.

Clearly, she didn't want to be here.

He slammed shut the door on those thoughts. Sophie was gone. She didn't get to live in his head.

Settling back against the wall, giving the man beside him all the space and time he needed, Judah said, finally, gently, "Tell me about the baby, Billy Ray. How did you help her? Because you did, didn't you?"

Billy Ray told him.

It was a long telling with many starts and stops, many side trips.

At the end, Judah rested his head against the wall and shut his eyes.

Mankind.

Man-unkind.

Stupid, all of it. Stupid. And a dead woman and a homeless child at the end of it all.

Outside the window of Sophie's grandmother's apartment, flurries of snow whipped in the dark against the sides of the yellow Chicago brick buildings. The gangways between them were so narrow that Sophie could have reached from her Bushka's steamy kitchen into the rooms of the building across the way with a short pole.

Living practically in the neighbors' pockets had once felt cozy. Now, though, missing the endless pulse of the Gulf outside her Florida house, she felt confined, as though she couldn't get a deep breath. She wanted to breathe in the tang of salt and sea, the smell of pale dirt and oranges. Since the moment she'd deplaned into O'Hare Airport's briskness, she'd yearned for that damp, rich smell of the tropics, the sensuous heat that loosened her muscles and made her yawn.

Unexpected, this longing for the sandy soil of a place she'd expected to be temporary, nothing more than a way station, a stopping place on the road to— Where?

She'd never planned for what would come after the job at Poinciana Hospital, never considered it as a permanent... *home.*

Her hands smoothed over the floured surface of the kitchen table. Her Bushka had already laid out the dough for the walnut rolls on the old kitchen table. The old table was square and heavy, the enameled paint that Sophie remembered from her childhood worn away by years of use. On the stubby legs of the table, remaining bits of brilliant red caught the light from the overhead fixture, their glitter a reminder of times past.

Letting her thoughts drift with her movements, Sophie

rolled the dough thinner and thinner until it almost covered the table top entirely.

Cracking walnuts at the kitchen counter, her grandmother hummed along with the Christmas music from the CD player, Sophie's gift to her the previous Christmas. It had replaced an ancient record player from the fifties that her grandmother had nursed along when everyone else had moved on to eight-track tapes, cassettes and then CDs.

At the time, Sophie had wondered if Irina Romanov would ever use the player.

Because, like the kitchen table, some things didn't change.

But, clearly, given enough time and inclination, some things did.

"There." Brushing the hulls aside, Irina tossed the ancient nutcracker onto the counter. "Finished with that job." She dusted her hands together, picked up the chopping knife. "When are you going to tell me, Sophie mine? About whatever has put those shadows under your eyes and the trouble in them?" Her elegant, husky voice held only a trace of the Russia of her childhood. A professor of Russian literature at Northwestern, she'd made her speech patterns mold to American life. "I would guess a man if it were anyone but my Sophie."

Sophie couldn't hold her Bushka's steady gaze.

"I see. Tsk." Irina Romanov moved the knife briskly over the nuts, chopping them finer and finer. "You have made a wonderful life for yourself, and now a man is playing topsy-turvy with your plans for the first time, yes?"

"It's not the man who's turning everything crazy. Not exactly." Sophie swooped the rolling pin diagonally over the dough, smoothing it into a glistening sheet of pastry rich with butter. "Anyway, I've never been much of a one for long-range plans, Bushka. You know that."

"I know. Oy. To lose your parents so young leaves a scar. You have always lived for the moment. But…" Irina stopped for a moment. "My poor Tatiana, so young… Well." She slammed the knife down on the kernels.

"It's complicated, Bushka."

"Sometimes life is. Sometimes, not so much. That never changes." *Chop, chop,* the rhythm of the knife against the cutting board invited Sophie to share.

Sophie rolled against the dough, making it as thin as she could without breaking it. "As for the man?" Thinking of Judah, an enigma definitely wrapped in a riddle as the old saying went, she laughed. "He's temporary. There's absolutely no future where he's concerned, but—oh, shoot." She laughed again, wryly. "Oh, Bushka, it's so darned *complicated!*"

"So you keep saying, my darling. Like the Irish and their love of stories, complications are part of our Russian nature. We thrive on them." Irina scooped up the nut pieces by the handful and tossed them into a cream-and-blue striped bowl. "But what you are telling me seems not so complicated. I don't understand what is different about your situation with this temporary man. You have always preferred temporary, my Sophie."

Sophie laid down the rolling pin. Scooting a three-legged stool over to the table, she sat on it, curling her feet under its rungs as she had during the years she'd lived with her grandmother after the death of her parents.

Eight years old, she'd come to live with Irina Romanov. Irina's love for the lost child Sophie had been triumphed over their shared loss and swamping grief. Only as an adult had Sophie finally understood the effort Irina had made to put aside her own devastation in order to create laughter and joy for Sophie, to make a life filled with color instead of unending gray.

Irina had given her a gift more precious than the Fabergé egg that sat in the dining-room hutch in its place of honor.

Where Irina was, was safety and security. A permanence that had freed Sophie to sail on the updraft of whatever winds she chose.

And yet now, that safety and security were shadowed by

these other wants, these other needs that came from miles to the south.

"Here's the deal, Bushka."

"Oh, a deal, is it?" Irina smiled and thumped cheerfully on the remaining walnuts, her slim arms flashing with her vigorous movements. "Deals are good. Give a little, get a little. Everybody wins. As the students say, works for me."

Sophie grinned back at her. "Oh, stop it, you. It's not that kind of deal. There's no negotiation involved."

Irina's voice was serious. "Sophia, there is *always* negotiation. In everything. We don't necessarily see the possibility, but it is there. Even with death, sometimes we can negotiate." She bent her head to her task. "Sometimes."

A sick tremor ran through Sophie. "Are you trying to tell me something, Bushka? You're okay? Yes?"

Her grandmother lifted her head and stared at her. Short, still-dark spiky strands framed her Slavic cheekbones. The faint buzz of the refrigerator seemed to fill the room as Sophie waited for whatever was coming.

"I am fine, my Sophia. What I am trying to say to you is that I am not young anymore. I will not be here forever, you know, darling child." Elegant Irina made seventy-three look like a perfect age for a woman who could live forever.

But she was reminding Sophie that she wouldn't.

Sophie swallowed.

"It would make my heart happy to see you—"

"Settled, Bushka?" Sophie managed a smile.

"Ach. No. Heaven help me, I think I am not yet that clichéd, *moye zoloto?*"

My gold, my treasure. Irina had called Sophie that from the beginning. *From much sadness, my Sophia, you are my treasure. God's golden gift to me.*

"No, not settled, Sophia. That is not quite what I meant. Not so lonely. That is all. Just…not lonely and alone."

"I'm not lonely."

Irina fixed her clear gaze on Sophie. "Yes. You are. And it will be worse when I'm no longer here. Many tomorrows from now, God willing.'' Irina returned to her chopping, wielding the knife decisively.

"Maybe I'm lonely, Bushka, but in a strange way. I don't have words to describe it. I'm happy, I'm busy, but it's as though there's this void inside me, this *place,* waiting to be filled with *something.*'' Sophie dragged her index finger over the floury surface at the edge of the table. "Here's the big, hairy deal, Bushka darling. What would you think about becoming a great-grandmother?''

Irina's flying hands went still. She turned to Sophie and leaned against the counter. "Tell me.''

As always Sophie marveled at her grandmother's ability to cut to the bottom line. No fussing about how in the world Sophie, who couldn't have children, thought she was going to make Irina a great-grandmother, and what did a temporary man have to do with this hypothetical great-grandchild? Nope, Irina Romanov would never dither, never crowd. She allowed a person space.

While the snow swirled outside in the darkness and beat against the kitchen windows like tapping fingers, Sophie told her about the emptiness of her beach home, about her sense that Angel was hers in some inexplicable karmic balancing.

She told her, too, about Judah.

Explaining Judah was hard—because she and Judah made no sense.

Her brain knew that.

Her heart, poor, confused, aching thing, didn't.

When Sophie finished her disjointed explanation, her grandmother enveloped her in a tight, wordless hug, rocking her back and forth on the stool as she murmured, "Ach, such pain.'' Sophie wrapped her arms around her Bushka's shoulders and clung to her, tears streaming down her face and puffs of flour rising from her hands against Irina's red-and-gold blouse.

"And what do you want, *moye zoloto?*''

"I want both. The man and the baby. The baby needs me, Bushka. I don't think the man does, not really.''

"But what do *you* need?"

"Both, I think, and I don't see that happening."

"Yes, my Sophia, what you want, what you hope for, is complicated, and your temporary man holds a part of your heart, permanently, I suspect. How much of your heart? Tsk. This business between you and him over his partner's death makes whatever is going on with you two a tricky negotiation because this Judah does not sound like a man who has forgiveness in him. And that will turn a soul dark and bitter," Irina said as she stepped back. "I am Russian. The river of history flows over me, and I have learned about forgiveness, if nothing else. Forgiveness. Redemption. Sometimes they are possible. Sometimes not. But we will figure out this problem. We always have. We can do anything, remember?" She tapped Sophie's cross.

"You really think I can make some of this work?"

"If this baby is what you want—and need—Sophie, we will find a way. The man?" Irina waved a hand, and bits of nuts spattered onto the floor. "Men are a mystery. Always. This man in particular seems to me to be…complicated." She sputtered with laughter, her short hair, sprinkled with shiny bits of nut meats and flour, moving with her laughter.

Whooping, Sophie blotted her eyes with the back of her hands. "Bushka, even if down the road I'm approved as a single woman to adopt this baby, I have to figure out how to work and still mother her. I want to mother this baby, to give back to her a little of what was ripped away from her, to love her, to—" Sophie stopped. *I want to make her safe the way you did me.*

Irina patted her cheek. "Yes," she said, acknowledging the unspoken words, knowing as always what was in Sophie's heart. "But it doesn't all have to be figured out this minute. We have nut rolls to make tonight."

They spread the walnut filling over the pastry and then rolled up the dough into one long roll before dividing it while the majestically soaring notes from the CD slid over Sophie's turbulent spirit and eased the yearning for Judah and Angel.

The need for them was so powerful in her that it was as if she could see them in the kitchen with her, could reach out and touch them.

With the snow still coming down in lazy drifts and the apartment fragrant with the smells of baking, they were in Irina's dining room having borscht and tea from the ancient samovar when the phone rang. They glanced at each other and then at the clock on the sideboard.

"So late. Tsk. But you are expecting a call, perhaps?"

Sophie shook her head. "No, but the hospital has my number. I don't have any cases pending, though."

"Well." Irina went to the kitchen to answer the phone and to check the cookies they'd put in after the walnut rolls.

When Irina came back, mischief danced in her blue eyes. "It is for you, Sophia. But not your hospital. This man, he calls himself Judah, and he wants to speak with you. He apologizes very nicely for the lateness of his call."

Sophie blinked. "Judah?"

"Yes. So he said." Irina lifted her soup spoon and swirled the sour cream into the borscht. "Cold borscht is good in summer, not so good on a cold night. I will go ahead with my soup if you don't mind?"

Her grandmother's words trailing behind her, Sophie raced into the kitchen, her heart beating so fast that she was breathless. "Judah?" she breathed into the receiver. "What's wrong? What do you want?"

The silence lasted so long that had there not been the hum over the wires, the hissing static from the storm, she would have thought he'd hung up.

"How's the weather in Chicago?"

"Snowy. You called to talk about the weather? Judah, it's eleven o'clock in Poinciana, ten here. What's going on? Is Angel all right? Is that why you're calling?"

"Angel's fine. But I have some news I thought you'd want to hear."

Sophie pulled up the stool, leaned her elbows on the counter, and felt her bare toes curling around the rungs of the stool. *Judah.* His voice over the line curled into her ear and she felt her belly go soft with a hunger that borscht and tea couldn't satisfy. "News?"

"Billy Ray Watley—"

"What?"

"*Watley.* Are we playing a version of the Three Stooges here, Sophie?" An almost-chuckle tickled her ear.

"What about Billy Ray? Why on earth would you call to talk about him? And the weather, for Pete's sake? Judah, are you drunk?"

The almost-chuckle became a real one. "Not at the moment. But I might be, later."

"How did you get my number?" she added as that thought struck her.

"Poinciana didn't hire me for my looks, Sophie."

"The hospital? It's not supposed to release personal information."

"The hospital didn't. The lovely personnel administrator withstood all my charms."

"Cammie, then."

"Cammie," he agreed.

Sophie stuck her finger through the coils of the phone cord. She'd accused him at Charlie's about not knowing what it was to play, to have fun. She was learning that in his own way, though, Judah could play. "So, explain to me about Billy Ray."

"He knew about Angel."

"What?"

"There you go again."

"Judah, stop it! You do sound six sheets to the wind. Tell me what's going on."

"I had a conversation with Mr. Watley after you left this afternoon. He was very helpful in our investigation."

"You bullied him, didn't you?" She pushed free of the stool and paced the kitchen, tethered to him at the other end of the wire. "Billy Ray's easily frightened, and you can be damned intimidating, Judah. You know that."

"Billy Ray and I came to an understanding. I didn't hurt him." Judah's voice was like warm chocolate sliding over her skin.

She shivered. The man had a criminally sexy voice, even when he was talking about nothing. Underneath the sexiness, though, she heard a tone she would have described in anyone else as playful. "All right then, Judah. Clearly you're bursting with news. Spill it."

"Billy Ray spilled it, actually. He gave us the name of the informant who called in the location of Angel the night she was left in the manger at the church. Seems Billy Ray and the informant are neighbors."

Sophie stopped midpace. She gripped the phone so tightly her knuckles were white. "You found the murderers?"

A sigh slipped over the wire. "Not yet."

"Oh." She sank against the counter. "But you know who they are?"

"No."

"Then what good is it to know who notified the police with the information about Angel? I'm missing a transition, Judah. Help me."

Again that staticky confirmation down the wires, a hiss of sound that linked them. "We're close. Tyree and I know where this Tommy Joe Dorgan lives. He's the informant. Tyree and I had another tip this afternoon after you left. We went out to The Palms, a trailer court. There was an incident. We encountered two men. They got away."

"An incident?" She rubbed her eyes. "Who got hurt? You or Tyree? Tyree's all right?"

"I'm touched by your concern." Again there was that slightly playful note. "We're both okay."

"What about the guys who shot you?"

"Well, shoot, Doctor Sugar, unfortunately, they're okay, too."

"Was this Tommy Joe one of them?"

"Nope. Wrong age. He's a kid. From what we found out, he's in the wind now, running from some real bad dudes.

And from us. From what we got from Billy Ray, Tyree and I believe Tommy Joe might have been one of the three boys at Le Duc Nhu's. We'll know what his role was when we find him. And we'll find him. And then we'll get the guys who killed Angel's mother. I figured you'd want to know. Closure and all that.'' There was an odd note in his voice as he said the last sentence.

She glanced out at the snow dancing along the window ledge. "I *am* glad you called. You were right. I like talking to you, Judah." *But I wish you were here.*

"Me, too." The sound of footsteps more than a thousand miles away. Silence again. "What are you and your grandmother up to?"

"Cooking. Drinking tea. Eating borscht."

"Ouch. You have my deepest sympathy."

"Borsht is soul food. Especially with sour cream."

"So's fried chicken. And it's not beets." More pacing, a pause as he stopped. "We're very different, Sophie."

"We are." Tucking the receiver between her chin and shoulder, she went to the oven and removed the last sheet of lemon cookies while the silence stretched between them. Oddly, though, it felt comfortable. Companionable, even with the elephant-in-the-living-room presence of his partner, a presence they'd been careful to avoid these last days. Still, this easy teasing was cozy, restful.

Then Judah's voice came sliding into her ear, lower now, and his voice wasn't restful at all. And definitely not cozy. Raspy, with an edge of need, just the sound of it made her nipples tighten. "What are you doing, right this moment, Sophie? Give me a picture. Please tell me you're wearing another version of that lacy stuff you had on earlier?"

"Like they say, in your dreams."

"Yeah, there, too."

She slid the cookies off the sheet onto cooling racks. "Sorry. I have flour all over my face, the kitchen floor, and I'm wearing my Northwestern sweatshirt. Big and baggy."

"Nothing but the sweatshirt?" An inhalation whispered

down the line. "That has possibilities. I can almost see you with all that flour spilled everywhere and you with nothing on under that shirt so easy—"

Her hand shook. A cookie slid off the spatula onto the floor, shattered.

"Judah—"

"I want to touch you, Sophie. I had no idea how much. And I can't."

Her mouth went dust-dry.

"I need— I want—" He stopped. She heard ice clatter into a glass. "You, Sophie. *You.*" There was the sound of liquid pouring, then nothing more for a full minute, only the sound of his breath, hers, joining through the miles before he added, "Sophie, come home. Please. Soon."

Home.

Chapter 15

After four days of endless snow, a pretty snow that had furred the trees and made driving to the old Russian section of their cemetery treacherous, Sophie walked out of the Sarasota/Bradenton airport into the soothing embrace of a warm December afternoon in Poinciana.

She couldn't help smiling.

Vacation over, sun-broiled tourists with bags of oranges and plastic alligators were huddled glumly in the waiting area as she'd passed. It felt mean to feel so giddy that she was strolling toward blue water and sun while they were headed back to gray skies and sheets of snow.

She set her suitcase beside her and gathered up her hair into a twisted clump on top, securing it with a pen from her purse. Looking up, stretching her arms, she saw the white contrails of airplanes vanish into blue brilliance. She could never have guessed that all this sandy dirt and humid summers would feel like home.

But here she was. Home.

And downright giddily silly about it.

As she picked up her suitcase, she turned straight into Judah's arms. Her smile stretched so big it hurt her cheeks.

"Hey, you. Where did you come from?"

"I was in the neighborhood." He scooped up her carry-on and suitcase. "You happened to mention what flight you'd be on. I'm real positive that was a slip of the tongue." He patted her in a brotherly fashion on her back. "Thought I'd drop in."

"Of course you did." Nothing brotherly in the way his hand slipped to the curve of her hip. "Certainly any mention of arrival times was purely accidental." She let her hip sort of wiggle into the shape of his palm. Touching him, even her body felt at home. "So, tough guy, what's going down in this neighborhood? And, after several days away, you notice how well I've retained my Southern and cop lingo, I hope?"

"You're a whiz, Yankee Girl. And, to answer your question, not much." His lips twitched as he glanced down at her. "Except—we finally picked up the informant Billy Ray gave us."

Sophie stopped so quickly that Judah bumped into her. "That's wonderful! When?"

"A couple of hours ago. Tommy Joe Dorgan's at the station downtown. Tyree's waiting for me. Thought I'd give you a ride home first, though." His lips did that goofy little twitch again as she grabbed his arm. "You don't want to go home. You want to see him, don't you? You can't stand not knowing what he's like, can you?"

"Gosh, how'd you figure that out, detective?" She couldn't help the excitement ripping through her. "Can you make that happen?"

"Depends." He guided her through the crowd with another of those casual touches that seared her skin. "I could be bribed."

"An upright cop like you?" She patted her chest and fluttered her eyelashes. "I'm shocked. Speechless."

"Not yet, but give me a minute. Or two."

She giggled.

"Where are you parked? We'll see what we can make happen."

"Promises, promises." Beeping the lock on her car, she almost missed the shadow that passed over his face. "What is it, Judah?"

He held the car door for her. "I went to see Angel."

Half stooping to enter, she froze. "You did? But you don't like kids."

"She's a witness." But he didn't smile. "And a victim. I was already at Poinciana General. I don't know, Sophie. It seemed the thing to do at the time. So I went. Make of it whatever you want to. But I promised her I'd find the scum who murdered her mother. I keep my promises."

Straightening, Sophie brushed his face. "You will, Judah. I have faith in you."

His eyes turned that stormy blue that she'd learned meant he'd walled himself off from her. From everyone.

"More than you have in yourself, I think."

"Yeah? How nice of you. But I don't want your faith, Sophie. Your body? That's never been in question, has it?"

"Don't work the attitude quite so hard, detective. I know what you're trying to do." With that, she slid behind the wheel, clipped the seat belt, and pressed the release lever for the trunk. Resting her forehead on the wheel in spite of its heat, she gathered herself together before looking up at him. In the glare of the sun, he was a tall silhouette, his features unseeable, his heart perhaps unknowable. "You unsettle me, Judah. But you don't scare me. There are things we need to talk about. We need to clear the air."

"Do we?" His question was silky-smooth and sharp as a stingray's sticker. "Now?"

"No. I'd still like to see the interview."

He placed her luggage in the trunk and then came back to her. "You know the way. I'll leave a pass for you at the front desk."

"Thank you."

She'd rolled down the car window, and he rested his hand

there, inches from her own. He didn't touch her. He lifted one finger, pressed it against the hot metal of the window frame, left it there. "Sophie?"

"Yes?"

"I—"

"You what, Judah? Apologize? Missed me? Is either of those so hard to say?"

"I apologize. And I—missed you." He took his hand away. "I told you, you've turned me inside out. You and this case. Lack of sleep. The timing. Pick any or all of the above." The side of his finger skimmed her hand. "I swear I don't even know who I am these days. Don't even know what I think—or feel—half the time. Bear with me?"

"I can do that." She left her hand near his. "For a while."

"Sophie, lately I feel like I'm sliding down an ice mountain and hanging on with my fingernails."

She heard the thin edge of despair in his voice. "Judah, I'm a doctor, but I can't fix that. I wish I could."

He shrugged. "You're right that we have to clear the air. But later. See you at the station."

When she entered the interrogation area, Judah motioned her toward the one-way window. Behind it, Tyree and a wide-shouldered guy, a kid, really, not more than sixteen, sat at a metal table bolted to the floor. Arms folded over the back of his chair, Tyree faced the kid. Neither one was saying anything.

"Stay here. This is unusual, but it's my case, my call to let you watch." Judah strode to the door, stood a moment, then opened it and walked easily into the room.

She didn't recognize this man who circled the kid, paced in back of him until she thought the kid's head would corkscrew right off. Once he smacked the back of the kid's head, a light, stinging slap. It was obvious that the slap didn't hurt, but after that, every time Judah passed in back of the youth, the kid flinched.

Good cop, bad cop. She knew the routine. Anyone who watched television or went to the movies did. Seeing it in action, though, was a whole other ball game. This Judah would have scared her had she been sitting in the kid's chair. There was something implacable, inexorable about Judah as he strolled casually around the room, not touching the kid again, but drifting close to him, leaning in until Sophie realized that the kid's eyes now never left Judah. As Judah nodded, the kid's head began to mirror Judah's movement.

Tyree left, came out into the room where she was, nodded to her. "Nice to see you, Dr. Brennan. This won't take much longer." He ambled out, headed down the hall.

Behind the glass, Judah sat on the edge of the table, one leg braced on the floor, his other swinging idly back and forth. Each time he leaned forward, almost in the kid's face, the boy tried to lean back.

Tyree returned and carried a couple of colas into the room. Judah must have toggled a switch in the room because she could hear what they were saying.

"Yeah, I was hanging around the church. So what, man?" the kid blustered. "Maybe I was getting religion, you know?"

"Could be." Judah nodded agreeably. "Don't think so, though. You, Detective Jones? You think Tommy Joe was getting religion?"

"Not at my church, he wasn't." Tyree handed the boy a cola. "Getting thirsty, Tommy Joe?" He watched as Dorgan sipped from the can. "Thought you might be. Gonna be a long night in here. A long, thirsty night." He stretched and sat back down in his chair. "You know, Tommy Joe, you look like a kid who's got a chance to do the right thing for himself. You look like a guy who's smart enough to see that."

"Not this guy." Judah swung his leg hypnotically. "He thinks he's being smart by not telling us what he knows about a lot of things. Like the graffiti around town, the bag of burning crap left at the A.M.E. Church. About the attack on the Vietnamese woman, for instance."

Cola dribbled down the boy's chin.

"That's not smart, Detective Jones. That's plain stupid."

"I think he's scared, not stupid. That right, Tommy Joe? Somebody got you so scared you can't see what's right in front of your nose?"

"That he's the one left taking the fall?" Judah patted Tommy Joe on the head and ignored the way the boy pulled into himself. "Fine with me. I don't care who goes off to prison. No skin off my nose. All those years in prison. How about you, Tommy Joe? It's going to be the skin off your nose, though, isn't it?" He touched the boy's nose, and the kid fell forward, sobbing, his hands over his head.

"I never meant anything bad to happen. Solo and those other dudes thought it would be fun to scare her! She's not one of us! I thought we were going to egg her house, maybe chuck a stone at her window. I didn't know they were going to break in! I didn't! I didn't! I saw how scared she was, and when I heard the baby, I got so scared I peed in my pants and Solo laughed. He laughed! I grabbed that baby and ran and ran."

Sophie covered her mouth with both hands to keep from crying out.

Judah's shoulders drooped for a minute. Then, so softly Sophie had to lean forward to hear, he asked, "That how it went down? Were you there when they beat the woman to death, Tommy Joe?"

"No!" The boy's whole body shook with his sobs. "I heard about that the next day."

Sophie could see the raw edges of his fingernails.

"I ran with the baby, that's all. She was so little. So quiet. And there was all that noise. I didn't want her to make more noise. I thought she would be safe at the church."

"And that no one would know you were involved, right?"

"I didn't want Solo and Ace to find her. I was scared Solo was going to do something awful to her, and then when I ran out, I knew he would kill me if he found me. Because I'd been there. Because I knew."

As he lay with his face cradled in his arms, Sophie felt

immense sorrow. For the woman she'd treated, for Angel. For this kid who'd tried to do the right thing but not soon enough. She felt sorrow for Judah, too, for the look in his face, a look that said so clearly what he was thinking: Tommy Joe Dorgan was one more proof of mankind's ugliness.

Suddenly Judah kicked the leg of the table and left the interrogation. Through the open door of her room, Sophie watched as he leaned against the wall outside.

Eventually Tyree and the boy walked out. Tyree crooked a finger at a uniformed cop who came over, cuffed the kid, and walked him away.

Sophie stayed where she was.

As Tyree and Judah came toward her, Tyree grabbed Judah's shoulder, stopping him, and said, "Look, Judah, he *is* stupid. Ignorant at the very least."

"You're defending him?"

"I'm saying what I see. He was in over his head, not smart enough to know how to handle the situation, but he saved that baby. You know he did. And you know what would have happened if he hadn't taken her out of there. He's just a mutt, just a kid."

"Mutts are dangerous—" Judah shook off Tyree's grip "—even when they don't mean to be. You know that."

"Yes. But this kid isn't evil. He made a mistake. Mean, stupid, dangerous. He'll have to pay for that mistake. But at the last minute, when push came to the proverbial shove, some goodness in him made him save that little girl."

"Not that I can see. Let it go, Tyree." Judah walked away.

When he returned, his face was still closed off and fierce. "All right, Sophie, I wanted you to see that. I wanted you to be face to face with what I deal with every day. I deal with scuzzy people. You know how the saying goes, 'lie down with pigs, get up smelling like one'? This is my life, Sophie. I'm not a nice guy."

"I never said you were."

"That's right. You haven't." His bark of laughter held no

humor. He leaned against the wall of the empty room as if he needed it to hold him upright. "Shocked now?"

"No."

"Ready to go clear the air then?"

Before she could answer, he swore and reached for his cell phone, listened, clicked it shut. "A patrol car spotted two guys who fit the description of those sterling gentlemen, Solo and Ace. Hell, why do you suppose mopes always go for names like that?" He glanced at her, away. Hesitant. "Afterwards?"

"Yes." She took a shivery breath. "Yes. But not at my house. On the beach near the pier."

He narrowed his eyes, understanding immediately. "That's how it's going to be? Neutral territory?"

She nodded. "Call first. I don't care how late it is. I'll meet you there." Trembling inside, she turned and left the room.

She had been shocked, upset by the violence. Nothing had been done to the boy. It was the violence in the atmosphere, what that emotional violence had done to Judah that left her shaking. Rooted as he was by his family and his faith, Tyree was fortified against the brutality and ugliness. Judah didn't have those resources. She'd had a glimpse of the way Judah tapped into himself, drew from whatever was, and soldiered on.

Every battle killed something in him, wounded him.

Soon there would be one case too many, and then the wound would be a mortal one. She suspected this case might be the one. The soul could only take so much.

He'd said earlier he felt as if he were hanging on by his fingernails. He was. She understood now.

Days passed. Judah didn't call. She couldn't believe how much she missed him, how shockingly lonely she felt without his teasing, without *him*.

She wondered, too, how far down his icy mountain he'd slid. But she didn't call him. She would give him time. Space.

But it was killing her.

But Jeannette called. She'd kept her word. Sophie had been approved as Angel's foster parent. The paperwork for the adoption had been started. It would, as all bureaucratic processes do, take time, Jeannette reminded her. "But, Sophie, I think by spring you can make her officially yours. For good."

It was for good, too. The sounds of Angel during the night, her soft cooing in the morning—all were miracles to Sophie, filling her with such happiness that she felt guilty.

Every morning as the sun touched the beach, she tucked Angel into a soft carrier in front and ran with her down the hard-packed sand, singing any song that came into her head. And Sophie talked to Angel constantly. An unending stream of words and stories. She told Angel over and over what a wonderful baby she was and how much she was loved.

Sophie talked to her, too, about Judah.

Whatever opinions Angel had about Judah, she kept to herself, quiet as usual, merely watching Sophie's face as she talked and wept and raged while Judah kept his distance.

On a reduced schedule from the ER, Sophie found she had time to read the paper, to discover that Henry "Solo" Moynes and Albert "Ace" Hershey had been arrested based on evidence from an unnamed witness and were awaiting trial. They had been found breaking into a trailer at The Palms. Bail had been denied. As the papers continued to be filled with more details about Le Duc Nhu's murder and the abandoned baby, Poinciana grew quiet with a sense of profound shame and something else that permeated the town, curdling it.

Sophie had thought that since the murder was solved and the attacks on the religious houses had stopped, life would return to normal.

But it didn't.

The crimes, with the hatred and intolerance that lay behind them, had left people stunned. No one seemed to know how to handle this horror that had tainted their lives. No one wanted to talk about the cause of the crimes because the underlying fear was that if you were different in Poinciana, you didn't know who to trust anymore.

There was still that ugliness simmering beneath the surface.

It was as if the murder and attacks had stripped away the pretext of civility. Shame, anger, and resentment made themselves at home in Poinciana, mocking its holiday decorations and symbols of love and peace on earth.

At the hospital and in town, Sophie watched as the people she knew and cared about treated each other with suspicion. Even Cammie seemed less open, less friendly with some of the other staff. Billy Ray, however, beamed at everyone through his stringy hair and mopped with a vengeance. He was the hero of the hour. Because he and Tommy Joe had lived in the same trailer park, The Palms, Billy Ray had been there the night the distraught boy had come running to the abandoned trailer Tommy called home. The *Coast Herald* reported that it was Billy Ray who'd told Tommy to call 911 and give the baby's location.

After Tommy Joe had made the call, Billy Ray figured he was responsible for Angel's safety and followed Judah whenever he was at the hospital, thinking in his confused way that Judah would take the baby away again.

A week after the arrests, the ministers from the A.M.E. Church and the Second Baptist met with the rabbi from Beth Israel and other religious and community leaders in Poinciana.

Something had to be done or there would be more violence. If not this week, this year, then the next. Hatred and suspicion and intolerance always, always resulted in violence—sooner or later. History and their own faiths had taught them that. Their religions, different in their specific tenets, shaped these men and women to believe that love could vanquish hate, that understanding could conquer intolerance.

As meetings were scheduled and committees formed, Sophie recognized some of the names that began to appear in the paper. Yvonna. Mr. Dai, the translator Judah and Tyree had used. Lolly, the nurse from the pediatric ward. People of optimism and hope, pushing back the darkness.

Just as she did, in her own way.

Judah called three days after the arrests. She'd given up expecting him to call and had tried with all her strength to cut him out of her heart. She'd understood too well why he'd allowed her to be present at the interrogation. He'd wanted her to see him as he saw himself. And then he'd regretted his decision and avoided her. She knew his patterns. Staying away was his choice. But in spite of her joy with Angel, Sophie found that Judah's absence was a constant ache.

But, as she'd promised, she met him at the beach near the pier after she'd taken Angel to the baby-care center at the hospital.

Long before she'd ever dreamed about Angel, Sophie had been the gadfly stinging the hospital administration into establishing the center. She'd finally sold them on the idea when she'd shown them statistics proving that in the long run it would be a cost-saving move. At the time she'd never expected to benefit from the idea. Now, with Angel, she could make it all work.

Judah was waiting when she drove up.

She wanted to slap herself for the jitters that ran under her skin as she walked toward him. She wanted to slap him for making her walk toward him.

"I'm surprised you came." He straightened from his slouch against the picnic table.

"I told you I would. Like you, I keep my promises." She wrapped her arms around her waist to keep from reaching out to him. "By the way, congratulations on solving several cases all at once. A real coup for you and Tyree. You know how grateful I am that Solo and Ace are behind bars. I have concerns about the boy, Tommy Joe, though."

"I heard you posted bail for him."

"I'm a fool, right? But Billy Ray told me about that boy, and I wanted to give him a second chance."

"You did what you had to do."

His stance and voice were so distant that Sophie wondered why he'd bothered to call. But she knew why she'd come to meet him, here in daylight where there was no possibility of succumbing to the pull of the chemistry between them. She walked straight up to him, unfolded her arms and took his terrifyingly distant, unbelievably dear face between her palms and bet the whole pot on the next few minutes. "We have to talk about George."

He jerked, but she didn't release him.

"Judah, maybe I *was* hasty with what I did the night I treated him, but I don't think so. If his death hadn't split us apart, I would never have thought twice about my actions of that night. But let's say I did act out of my dislike for him or out of annoyance with his constant crudeness. I've finally realized that if I had, that would be on my conscience. But my conscience feels clean. What about your conscience, Judah? Is it clean?"

"Low blow, Doctor Sugar." His fingers closed around her wrists, but he didn't try to pull her hands away from his face. "No. My conscience isn't clean. How'd you guess?"

"After you talked about your father, I figured it out."

"I loved that crude, rude, obnoxious son of a bitch, you know. I don't have a clue why I did, but I did."

"I know," she said softly and knew, too, that he wasn't talking about Calvin Finnegan, the man who'd almost destroyed him.

"He was impossible. He ate and drank too much, he pissed off everyone at the station. He didn't take care of himself, but he took care of me. He trusted me to keep his back, no matter what. And in his own way, he loved me."

"Of course he loved you." Sophie rested one hand against the steady beat of Judah's heart.

"But I let him down."

"How? Tell me."

"I should have stopped him that night. I should never have let him take off in the squad car."

"The car didn't kill him, Judah."

Off in the distance, lights from a ship on its way to the harbor in Tampa spangled the night, a holiday decoration against the movement of the Gulf on a starless night.

Judah sighed, and a shudder ran through him. "I know. But I still can't forgive myself."

"For what? For not taking away his gun? For letting George slide by with his misogynistic comments and self-indulgences? For not treating a grown-up man, one quite a few years older than you, by the way, like a naughty child and sending him to his room?"

"You can be tough, Sophie, can't you?" He rested his chin on the top of her head.

"Judah, George killed himself. Because he was empty at the core, because he was unhappy, because his ego had been stomped on. Who knows why, Judah? I doubt that he knew himself. George Roberts was a desperately unhappy man. And his emptiness was his own decision. But you can't forgive yourself for not being God. You're only a man, Judah. A wonderful man, but not God. Any God I'd believe in would be a forgiving one. That's not how it is with you. You don't forgive, Judah. Not yourself, not me. You can't forgive me. You keep nicking away at me with the knife of your anger. Because it's easier to blame me for George's failings, easier to blame yourself for your inability to save the world, than it is too blame George."

"Cruel, Sophie."

"Maybe. But it's the truth. Your father abandoned you. So did George. But you loved George, and so you can't forgive him for leaving you." Sophie stepped back, dropped her hands. "Unless you can find a way to forgive yourself, to forgive George and, yes, even your father, you're going to slide right off that mountain, Judah, right into the chasm. Think about it. Because you're at the edge. And as far as I can see, every time someone reaches a hand out to you, you chop it off. That's why you wanted me there at the interrogation. Your not-so-subtle way of trying to push me away one more time. It didn't work. Why? Because you were breaking my heart in there.''

"You don't know what you're talking about, Sophie."

"I know we have no future, Judah. Unless you figure this out."

"A future? I like what we have right now." He touched her throat, stroked down. "I thought you did, too."

"I do. But I don't like what's happening. What we have? It's nothing. A dead end, Judah. I've never liked dead ends. I want more. You should, too."

"I reckon that's how we leave it then."

She could see the shuttered look of his face, his rejection of what she was trying to make him see.

"I don't want this to end, Sophie. Not now. Not like this."

"Neither do I, Judah, but you're the one with the power to change the situation, not me. I learned in surgery that sometimes you have to cut away in order to cure. There's a kind of sickness with us right now. You're the only one who can change things. I hope you can."

She stood on tiptoe and kissed him, kissed him with hope, kissed him with regret.

Judah was so furious with Sophie that he stormed around until Sunday afternoon. Tyree literally threw up his hands and quit talking to him. The other cops saw him stomping down the hall and gave him a wide berth if he looked at them. It took that long for the heat to die down and Sophie's words to percolate through the layers of his anger and hurt.

It was the hurt that kept stunning him. It was the hurt he hadn't expected. Not like this, anyway. Not this searing knife-like pain that sliced through him every waking minute. He'd thought that when the time came, he'd be able to walk away from her without a second thought. That had always worked before.

It wasn't working now.

Anger eventually simmered down, died away. The hurt stayed.

At some level he knew he wasn't being honest with himself.

He'd known from the minute he'd seen her again in the ER that she was already under his skin, burrowing deeper into him, making herself at home in spite of all the reasons he hadn't wanted her there.

He had never expected to need her the way he seemed to. He'd had a taste of that need during the days she'd been in Chicago, but now? Chicago, as wrenching as it had been, was nothing compared to this desolation.

Sunday afternoon he drove to the cemetery. He had not been to his father's grave since the funeral. He'd thought he'd have trouble finding the site, but his feet took him there as if he made the trip every day, through the weeds and sand-spurs to the edge of the sandy plot where the remains of Calvin Finnegan lay.

There was no headstone. Only a flat marker in the grass.

Only the occasional birdsong broke the silence. The grave was indeed a quiet and private place.

"All right, Calvin. I'm here. You've got my attention. You preached salvation and damnation. Got anything to say about those topics now? Because if you do, I'm listening. Strike me dead, speak to me. Here's your chance."

Only the sighing of the wind in the pines answered him.

Judah didn't know what he'd expected in coming to the cemetery. In books and movies, folks always had a moment of clarity, an epiphany. He would welcome an epiphany now, that was for sure.

But the silence continued.

Judah squatted down on the grass around the plot, pulled up a clump. "You were a mean, vicious, unloving old man, you know. Did you ever realize that? You had to, I'd think. I hated you with everything in me. Did you hate yourself, too, old man? The way you hated everyone else? Because that's what all that ranting and raving was about, best as I could tell. Hate. Oh, you cloaked it in fancy words, like it came on a tablet from God, but you preached hate, lived hate with every breath. And you passed on that legacy to me, Calvin. How'd I let that happen, huh?''

He watched as the wind bent the grasses down, swirled a brown leaf.

No deep, booming voice came from on high.

He hadn't really thought there would be one.

For a long time Judah sat there under the blue, empty sky and listened to the silence, to the sound of nothing.

And what he longed for was the sound of Sophie's voice.

Chapter 16

In the days before Christmas, Sophie decorated her house. She and Angel baked cookies. Irina called several times a week and insisted on talking to Angel while Sophie held the receiver up to Angel's ear. Sometimes Angel gooed back. Mostly, though, she listened as Sophie's Bushka welcomed this new female to the family and made plans to visit in the new year.

Figuring Angel's quietness was a language issue, Sophie took Angel to visit Hoang Lan Thoa, the woman who'd identified Angel and her mother. There, Angel chattered in her own way while Sophie nodded and smiled. The Vietnamese woman cried sometimes, but she always opened her door to them with an offer of tea. Once she gave Sophie a mobile to hang high over Angel's crib. Tiny origami cranes dangled and moved with every draft of air. The cranes symbolized longevity, Sophie learned.

She planned, too, for the new year, wanting to give Angel what she could of her heritage. Sometimes when she visited Hoang Lan Thoa, Mr. Dai, the translator, was there, and Sophie took notes on everything the two of them told her about Angel's mother, about Angel, about Vietnam. She made an ever-expanding book for Angel, to give her when she was older. In the meantime, though, she showed Angel the pages and told her the stories. She began to hang pictures of unicorns, signifying wealth, and dragons, for power and nobility, in her beach house. Angel would need power. She bought fanciful pewter and silver figures of these creatures and put them on a high shelf in Angel's room to watch over her.

Sophie framed the blanket Angel had been wrapped in when she was found in the manger and hung it on the wall above the crib so that Angel would see it every day.

Sophie had no intention of allowing everything to be stolen from her daughter.

Jeanette prepared the preliminary papers to begin the investigation process for the adoption. She'd already gone to court on behalf of DCF to have Angel declared a dependent child of the State of Florida, thus leaving DCF with no notification of kin requirements. Sophie smiled, followed her friend's instructions, went to court, and floated along with the process that seemed to move with surprising smoothness, another gift, another miracle.

Most nights, Judah knocked at her door.

The first night, the Sunday after they'd cleared the air, she'd blinked at the sight of him.

"May I come in?" he asked with careful politeness.

"Why?"

"I'm trying to learn, Sophie. About forgiveness. About not being a straw man like George, a man who can't handle the first strong wind. I don't wasn't to be a hollow shell, Sophie."

How could she not open her door wide, welcome him with her arms and her heart?

Their loving was slow, exquisitely gentle.

Poignant.

They talked, their voices rising and falling during the nights they lay in each other's arms. They talked sometimes until Sophie's throat was sore. She told him her grand-mother's pet phrase for her, told him about the way Irina had turned sadness into golden joy, had made life rich for them both. Her soul hurt sometimes when Judah talked. She wanted to clap her hands over his mouth to stop the words, to erase his awful memories, the pain. She let him talk.

Because there was a sense of fragility to each encounter, Sophie tried not to think, tried not to *want* so much. But each night Judah was there, and Angel was in her bedroom, So-phie's heart expanded to the bursting point. The shadowy figure of Judah in the night as he went to stand at Angel's door, the way he carried her down to the beach on his shoul-ders—it was *everything* Sophie's heart craved.

But…there was everywhere that niggling sense of walking on eggs. In Poinciana, where the community committee didn't seem to be making much headway, and in her beach house.

The days drifted closer to Christmas. Judah went with her and Angel to pick out a tree and carry it back to the house. While he didn't decorate, he watched Sophie dance with An-gel around the tree while Sophie sang about Mommy kissing Santa. She pranced beneath the arch of the kitchen where a red-bowed sprig of mistletoe dangled.

She noticed that Judah almost laughed at the silliness.

She made plans for Christmas day: a late-afternoon open house and a bonfire down on the beach afterward. She sent out red invitations with extravagant calligraphy to everyone she knew. Billy Ray didn't think he should come since Tommy Joe was now living with him. She told Judah her plans and didn't say anything when he merely nodded.

She could see he was struggling.

At night she tried to let her touch, her body, speak to him, to tell him of the infinite possibilities of love and hope.

But…

On Christmas Eve everything came to a head.

Glogg was in a big pot on the stove, ready for the party the next day. She had spring roll ingredients chopped in a bowl in the refrigerator, and Angel was in bed, her wispy black hair spiking out around her face. In her crib, she clutched a purple plush dinosaur with both chubby hands.

She and Judah had made love again and again. There was something desperate in his touch, as though he couldn't get close enough, often enough. His desperation seeped through to her and made her jittery, anxious. Even though she was filled with him, she sensed that he wasn't there. When he lifted himself away from her, his finger trailing down her midline slowly, reluctantly, she sat up, the sheet beside her. If they were going to have this discussion, they would face each other with no walls of any kind.

"Sophie, I can't do this. I have to go."

"Go? I don't understand."

But she did. She'd hoped, but sometimes hope wasn't enough. She wanted to be cool and calm, but her heart still fought for what she'd dreamed was possible.

"I thought we were going to celebrate Christmas together. You, me. Angel. We bought the tree. Together." She waved frantically at the stubby tree in the corner. Silly thing, a tree, to carry the weight of so much hope. But it did. She, who'd never begged, would. For this, oh, yes, she would beg. On hands and knees if it came to that. "Stay, Judah. Please."

"I can't."

In the dim light, such pain and misery filled the long, narrow lines of his beautiful face that she couldn't stop weeping. For him. For the pain slicing through her with his agony-filled words. For what was never going to be. "Oh, Judah. How can you do this?"

"Because I have to. Because I can't *be* with you and Angel. Oh, God, Sophie, I want to. I've been trying so hard."

"Then *do*, Judah. Just...*do*. Be with us."

"It's this goddamned darkness inside of me. I wanted to kill Tommy Joe. Did you know that?"

"Yes." She batted her hands against his chest, and her tears dripped down onto his arms holding her at a distance. "I knew!"

"Even though he was the one who saved Angel. If I could have gotten my hands on him… I have no forgiveness in me, Sophie. I'm a cold, hard, unforgiving son of a bitch. Just like my old man. All this light I see in you, all that you can give Angel—I want it for me, too. And I'd turn all that love and joy inside out. I'd ruin everything. You'd hate me. I'd hate myself. I'd fill that beautiful child in there with this darkness I can't escape. I'm leaving while I still can. Because you're so much a part of me already that if I stay longer, I won't ever be able to leave you."

"You'll push us away, push me away? To protect me?"

"You saw how I let George's loss fester inside of me. You saw how I let it eat at me, how I let it distort everything. How I couldn't forgive you for doing your job. In my head I knew you'd done what you had to do. I knew up there," he smacked his forehead, "that it wasn't personal. But I couldn't forgive you, Sophie. I lost a whole damned year with you because I couldn't let go of my anger. That's who I am, Sophie—I see evil in the world, in people. I don't see anything else. Except in you. And I'd destroy you, one way or another. You said that earlier, and I tried so damned hard—" His voice caught. "But that's how it is. I'm my dear old daddy's boy."

Her heart, splintering into bits, bled a little more for the torment of this lost man she loved with everything in her.

Then he wove his hands through her hair, lifting the strands, studying them as if he were memorizing every curl, every shade. "I once accused you of being a fool. You aren't. You never were. I'm the fool. I can't change who I am."

"You can. If you love me."

"I thought I could change. But you saw me with that kid…."

"Judah, you *didn't* hurt him."

"Not this time, no."

"You were tough, yes, with him and with Billy Ray, but you had to be. You are not this, this *Prince of Darkness!*"

Laughter struggled with the scalding tears and lost. "You're not!"

"God, Sophie," and it sounded like a prayer, "you're the air I breathe, you're in every pore of my skin, every cell of my body—you're my everything."

"But?"

"But." He held his hands out helplessly.

"Angel. You can't see yourself being a father?"

He nodded. "I can't do this. I love her. I don't know when it happened, but it did. I would kill anyone who touched her. I love you, with everything in me, but I can't do this, Sophie. I want to. You don't know how much I want to. I can't."

She wanted to tell him to have a little faith. In her, in himself. In the two of them together. She wanted to tell him that they could make it work if he believed in what they had together. Instead, feeling as if a part of her were dying, she said, "I love you, Judah. You know that. I love you more than I ever thought I could love someone. You're in every breath I take, too."

He nodded in the direction of Angel's room. "She needs you. I want her to have your caring, your joy. I want all that, too. But..."

Sophie could feel her throat closing, the tears dropping onto her breast. She didn't know how to make him see what he was walking away from, what he was losing. "I love you," she repeated, her words tear-clogged.

"I know."

"Isn't that enough? Can't we build on that?" How could he be so blind? So stubborn. She wanted to shake him until his teeth rattled, until he understood. "I love you," she repeated. "You love me. I know this."

"Aw, Sophie." Wrapping her in his arms, he buried his face in her hair. She could feel the horrible pounding of his heart against her, and she thought she felt his own tears. "Love? A long time ago, in high school, we had to memorize this poem. 'Renascence,' I think it was. I never forgot it."

Low and killing, his words slid into the spaces between them.

> Love is not all: it is not meat nor drink
> Nor slumber nor a roof against the rain;
> Nor yet a floating spar to men that sink.

She held on to him with all her strength. "Are you sinking, Judah?"

"Oh, God, Sophie. I'm drowning, I'm drowning."

"Then hold on to me, Judah. Let me be your spar."

"I'd drown both of us." He unwound her arms and stood up. "I'll want you until the day I die."

"But not enough."

His T-shirt half pulled on, he stopped, frowned. "That's not true. You know I want you."

Naked, she faced him. "Not enough, Judah. You don't have any faith in yourself, not in what we create together. You think it's easier to walk away, safer. But it isn't. You're a coward."

"Probably."

"Hearts don't break, Judah, I know this, so why does it feel as though mine is ripping apart? I'll survive, but my world will be smaller without you. You need to know that, to understand what you're doing. To me. To Angel. To yourself."

She turned away before he could touch her. She didn't think she could bear it if he touched her. Not now.

There was nothing left to say.

She'd known she couldn't change him. That had never been in the cards. She'd hoped that with her he could find the path to change himself. As clearly as if she were watching a movie, she saw what the days ahead would be like. For her. For him.

And she feared for him, for the darkness waiting to consume him.

* * *

Judah hesitated at Angel's bedroom door. He couldn't go in. He'd thought he never wanted children in his life, but Angel— Well.

He shut the door of Sophie's beach house carefully, with a quiet finality, and somehow believed that by doing so, he showed respect.

Even though he tried not to, he looked back once. Sophie was in the living room, holding Angel. The hint of red in Sophie's hair caught the glow of the lamp as she leaned forward, her body curving over the baby's. Through the window as he watched, he saw Sophie stroke Angel's cheek. One russet curl clung to Angel's flailing hand.

His heart beat hard in his chest, and there was no room for it, his chest closing tightly around that poor organ until he believed he couldn't breathe. There, behind the glass, Sophie and Angel, caught in the amber spill of light.

He turned and moved into the darkness of Christmas Eve, walking away from everything he loved most in the world and everything that most terrified him.

Starting the engine of his car, he fought the impulse to turn off the key and run back inside, to run to the refuge of Angel and Sophie.

He drove, for hours it seemed, before parking.

The river flowed smoothly, darkly before him, its glassy surface glinting even in the pitchy night. For a long time he watched as the river, moving like a powerful muscle underneath glossy skin, pulsed toward the Gulf.

Sophie was right. The heart didn't break. But he'd had no idea that it could hurt, hurt beyond anything he'd ever known, aching until he pressed his fist against his chest and sank to his knees on the tough grass edging the riverbank. Loneliness he understood, but *this,* this awareness of being alone under the dark bowl of the sky went beyond loneliness.

Like an animal forced to its knees, he knelt there in the silent, chilly night.

Then, suddenly, barely heard, music drifted toward him.

Like tiny, distant bells, the music pierced him.

Angels singing in the night.

He was not a man whose experience had led him to believe in angels. Even so, it took him a minute to understand that the sound he heard, the music surrounding him, filling him, came from human voices, the voices of men and women lifting in an unbearably sweet harmony.

Following the river, Judah approached the center of town. A crowd of people—men wearing yarmulkes, women wearing the shawls of the Muslim faith, priests in collars—hundreds of Poinciana's people were gathered along Main Street. They held shielded candles in their hands. Luminaria lined Main Street and its side streets, a yellow glow down to the dark of the river's edge.

Off in a corner of the crowd, under the banyan tree of the Second Baptist Church, a boy-man stood alone, a stubby candle in his hand.

Tommy Joe. Out on bail that Sophie had provided. He knew Sophie had gone to talk with him from time to time, had arranged counseling, and had been the instigator behind the decision to allow Tommy to live with Billy Ray while his case was proceeding through the courts.

Sophie had believed in the kid, believed in Billy Ray.

But still, Tommy Joe, here with the rest of Poinciana, joined with some of the very people he'd said "weren't like us."

Judah looked again at the kid, thinking it couldn't be the same boy.

Tommy Joe nodded stiffly back at him.

The same boy?

No.

Judah found himself nodding back, acknowledging the need in the human soul for something higher.

It wasn't a question of religious faith. It didn't have anything to do with one religion or another. It was faith in the human heart. This was what he'd never understood. That it all came down to this—

To the small flicker of goodness inside each human heart. To the light of that tiny, sometimes barely perceptible flame casting its glimmer of hope into the darkness of an often bitter world.

There were evil and hate and cruelty in the world. God knows he'd fought them long enough. His whole life had been spent in those trenches where the worst of humankind lived.

And he'd forgotten.

Forgotten that sometimes religion wasn't used as a weapon. Forgotten that men and women could sometimes rise above everything to join together as they did now in a flowing river of light.

This was what Sophie had tried to show him.

And he hadn't understood.

Lifting his head, Judah watched the slow, now silent movement of all the different people in Poinciana as they merged into one.

His town.

His people.

Tommy Joe was there, too. Tommy Joe could change.

Standing there in the shadows, the lights flickering in front of him, sending a message in the face of darkness, Judah realized that if Tommy Joe could change, maybe he could, too.

What he'd tried to do alone, he could do with Sophie. And Angel.

If he weren't a coward.

If he could take that leap of faith that Sophie had talked about.

On Christmas morning, Sophie let Angel bat at the colored papers from presents that her friends in the ER had sent. Paper spiraled and clumped under the tree, across the floor into the kitchen. Irina had already called, and they'd both shed tears as Sophie related the events of Christmas Eve.

Sophie's eyes were swollen from crying. There had been no sleep during that long night.

But as Angel made her funny noises and the whisper of the incoming tide came through her windows, Sophie was at peace.

With her grandmother, she'd shed her final tear.

She touched her talisman on the chain around her neck. Some day she would pass it on to Angel, to remind her that while love didn't always conquer everything, it was the only thing that stood a chance.

Judah's presence was there with them in the remembered moments. It would be all she would have.

But she wouldn't dwell on the loss.

She would cherish the memories and let them enrich her life.

She would make it be enough.

Lost in the moment, absorbed in Angel's play, Sophie jumped when her door vibrated with the pounding on it. She tucked Angel into the playpen, another gift, and went to the door.

There, standing on her stoop, was Santa.

A Santa who'd seen better days, that was for sure. His red suit was much the worse for wear, torn and bloodstained. His cheap beard was drooping off his lean cheeks.

Santa, nonetheless, and bearing a brown bag.

Judah.

Gasping, laughing, crying, Sophie pulled him into her house. "Judah! You idiot!"

Behind her, Angel gurgled a word that perhaps only she understood, but it seemed to Sophie that Angel was communicating something, was welcoming the tall, tattered figure in front of her.

Seated on the floor beside Angel's playpen, Judah handed Sophie the brown bag.

"A present? After everything that's happened?" Her hands shook. That *Judah*, of all people, would be so whimsical as to appear in a Santa suit left her trembling inside.

"Wait. Don't open it yet. I have a story you need to hear." Still not touching her, he finally told her about going to the cemetery, about the silence he'd found there, the lack of answers. Then he told her what had happened after he'd left her, what he'd finally grasped. "I am stupid, Sophie. But can you find room in your life, your heart, for a stupid, work-obsessed fool?"

"What have I been saying over and over again, you goof?"

"You sure? All I can promise, Sophie, is that I won't walk away again. I'll do my best to learn how to be a husband and a father, to love you as you deserve. If you'll help me?"

"Oh, you fool! You know I will." She dragged the beard free of his well-loved face and covered it with kisses. "Judah, together we can do anything, *become* anything. That's all I wanted you to see. The possibility."

"All right. Open the bag. I'm sorry it's not exactly gift-wrapped."

"But the top is folded over so nicely. Such effort. I'm impressed."

He laughed, a free, unreserved, no-holds-barred roar. It was the first time she'd heard him laugh like that and it went straight to her heart. Angel shrieked. Then, waving a fist full of paper, she laughed.

"The kid has a sense of humor." Judah fidgeted, picking up bits of this and that from the floor as Sophie unfolded the bag slowly, wonderingly. "That's good."

Sophie thought he was nervous.

It made no sense.

Until she pulled out the first piece of paper inside the bag. One of those forms anyone could pull off the Internet, it was a marriage license. She blinked, blinked again as she looked at Judah's signature at the end.

"Please?" He tapped her knee. "Make it official? Make it real? Soon?"

She dipped her head and slowly removed the second folded paper. She'd thought Judah had made her cry for the last time, but as she opened the folds and saw what was there, she burst into tears.

Another Internet form, it was a sample request for adoption. Under Father, Judah had carefully filled in his own name.

She leapt into his arms, knocking him over backwards. His head bumped the edge of Angel's playpen. Through the webbing, Angel reached through and batted his face.

"No fair, kid, two on one." Half sitting, he reached in and lifted Angel out, settling her on Sophie's lap.

Judah rubbed his whiskery cheeks against Sophie's face and then nibbled her chin. "You taste so good. Maybe a little salty."

"I cried a lot."

"I'm sorry, Sophie. For that, for all the mistakes."

"Of course you are. And you'll make more mistakes. So will I. But we'll forgive them."

He held her in his arms, and she could feel him shaking.

"God, Sophie, I love the taste of you, the smell of you. You. *Moye zoloto*," he said, using her grandmother's name. "You're my treasure, Sophie. My gold."

Much later, after the party, after they'd settled Angel down for the night, Sophie led him to her room. There, in that room, in her body, her self, he found the sanctuary he'd never known he wanted or needed. In the quiet of a darkness pierced by the light of stars shining outside their window, they made slow, achingly sweet love and with each murmur, each touch, Judah, patron saint of lost causes, felt himself learning that with love, everything is possible.

Even hope.

* * * * *

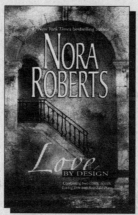

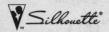

Your opinion is important to us! Please take a few moments to share your thoughts with us about your experiences with Harlequin and Silhouette books. Your comments will be very useful in ensuring that we deliver books you love to read. *Please take a few minutes to complete the questionnaire, then send it to us at the address below.*

Send your completed questionnaires to:
Harlequin/Silhouette Reader Survey, P.O. Box 9046, Buffalo, NY 14269-9046

1. As you may know, there are many different lines under the Harlequin and Silhouette brands. Each of the lines is listed below. Please check the box that most represents your reading habit for each line.

Line	Currently read this line	Do not read this line	Not sure if I read this line
Harlequin American Romance	❑	❑	❑
Harlequin Duets	❑	❑	❑
Harlequin Romance	❑	❑	❑
Harlequin Historicals	❑	❑	❑
Harlequin Superromance	❑	❑	❑
Harlequin Intrigue	❑	❑	❑
Harlequin Presents	❑	❑	❑
Harlequin Temptation	❑	❑	❑
Harlequin Blaze	❑	❑	❑
Silhouette Special Edition	❑	❑	❑
Silhouette Romance	❑	❑	❑
Silhouette Intimate Moments	❑	❑	❑
Silhouette Desire	❑	❑	❑

2. Which of the following best describes why you bought *this book*? One answer only, please.

the picture on the cover	❑	the title	❑
the author	❑	the line is one I read often	❑
part of a miniseries	❑	saw an ad in another book	❑
saw an ad in a magazine/newsletter	❑	a friend told me about it	❑
I borrowed/was given this book	❑	other: _____	❑

3. Where did you buy *this book*? One answer only, please.

at Barnes & Noble	❑	at a grocery store	❑
at Waldenbooks	❑	at a drugstore	❑
at Borders	❑	on eHarlequin.com Web site	❑
at another bookstore	❑	from another Web site	❑
at Wal-Mart	❑	Harlequin/Silhouette Reader	❑
at Target	❑	Service/through the mail	
at Kmart	❑	used books from anywhere	❑
at another department store or mass merchandiser	❑	I borrowed/was given this book	❑

4. On average, how many Harlequin and Silhouette books do you buy at one time?

I buy _____ books at one time	❑
I rarely buy a book	❑

MRQ403SIM-1A

5. How many times per month do you shop for any *Harlequin and/or Silhouette* books?
One answer only, please.

1 or more times a week	❑	a few times per year	❑
1 to 3 times per month	❑	less often than once a year	❑
1 to 2 times every 3 months	❑	never	❑

6. When you think of your ideal heroine, which *one* statement describes her the best?
One answer only, please.

She's a woman who is strong-willed	❑	She's a desirable woman	❑
She's a woman who is needed by others	❑	She's a powerful woman	❑
She's a woman who is taken care of	❑	She's a passionate woman	❑
She's an adventurous woman	❑	She's a sensitive woman	❑

7. The following statements describe types or genres of books that you may be interested in reading. Pick *up to 2 types* of books that you are most interested in.

I like to read about truly romantic relationships	❑
I like to read stories that are sexy romances	❑
I like to read romantic comedies	❑
I like to read a romantic mystery/suspense	❑
I like to read about romantic adventures	❑
I like to read romance stories that involve family	❑
I like to read about a romance in times or places that I have never seen	❑
Other: _____	❑

The following questions help us to group your answers with those readers who are similar to you. Your answers will remain confidential.

8. Please record your year of birth below.

19 ____

9. What is your marital status?

single ❑   married ❑   common-law ❑   widowed ❑
divorced/separated ❑

10. Do you have children 18 years of age or younger currently living at home?

yes ❑   no ❑

11. Which of the following best describes your employment status?

employed full-time or part-time ❑   homemaker ❑   student ❑
retired ❑   unemployed ❑

12. Do you have access to the Internet from either home or work?

yes ❑   no ❑

13. Have you ever visited eHarlequin.com?

yes ❑   no ❑

14. What state do you live in?

_____

15. Are you a member of Harlequin/Silhouette Reader Service?

yes ❑   Account # _____   no ❑   MRQ403SIM-1B

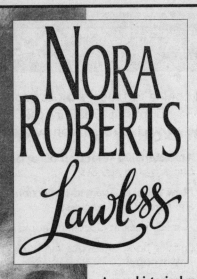

COMING NEXT MONTH

SIMCNM0903